W9-CHQ-557

Praise for

GINI ANDING

and the

AMY PAGE / JEAN-MICHEL JOLIVET "WITNESS" SERIES

WITNESS ON THE QUAY

"A richly detailed, authentic travelogue centered on the historic Ile Saint-Louis in Paris. . . . A compelling, immediate, exciting story."

—Steven W. May, Amazon.com

"For aficionados of mystery-detective-espionage thrillers, Gini Anding offers both a new take on the genre and—best of all—a distillation of the finest features of whodunit fiction."

—Robert Griffin, Amazon.com

"Wise, witty and winsome, Witness on the Quay testifies warmly on France and things French. . . . Anding does for the City of Paris what Dan Brown does for the Eternal City!"

—Jacques Otrebor, Amazon.com

"A genuine page-turner. . . . The author nails Paris (and the French) in a way that few American writers are able to do. . . . Most important, we see that love and passion can bloom in the lives of people over fifty."

—Robert W. Greene, BarnesandNoble.com

"Amy is an unusual, fun, middle-aged heroine that the reader will fall in love with immediately. . . . It's fun to read about an intelligent, talented, and yes, sexy older heroine."

—Writer's Digest

WITNESS AT THE BRIDGE

"*A fast-paced mystery involving murder and the international drug trade, a heartwarming love story, a meticulous guidebook to Paris and especially to the Ile Saint-Louis, and a compendium of information about French history, cooking, and assorted customs.*"

—Barbara C. Bowen, BarnesandNoble.com

"*A delicious mix of mystery, romance and traditional whodunit.*"

—Heather Froeschl, BookReview.com

"*[A] crash course for Francophiles, history buffs, pop culture aficionados, cuisiniers and chef wannabes, and fun reading for anyone who loves a contemporary, mature, and Gallic-spiced romance.*"

—Katherine C. Kurk, Kentucky Philological Review

"*A delightful romantic mystery set in Paris. . . . Plenty of action and surprises to keep the reader turning pages until the delightful end.*"

—Writer's Digest

WITNESS IN THE SQUARE

"*A fun read. . . . A multilayered take woven into a cleverly plotted tale.*"

—Anne K. Edwards, MysteryFiction.net

"*In the reflective tradition of Agatha Christie . . . this is not your typical murder mystery.*"

—Heather Froeschl, BookIdeas.com

WITNESS BY THE CHURCH

"*This mystery series seems grand fun. Written by an expert in French language and culture, it features a romantic angle seen not often enough in mystery.*"

—Writer's Digest

"If you like action and intrigue, this is a tale that will please you. . . . Lots of mystery . . . a secret society . . . a lost treasure, spies, a murder in a church . . . blended together to give the reader lots to consider."

—Anne K. Edwards, MysteryFiction.net

"[Anding] takes you to some wonderful places in Paris. . . . Vivid descriptions bring everything to life. . . . For a fun, romantic mystery, Witness by the Church is the perfect pick. Romance reader groups will especially love it!"

—Paige Lovitt, Amazon.com

"[Anding] has dedicated such energy and intellect to the details that she makes the settings as real to the reader as to the visitor."

—Julie Costich, Amazon.com

WITNESS FROM THE CAFÉ

Amy Page / Jean-Michel Jolivet Novels by Gini Anding

Witness on the Quay

Witness at the Bridge

Witness in the Square

Witness by the Church

Cookbook by Gini Anding and Amy Page

The Amateur Gourmet

**Nonfiction Books
Under the name Virginia A. La Charité**

*Bonaventure des Périers's
Novel Pastimes and Merry Tales*
(with her husband, Raymond C. La Charité)

The Poetics and the Poetry of René Char

Henri Michaux

The Dynamics of Space:
Mallarmé's Un coup de dés jamais n'abolira le hasard

Twentieth-Century French Avant-Garde Poetry,
1907-1990

Visit her website at
www.GiniAnding.com

WITNESS FROM THE CAFÉ

A Novel

Gini Anding

iUniverse, Inc.
New York   Bloomington

Witness from the Café
A Novel

Copyright © 2010 by Gini Anding

*All rights reserved. No part of this book may be used or reproduced by any means,
graphic, electronic, or mechanical, including photocopying, recording, taping or by
any information storage retrieval system without the written permission of the publisher
except in the case of brief quotations embodied in critical articles and reviews.*

*This is a work of fiction. All of the characters, names, incidents,
organizations, and dialogue in this novel are either the products
of the author's imagination or are used fictitiously.*

iUniverse books may be ordered through booksellers or by contacting:

iUniverse
1663 Liberty Drive
Bloomington, IN 47403
www.iuniverse.com
1-800-Authors (1-800-288-4677)

*Because of the dynamic nature of the Internet, any Web addresses or links contained in
this book may have changed since publication and may no longer be valid. The views
expressed in this work are solely those of the author and do not necessarily reflect the
views of the publisher, and the publisher hereby disclaims any responsibility for them.*

ISBN: 978-1-4502-2399-7 (sc)
ISBN: 978-1-4502-2400-0 (ebook)

Printed in the United States of America

iUniverse rev. date: 04/12/10

Author's Note

The French café is a venerable institution. Literally, a café is a coffee house, originally established to serve coffee at small tables. Today when a café also serves food, its little round tables set it apart from all other establishments, such as bistros, brasseries, and restaurants. History has long maintained that the Soleiman Aga introduced coffee as a drink to King Louis XIV in 1669, and the first coffee house appeared in Paris shortly afterward: Le Procope on the Rue de l'Ancienne Comédie in 1686. Of course, trivia lovers know that the first authentic café in France was founded in Marseilles by a Sicilian, Procopio dei Coltelli, in 1654.

The café is a neighborhood social club that acts as a gathering place for serious discussions of the arts, sports, politics, and economics. It is a landmark where friends as well as lovers meet and where the residents of a given quartier feel safe and secure, for café habitués usually work and/or live nearby. The institution of the café appeals to all socio-economic groups, all political persuasions, all philosophies, and all religious beliefs. The clientele ranges from manual laborers to the so-called artsy crowd. Some are visited by just the right wing, others by only the left; some are frequented mainly by journalists or university students, and others appeal primarily to businessmen or serve as an established forum for the exchange of ideas among the intelligentsia.

The eighteenth-century *philosophes* met regularly in the café Le Procope, and the famous *Encyclopédie* was actually conceived there. Much of Baudelaire's *Les Fleurs du mal* was written in the Café Voltaire, and it is well known that the Impressionist artists met regularly in the evening in certain cafés along Hausmann's newly created *grands boulevards* when there was no light for painting. During the Roaring Twenties, what the French call *Les Années Folles*, the Surrealists gathered twice a day in cafés to criticize each other's work and plan outings as well as exhibitions.

When the artistic center moved from Montmartre to Montparnasse and the workshop area known as La Ruche, painters and sculptors alike tended to favor La Coupole and La Rotonde, while the English and American expatriates preferred Le Dôme and Le Sélect. Down the Boulevard Montparnasse in La Closerie des Lilas, Ernest Hemingway wrote most of *The Sun also Rises*. Because of a serious fuel shortage during World War II, Jean-Paul Sartre and Simone de Beauvoir went daily to Le Flore or Les Deux Magots in Saint-Germain in order to write, undisturbed, in a warm place.

Above all, a café is congenial, with a well-established code of behavior. A customer is always welcome. The ritual begins with shaking hands with the proprietor and all acquaintances. After the exchange of pleasantries, the client—and one is more of a client than a consumer—chooses a table that he or she literally owns for the duration of that visit, which can last all day. Indeed, one doesn't go to a café so much as one visits it. Café time is a time for thought and meditation, a time for reading a newspaper or full-length novel, a time for *bavardage* and catching up on the latest gossip, or a time for just being idle, just sitting. Watching people is the major sport, enjoyed by all. In a café, one is at home and simply relaxes.

While there are luxurious cafés, the average one serves very simple food and drinks. Service is always included in the bill. The least expensive fare is found at the stand-up zinc bars, where there are no stools for sitting; the most expensive fare is found outside on the terrace. There are over 8,500 cafés with terraces in Paris, and they range from small to large ones, from just a few tables to fifty.

The café can always be depended upon to offer breakfast, lunch, dinner, and *le snack*. While some have slightly more elaborate menus than others, all offer coffee, wine, beer, and soda, along with croissants in the morning, sandwiches, salads, and omelets at noon, and usually a two-formula plat du jour in the evening (first course and main dish or main dish and dessert). Some cafés are splendid and elegant, while others are plain and unadorned, but, regardless of size and location, all cafés are hospitable and make the visitor and regular customer equally welcome.

On her beloved Ile Saint-Louis, Amy is a regular visitor to all three authentic cafés. Only occasionally does she go to the *salon de thé* or tearoom, which in addition to tea and pastries serves lunch, but no other meals.

She and Jean-Michel enjoy the only brasserie, across from the Pont Saint-Louis, and she has learned that a brasserie is more informal than a restaurant yet different from a café in that it is invariably noisy and never serves breakfast. The French brasserie is known for hearty cuisine at reasonable prices, fairly fast service, large offerings of beer, although not necessarily draft beer, and the fact that the waiters are usually men only.

A bistro—and there is one on the Ile—is also known for hearty food, especially home-style dishes dictated by what is available in the market. Only a bistro will serve a *plat ménager*, a housewife's dish and homemade terrines and soups, items not found in cafés, brasseries, or restaurants. While a bistro is generally less expensive than a brasserie, it offers a much broader menu than a café, and it is usually much livelier as well.

Seated in the corner of a café with an espresso on the table before her, Amy ponders the French sense of classification. Everyone knows just what a café is and why one goes there. Everyone also knows that brasseries are Alsatian in origin, while bistros owe their name to the Russian soldiers in 1815. By default, a restaurant is then considered a more elegant and formal eatery. Some serve dinner only, while others are also open for lunch, but never for breakfast or *le souper*.

However, to make distinctions all the more confusing, Le Lipp in Saint-Germain is usually described as a café-brasserie-restaurant because it combines the characteristics of all three.

Looking through her notebook, Amy sees that she has also listed other variants: café-concert, cabaret, café-chantant, café-théâtre. Then there are all kinds of bars: wine bar, beer bar, dance bar, music bar. She groans when she comes across that real oddity, the bouchon, which is a small family-owned restaurant specializing in cuisine from the city of Lyons.

"Oh, hello, Gini," she says with a smile. "Sit down. You'll never guess what I've found out about the French café. Did you know that—"

* Œufs durs mayonnaise   3,10
* Poivrons rouges grillés   4,20
* Filets de hareng, pommes à l'huile   4,30
* Avocat aux crevettes   4,30

* Salade Bressane   9,50
* Salade Exotique   9,50
* Salade Auverguate   9,50
* Salade Nordique   9,50
* Salade de Chêne au basilic, salade   8,20
* Quiche du Jour, salade   9,00
* Bruschetta   10,00

* Poêlée de gambas au basilic, riz 3 parfums   13,20
* Pièce du boucher sauce poivre, frites et salade   13,50
* Confit de canard, pommes sautées à l'ail   13.
* Paupiette de veau, spaghettis   12,50
* Roasbeef, gratin de choux fleurs   13.

Prix Nets

CAST OF CHARACTERS

Amy Page: widow from Charleston, SC; columnist for the *County Chronicle*; author of cookbook, *The Amateur Gourmet*; mother of Jack and Mary E.; sister of Carter Taylor, United States government agent

Jean-Michel Jolivet: former inspector for the criminal division of the French police and director of the International Bureau of Security; comte de Bourdonville; son of Hélène Rochefort; brothers Yves and Alexandre manage the family estate and winery; two sisters are Emilie, a pediatrician, and Denise, an artist and historical preservationist

Inhabitants of the Ile Saint-Louis

Corinne Avouche: owner of the Café du Coin

Paul Champion: fisherman

Claude: majordomo for Jean-Michel Jolivet; wife Aline

Auguste Jolivet: chef of Chez Ma Tante restaurant; wife Toinette; daughter Léonore

François Lacour: owner of map and chart shop; wife Maryse repairs dolls

Tiago Luiz: chess master

Léon and Yvette Machaut: house staff for the Hôtel de Rochefort; son Pascal, computer expert

Jacob Poncet: dog walker

Caroline Rochefort: unmarried aunt of Jean-Michel Jolivet; amateur historian and artist

Members of the Interpretive Cultural Committee

Natalie Darcet: historian and museum curator

Félix Dubois: retired physical education teacher

Hortense Gallifet: lawyer

Bernard Gourdon: actor

Philippe Jammet: banker

Camille Maréchal: new assistant priest

Marcel de Montvalont: urban planner; brother of Marianne Rochefort

Tristan Moreau: priest of the Eglise Saint-Louis-en-l'Ile

Pierre Richard: retired concierge

Members of the Police

Rémy Legrand: successor to Jean-Michel Jolivet at the International Bureau of Security

Hervé Mathieu: police inspector

Others

Archangels (secret group of investigators): Raphaël, Uriel, and Gabriel; Achille, Raphaël's cousin and team member

Sylvestre Ballanche, marquis de Granvelle: Jean-Michel Jolivet's best friend; toothpaste magnate; married to Véronique

Foster: editor of the *County Chronicle*; married to Dory

Clovis and Clotilde Leroy: owners of the bar Le Singe Vert

Serge Longuet: journalist; Jean-Michel Jolivet's nephew; girlfriend Justine

Pip (Payton Iverson Pommelton): retired British government agent

Nikki Raymonnet: security expert; son Didi, engaged to Léonore Jolivet

Laurent Rochefort: Jean-Michel Jolivet's first cousin; physician; married to Marianne de Montvalont

I

Amy Page frowned. She looked at the grand café crème on the table in front of her. It was her favorite way to have coffee whenever she was in a café in the morning. Back in the apartment she shared with Jean-Michel Jolivet on the Quai de Bourbon, morning coffee was au lait.

Of course, she knew how to make a café crème. After all, she was a food writer and author of a cookbook, *The Amateur Gourmet*. It was just that she had never actually made one, preferring to order it in cafés.

It always came in a large cup. A small bowl, actually, with a handle on it. She had six of them in the apartment, even though she knew that in French families the morning café au lait was served in cereal bowls without handles.

Hmm, she thought to herself. Maybe she could get an article out of cups. Tea cups versus coffee cups. French café au lait bowls versus café crème large cups versus demitasse cups. Espresso was always served in demitasse cups. Then there were chocolate cups that were just a bit larger than demitasse cups. Russian tea was served in glass mugs. There really were all kinds of cups—

"Excuse me, Madame, but do you have any aspirin? I am having one of my headaches and I don't seem to have my medicine with me. Just how long do you think the police are going to keep us here? You don't think we are suspects, do you?"

Amy looked at Natalie Darcet and nodded.

Natalie was clearly miserable. Compared to the slightly plump Amy, Natalie was rail-thin. Amy knew that she was a dedicated vegan and wondered if the restricted diet was responsible for her constant stream of ailments. The room was either too cold or too hot. The weather affected her rheumatism or her liver. Her allergies included the whole spectrum of the world around her: pollens from flowers, vines, grass, bushes, trees, and all sorts of foods. On the other hand, she was a well-trained historian and would be an excellent curator for the new museum on the Ile Saint-Louis. Sometimes, fussiness and overzealous attention to detail were assets.

They really were a motley crew in this corner of the Café du Coin.

For what seemed like the hundredth time, Amy surveyed the room. It was probably the most typical, ordinary, mundane, and uninteresting café in all of Paris. Those were the very reasons Amy loved it.

She still went to the Café du Patriarche on the corner of the main crossroads of the Ile to have coffee with Pierre Richard, the retired concierge, who was always a fount of interesting bits of gossip, but now that she lived on the Quai de Bourbon, she usually frequented the Café du Coin. It was on the prized corner at the end of the rue Saint-Louis-en-l'Ile. From one of the very few tables crowded on the sidewalk on either side of the front door, one could see the Pont Saint-Louis and the back of Notre-Dame, and the backside was supposed to be the best view.

The front room of the café was hardly a room. It was just big enough to contain the entry and the bar where workmen came and stood to have a coffee in the morning and a glass of wine on their way home at night. Sometimes businessmen had their evening apéritif on one end of the bar. It was the domain of the owner, Corinne Avouche.

She was reported to be a former madam from Pigalle, so the rumor mill said. Amy had once asked Jean-Michel if the rumor were true, but he had merely shrugged his shoulders and said that she had bought the café well before he had returned to live on the Ile.

Amy had then asked Charles Pichon, the antique dealer with whom she had dinner at Chez Ma Tante every other week, and he had smiled mysteriously and said he didn't think she had been a madam. That enigmatic answer had led Amy to assume that Corinne had probably been in the business and was very likely a friend of Artemis, the queen of Pigalle.

Amy had never met Artemis, but when Jean-Michel was shot and again when he had a bad case of pneumonia, an enormous flower arrangement had arrived with a card signed in hot pink, "Artemis." She had then asked Roger Gramont-Rochefort, Jean-Michel's uncle, just who she was, and the art critic had replied somewhat dismissively that all men of a certain social strata were acquainted with Artemis. She was one of those women of importance and means to whom he had sold some very expensive pieces of art. He thought he had met her through Charles Pichon, who helped her with her famous collection of snuffboxes.

Not even Florian Renan, the flamboyant second-rate actor who had roles in sex shows in Montmartre, was of any help. He claimed that she was an important theater person well before his time, but he didn't know her.

The chair was getting harder. Amy shifted on the chair, then uncrossed her legs and then crossed them again.

Maybe I should write an article on the typical Parisian café, she wondered, one that the locals frequent and not one that is sought out by tourists and foreign students. That's it. Before doing cups, I'll do a café. I'll describe this one.

She rooted around in her tote bag and took out a small notepad and pen.

Let me see, she mused. The café has only two public rooms: the front entry, with no stools or chairs, and this large room with . . . let me count, six tables that will seat four each and six small tables for just two people. A small aisle divides the room and leads to the unisex toilet on one end and a street door on the other. That side door could only be used for leaving, never for entering. That's odd, Amy thought. After all, the door opens both ways. Maybe there was a story there.

Looking around, she noted that there were no decorations, except for the paper place mats that are always a deep burgundy color. In the evening, large red wine glasses hold large paper burgundy napkins. Corinne handles the bar, so she only needs one waiter at a time.

The china is that solid serviceable restaurant white. The small condiment caddy holds salt, pepper, a small dish of white and brown sugar cubes, and a little pot of very hot Dijon mustard. If the customer is a regular who requests sugar substitutes, the waiter puts a small white dish with yellow packets on his table.

Next to the street door, Amy saw the tall glass case that contains whatever pastries Corinne picked up that morning. At lunchtime, a runner from one of the pastry shops would arrive with a tray of tart slices for dessert.

The printed menu is inside, while the plat du jour is listed outside on a chalkboard. Regulars never use the menu, and some automatically take the special of the day, no matter what it is. But regular or visitor, Corinne greets each one with a smile.

Amy smiled. Yes, that is . . . so café. The owner or whoever is behind the bar smiles and gives a cheerful welcome to each person who comes in, but the waiters never smile. It's as though it's an unwritten rule. Come to think of it, it's the same with bistros, brasseries, and restaurants. Even in her favorite restaurant, Chez Ma Tante, where she knew everyone well and sometimes helped out, only the owners smiled. Never Emile, the head waiter.

Dourness was obviously a requirement. She'd have to ask Pierre Richard.

"Ladies and Gentlemen, we regret the delay, but I must ask you to be patient for a little while longer. Madame Avouche has agreed to serve you if you wish something more to drink. I've promised her that we'll be through processing the crime scene in time for the dinner crowd. When we finish here, you'll have to follow me to the Préfecture and file official statements. It might save time if you started now to write down what you saw."

Inspector Hervé Mathieu spoke patiently. He'd never had a murder with so many witnesses on the spot. This was also a group of intelligent witnesses. He should be able to get some good leads from them. He just needed Jean-Michel to get here from his meeting in La Défense. Jean-Michel knew all these people and would be a better interrogator. Especially of Madame Amy Page, who seemed to be a witness in every important case that happened on the usually quiet Ile Saint-Louis. Funny, he still thought of her as Madame Page.

Amy set aside her notes for an article on cafés and tried to think about what she had seen.

Not much.

General Sébastien Reboursier had simply dropped dead. He had keeled over. Right onto his half-eaten croissant.

Félix Dubois and Marcel de Montvalont had jumped up. Marcel said he remembered his army training and Félix said he knew CPR because one of his duties at the lycée had been to teach first-aid. They immediately said that the general was dead and it was probably poison.

Both priests had then knelt by the body and said they agreed. The general was dead.

Corinne had immediately telephoned the Préfecture and announced calmly that someone had been murdered in her café. Because it was the Ile, Mathieu was promptly notified. He arrived with several others within a few minutes, and they were soon followed by an ambulance from the hospital on the Ile de la Cité.

Mathieu wanted to know first off why Corinne had called the police. Why did she think it was a murder and not a death from natural causes, such as a heart attack?

Corinne Avouche had answered Mathieu in a commanding voice.

"Two reasons. First, Félix Dubois and Marcel de Montvalont shouted that the general's skin was bright pink, a sure sign of cyanide poison, and Pierre Richard and Father Moreau agreed. Second, there's his medical history. Ever since his wife died last year, the general has come here for breakfast every morning. He always orders a large orange juice, café au lait, two croissants, and marmalade. Always. He arrives promptly at 9:00 a.m. with a copy of *Le Monde* and he sits at table number 3. Always. And each morning I ask him how he is. Last week he told me that he had just seen his internist and that he was in excellent shape for his age, although he should try to lose fifteen pounds. He hoped I had a sugar substitute for his morning coffee and said he would also omit marmalade on his croissant. He planned to extend his walking path to include not just the two islands but the quays on the other side of the river. Combine that with the odd skin color, Inspector! I'm just sure he didn't die of natural causes, so someone must have killed him, but I don't know who. And why here in my café?"

"I see," Mathieu said slowly. "I need you to list everyone who was here right before the general collapsed. Include anyone who has already left. What about your waiter? I don't see one here."

"I don't know what happened to Fernand. He's been my day waiter ever since I bought this café," she replied. "He called in sick and said he was sending his cousin over in his place, and he did. Oscar . . . I didn't get his last name, but he came and turned out to be a very good waiter. I don't know when he left. Anyone can go out the street door, you know."

"I notice that the table next to the toilet hasn't been cleared. So who was there?" Mathieu asked.

"Table number 5. That was François Lacour. You know. He owns that odd map and chart store on the Rue des Deux-Ponts, right next to the grocery shop. His wife repairs dolls. You know. Makes their eyes blink and gives them new wigs. That sort of thing. Monsieur Lacour is the first client every Tuesday and Friday morning. He always sits there at that table in the corner and reads several newspapers. He once said he liked that table because he could prop up his bad foot and bad hand. He wears a glove, you know. I think he was in an automobile accident. How else could he have lost an eye and been so banged up on one side?"

"If you think of anything else, Madame, please tell the officer I'm posting at the door. I'm sorry that we have to shut you down for a while, but in the long run, it will double your clientele. People are always drawn to crime scenes."

Mathieu went back into the main section of the café. He quickly took note of the people seated at various tables: an elderly English couple, priests from Notre-Dame, the deaf and nearly blind Madame Biron from the Rue Poulletier, and Monsieur Valbelle and his daughter Nina, who was visiting from Cahors.

And herded away from the back two tables to the two tables between the toilet and the kitchen sat the interpretive culture center committee. Twelve stalwart citizens, now reduced to eleven. And although not present physically—but as Mathieu knew only too well—there stood behind the committee an even more formidable group of important people, who just happened to be native inhabitants of the Ile and who were connected to all the shakers and movers in Paris.

His first phone call had been to René Legrand, Jean-Michel Jolivet's successor at the International Bureau of Security on the Quai des Orfèvres. He would find Jean-Michel and send him immediately to the Café du Coin.

"*Bonjour*, Corinne. I hear you've had quite a morning. I was told that General Reboursier was murdered? The hen grapevine is probably working overtime already. It might even be enough to get Margot out of her hospital bed. We'll talk later, providing you break out that magnificent bottle of cognac you've got hidden back there! *A tout à l'heure.*"

"Oh, Jean-Michel!" Amy called loudly. "I'm so glad to see you. Tell Mathieu to let us go. We've been stuck in this corner for hours and hours. Not even allowed to talk! Poor Mademoiselle Darcet has one of her dreadful headaches, and I need to . . . well, you know. They've told us we're witnesses. We're going to have to walk over to the Préfecture and make official statements. Well, we didn't kill the general. And we don't know who did. We didn't even know he'd been poisoned until Marcel de Montvalont pointed it out. We thought it was a heart attack, but Marcel said no because of something about pink skin, profuse salivation and the involuntary release of something or other. The smell is just terrible. I don't know how he knows about poisons, but then Bernard Gourdon said he agreed with Marcel and Félix that it was probably cyanide. You probably don't know him, but Bernard is an actor friend of both Godefroy Quinault and Arthur Tessier. He said he once had to play a poison victim and expire on stage exactly the way the general did."

Jean-Michel looked at the miserable group. Indeed, several were quite pale. The odor wasn't as bad as they thought, but then they weren't used to having their nice, tidy, protective world invaded by such ugliness.

"Who is the spokesperson for the committee?" he asked

The group responded in chorus, "It was the general."

"Then, who was his second-in-command?"

Philippe Jammet, the banker, answered. "This isn't a committee in a formal sense, Jean-Michel. The general was to be the overall director of the board, which will run the center. But that actual board hasn't been put together. This is an *ad hoc* planning group. We're mainly consultants trying to get the center off the ground. Natalie Darcet is the only one so far who has accepted a paid position: curator-historian. The rest of us are volunteering our expertise. Ultimately, we hope to hire in more positions, such as a canteen manager, a custodian to tend to the physical appearance and upkeep of the facility, and maybe an activities organizer. In the meantime, I am handling the financial end of things and working with Julien Turenne to establish a permanent foundation."

Jammet paused and looked at the group. No one spoke, but all nodded, indicating that he was to continue to speak for them.

Jammet cleared his throat. "One of our goals is to involve young people, give them a place to use up that pubescent energy, so Félix is going to teach swimming and tennis for starters. Bernard wants to expand the youth activities into dancing and dramatics, and he'll use his theater experience to train the guides. It's obvious why our parish priest, Father Tristan Moreau, is here. This morning he brought his assistant, Father Camille Maréchal. Marcel's job as our resident Ile urban planner is to convince contractors to work for cost. I think his plan is to use mainly apprentices for the physical overhaul of the building that will house the center and so save us a considerable amount. Right now we're operating on seed money from various residents such as yourself."

It was Jean-Michel's turn to nod in response. Jammet sighed and polished his glasses. No one said a word.

After a long and awkward pause, Jammet looked at Jean-Michel and said: "You know everyone here. It's obvious why the lawyer Hortense Gallifet is on board. Pierre Richard is here because he is representing Margot, who is ill, and her food services project; all the cafés and restaurants are going to help supply the canteen with sandwiches, salads, and soups."

Jammet took a fine linen handkerchief from his breast pocket and mopped his brow. He looked at Jean-Michel, who merely cocked his head in invitation for the banker to continue.

"As I was saying, your uncle Roger rarely misses a meeting, but today he's involved with some gallery showing of art featuring musical instruments. He's already located an entire collection of nineteenth-century paintings of the Ile. Charles Pichon has been drawing on his contacts in the antique business to gather items for what are called, I believe, rotating displays."

Again Jammet stopped, hoping that someone else would speak. And again he was met with silent nods.

"Well, Jean-Michel, that's about it. We've even gotten you to participate. We're most appreciative of your generosity in lending us much needed secure storage space in your new office and, I might add, for getting Pascal Machaut to volunteer his time in designing and running a computer program for our operation. So you see, it's really quite simple. Everyone involved has a role and there is no particular chair for this group. But to go back to your question and answer it as best I can, I have to say that our actual chair is your aunt, Caroline Rochefort. She's the one who started this project and so she is to my mind very much the person in charge. While she may have convinced the general to serve as Chairman of the Board of Directors, she's the real commander-in-chief. Yes, Jean-Michel, I'd have to say that the general was only the second-in-command. Your aunt is the driving force behind the center, so our leader here, *in situ* if you will, must be her representative, Madame Amy Page. Excuse me. I mean the Countess of Bourdonville."

"Who?" Amy gasped.

"You," the group answered all together, looking at Amy and nodding their heads in agreement with each other.

Of course, Jean-Michel thought. His bride. Why wasn't he surprised? Somehow, if there had to be a murder on the Ile Saint-Louis, it was inevitable that Amy would be involved. They had met because of a murder and their romance had developed in the midst of others, maybe even because of others. He didn't know. He just knew that the woman he loved beyond all reason and had married just three weeks earlier had managed once again to be a witness to a capital crime, and one whose ramifications probably extended far beyond the Ile and the city of Paris.

No wonder Mathieu had called him. It wasn't because the Ile was involved. Oh, no. It was because of Amy.

Jean-Michel glanced at Mathieu, who was secretly congratulating himself on seeing to it that Jean-Michel was on the scene.

"Thank you, Philippe, for clarifying the roles and responsibilities of this group. I now have a real understanding of why each of you is here. I'm confident that because of this group and their respective talents and skills, the center will be a huge success."

The committee members smiled for the first time. Jean-Michel's compliments meant that despite the death of the general, the committee's work would be able to continue, uninterrupted by the investigation. All but Amy visibly relaxed, confident that the ordeal of the morning was over and that they could now leave the café.

"By the way, I agree with Inspector Mathieu," Jean-Michel added. "It is important now that you follow him to the Préfecture for more formal interviews. They won't take long and then you can all go home or to your place of business. Before you ask, yes, I'll be there. And, yes, the other customers are leaving as soon as they complete their written statements for the police."

"Ah, Uriel," he said to the tall man who had just entered. "I'm glad you got here so quickly. Yes, I see that you already are thinking cyanide poisoning because of the bright pink color of the skin. I agree. Call me the minute you complete the autopsy and a preliminary toxicology test."

With the arrival of Uriel, the forensic pathologist, Amy got up along with the other committee members and meekly followed Mathieu out of the café.

With Jean-Michel and Uriel on the scene, she was now convinced that the general had been murdered. She just couldn't figure out how it had happened with all of them at the same table. Maybe it was a mistake. Maybe the general wasn't the real target. The general was really a very kind person, but if not the general, then who? Indeed who? And how? And why? Just what was she a witness to?

II

"I've never been so tired in my entire life," Amy moaned. "It's really been the most exasperating day! I can no longer think. Why did I ever let your aunt Caroline bully me into being on the committee for an interpretive culture center on the Ile? I don't know anything I should know. Everyone has an area of expertise, except me. If we were in the States, the committee could meet in private homes. It could meet here in the Hôtel de Rochefort and Caroline could then preside. But oh, no, that's just not how it's done. If there were a big business on the Ile, we could use their boardroom. Instead we meet at the Café du Coin. Out in public!"

Jean-Michel cocked his head, as Amy vented. He knew that she would have done anything to be on the committee. She enjoyed being in the midst of life on the Ile, and an interpretive center was the perfect venue for her boundless curiosity and enthusiasm. She knew almost as much about the Ile as Caroline Rochefort, his reclusive aunt, who had written its definitive history and who headed a formidable intelligence-gathering network.

Nothing happened on the Ile that wasn't reported to Caroline and her hens. Without being aware of it, Amy had become one of them and an invaluable link in the gossip chain. Now that the hotel owner and Caroline's primary link to happenings on the Ile was in the cardiac unit of the hospital, Amy's position in the Ile network had become all the more important.

"I rather thought you enjoyed meeting in the café. I remember your saying that the café atmosphere automatically put everyone at ease and in a convivial mood. The perfect icebreaker was how you put it."

"Well, yes, I did say that. And it's true. Getting a group of twelve strangers to sit down together and order coffee and perhaps a tartine does have a way of forming a bond. We get along quite well and we have become a congenial group. When the idea for such a center was born, I had no idea that so many experts in so many areas could be found so quickly. It's also amazing that all are volunteers, except for Natalie Darcet. Do you know what's truly remarkable about this group, Jean-Michel?"

"The fact that they are enjoying the challenge of the project?"

"Of course. That's a given. No, it's that there is no rivalry, just respect for what each one is bringing to the project. I've been on lots of committees in my day, but this one is . . . I guess genteel is the right word. Isn't that a strange way to describe a committee?"

Jean-Michel laughed. He sat on several boards in Paris and in his native Burgundy and was all too aware of the underlying tensions among various members. His best friend, Sylvestre Ballanche, the marquis de Granvelle and chair of the largest toothpaste industry in France, frequently complained about committees. According to Sylvestre, the reason he insisted that Jean-Michel be on his board was because he didn't want to and because he didn't have a hidden agenda. It had nothing to do with ability or credentials. In fact, the most able were usually the most difficult team players.

With that in mind, Sylvestre had divided his employees into three camps.

On the one hand, there were the workers, who were well rewarded for their mastery of a given skill, loyalty, and hustle in his factories.

In contrast, he had a stable of creative oddballs whose sole job was to dream, think, and experiment so that the third group, what he called his facilitators because they actually ran his industry, could keep it on the cutting edge of dental products. The board then reviewed everything, but actually supervised nothing. That was Sylvestre's job, and he was very good at it.

In all truth, Jean-Michel enjoyed serving on Sylvestre's board. It didn't meet in the boardroom, but in fine restaurants every two months. "A matter of atmosphere," Sylvestre declared. "Now you know why my team of dreamers usually don't have offices. They work wherever it's comfortable. One has a warehouse loft, another a favorite café, a third is in a proper studio in a castle outside of Paris, and so on."

Suddenly it dawned on Jean-Michel. His aunt Caroline had asked Sylvestre how to go about setting up her operation and there it was. Right out of Sylvestre's sense of organization. There were the workers: the actor, the athletic coach, the museum curator, and Margot, the hotel proprietor, now replaced by an experienced concierge. Then there were the dreamers: the antique dealer, his own uncle, the parish priest, and, of course, Amy. The third group, the facilitators, was obvious: the banker, the urban planner, the lawyer, and the general, who was going to be the official chairman of the board. Jean-

Michel saw clearly that one of the members of the board would ultimately be the marquis de Granvelle. Titles were important in Caroline's world.

Amy's voice interrupted his thoughts.

"Now we have to replace the general. He was so good at setting priorities, formulating agendas, working out timetables, and conducting a meeting. He expected each person to attend each meeting and come with a prepared report that was then handed to the recorder. Frankly, some of the reports are boring, but the general insisted on details. In fact, he wanted detailed details!"

"Remember, Amy, that old adage: 'The devil is in the details,' as the general well knew. But what about this recorder? Does that mean there are minutes and copies of all reports somewhere?"

At police headquarters, none of them had thought to ask how the committee was structured and how it operated.

"Who is your recorder?"

"At first, it was Margot. Then she had the heart attack, and, since we had already hired Natalie Darcet, it seemed natural to give her the job."

How logical, Jean-Michel thought. A committee chaired by General Reboursier would naturally have a company clerk, or in this case a secretary, to take notes and file reports. A system of meticulous recording and filing would have been automatically required by several members of the committee, not just a general, but also a banker, a lawyer, and most definitely, his aunt Caroline. He had given the committee storage space in his office, so he already had all the reports.

He felt like a dunce. Neither he nor Mathieu had thought to ask about committee actions and decisions leading up to the general's murder this morning.

The more he thought about the make-up of the committee, the more he had to admire his aunt Caroline. She had put it together. With Sylvestre's input. Half the members actually lived on the Ile; the other half were linked to someone who lived on the Ile. Félix Dubois, the retired lycée coach, was a cousin to Madame Giraud, who ran the florist shop. The actor Bernard Gourdon was an associate of Godefroy Quinaut, who was not only a well-known retired member of the illustrious national theater, La Comédie Française, but also along with the antique dealer Charles Pichon and now the retired concierge Pierre Richard, a member of the Comité des Douze that virtually ran the Ile.

Jean-Michel silently saluted his aunt. Charles Pichon was not only on that all-important local committee, as well as this one, but was also the half-brother of Julien Turenne, Jean-Michel's godfather, one of the wealthiest magnates in France and his aunt Caroline's former fiancé. Amy had a standing dinner date at Chez Ma Tante with Charles and Julien every other Thursday.

Of course, it made sense to have his uncle Roger Gramont-Rochefort on the committee because he was so prominent in art circles. And, adding the parish priest somehow gave the committee a certain stature, if not an actual blessing, as the hens might put it.

"Tell me, Amy, when does the committee think the center will open? It's already the middle of April. Do you think the center will be ready this summer as originally thought?"

"Yes, I do. We've targeted Bastille Day for the Grand Opening. A lot has already been done. You'd be surprised at the help we're getting. The Ollier workshop has already finished about a dozen or so costumes for the guides. Félix has gotten several of his friends to donate soccer balls, tennis rackets, and things like that. Then before her attack, Margot had convinced all the cafés, restaurants, and food shops to help man and stock the canteen. The canteen is not going to be a place to eat a full meal, just simple snacks and drinks, things that kids and tourists like. Caroline is quite adamant that there should be no vending machines, but there does need to be a place where a visitor can sit down and have a cup of coffee or a glass of lemonade. Pierre Richard is working on a schedule so that the rotation of responsibilities is fair. Toinette and Auguste from Chez Ma Tante are going to handle the canteen for the opening. Isn't that terrific?"

"I am impressed, *chérie*. But I am surprised to see Marcel de Montvalont there."

Amy laughed.

"Imagine how surprised I was to meet him and learn that he is your first cousin's wife's brother! I thought Marianne only had sisters. I can't believe that he's related to you by marriage, lives on the Ile, and I've never run into him or met him or even heard of him!"

"Marcel is about ten years older than I, so I don't know him very well. I think he went to school with Tristan. He's always been quiet and reserved. His wife, Blandine, has been sickly for a long time. She rarely goes out, and to my knowledge none of their three children lives on the Ile, which is a shame. Their mansion on the Quai d'Anjou is one of the oldest and most elegant private residences on the Ile. When old Madame de Montvalont died, Marcel and Blandine redid it completely, but also managed to keep all of its former splendor. Marcel knows most of the architects in Paris and probably had no trouble hiring one who specializes in restoration. The family has been on the Ile since its beginnings, so I am particularly delighted to see that Marcel is getting involved with its life. I really don't remember the last time I saw him or Blandine. I had just moved to Paris when the renovation was finished and Marianne gave me a tour. You would enjoy it."

"I'd love to get inside the mansion," Amy said. "I've read that it's a perfect example of *le style ludivicien*."

"What's that? I've never heard the expression. *Ludivicien* refers to a person whose family roots date back to the earliest days of the Ile Saint-Louis, the seventeenth century. People like Marcel and me. Its news to me that there's a style by that name. Where did you pick that up?"

"I read it somewhere. Probably in a book on seventeenth-century architecture. Marcel and Natalie both use it all the time. It refers to those buildings on the Ile built between 1614 and maybe fifty years later or so. On the outside, the mansions were very solid and regular in appearance. Some even use the word *stolid*. Modern for their time, they had multiple stairways with as many as four landings, and they were built around a central space or courtyard. What was very new and avant-garde and totally non-Parisian was their insularity. They were built on quays, facing the river, and their courtyards and gardens were in the back. They had lots of vestibules for passageways because they were so spacious, with lots of rooms and antechambers, especially dining rooms, which were a novelty at the time. The exterior didn't use brick or stone, but some form of gray masonry, concrete, I think, and massive paneled entry doors. The outside is Louis XIII in style, but the interiors are Louis XIV. Really sumptuous."

"Sumptuous?"

"Yes, sumptuous, with large rooms, painted galleries, ballrooms, libraries, reception rooms, and all sorts of other rooms like *pavillons* and *grands cabinets*. And to top it all off, they had luxurious furnishings, tapestries on the walls, ceiling murals, painted wooden beams, and brocade curtains. And it all happened within about fifty years. The Ile is the first truly urban undertaking and this *style ludivicien* is considered stately, majestic, and elegant, built for privacy and comfort. You should hear Marcel on the subject."

Jean-Michel smiled. Amy was one of the Ile's greatest admirers and defenders. But he needed to get her back to the subject of the interpretive center committee and the events of the morning.

"I'm sure that Marcel knows what he's talking about. As for the committee, I now understand that each member has a specific area of responsibility."

"Yes, that's how it was put together."

"What's your role, Amy?"

"Funny you should ask. I'm not the one in charge, that's for sure. I could not believe that Philippe Jammet said that I am. Absolutely not! General Reboursier was the chair because he's the only one of us who was going to be on the real board of directors."

"So what is your job?"

"I haven't a clue. I'm sitting in for Caroline, but that's just because I live in the same mansion and I guess I'm now one of her in-laws."

Amy started to laugh.

"I am, aren't I? A Rochefort in-law?"

"Yes, you are. But what do you do on the committee?"

"Nothing. I just sit there. I think I'm the only one who's had any experience with an interpretive center. When Caroline had the idea, she didn't know what such a place should entail. I'm the one who suggested that it not be just a youth center, but also a place to showcase the history of the Ile and involve young and old people in special activities, exhibits, projects, and that sort of thing. I had hoped that we could have tours of some of the mansions. Well, not just the old mansions, but also those places that represent changes made in the eighteenth, nineteenth, and twentieth centuries. We have a list, but so far no one is willing to open their doors to us. The city of Paris won't even discuss opening the Hôtel de Lauzun. Gautier lived there, so did Baudelaire, Rilke, even Wagner."

"Yes, I see, but then the residents of the Ile are being true to history, aren't they, by being protective of their privacy? I'm not surprised that no one wants to be toured by the public."

"I get your point. I hadn't thought of it that way. We certainly wouldn't want people tramping through the Hôtel de Rochefort."

"No, we wouldn't, but to get back to the committee. I think you're on it because of your familiarity with the Ile. You can easily put together a list of famous people and where they lived. In fact, I think you already have such a list, so using your list, you can create specialized tours by century or field. For example, Baudelaire lived in several different places on the Ile. Do a tour of writers and artists. Then you can do one of the English and American celebrities who lived here. You're always talking about Nancy Cunard. Here's a chance to tell other people about her. Maybe Marcel can do some models of buildings as they were in the sixteenth century and the changes that came after, like all the ironwork, and the cemetery that no longer exists. That sort of thing. It can be just as rewarding."

"The buzzword, Jean-Michel, is interactive. Different kinds of tours would be perfect. Marcel is going to get someone to build models of the various old mansions, including the grandiose Hôtel de Bretonvilliers that was the largest and grandest of all. We hadn't thought of doing interiors, but we could."

"There you go."

"We could create shadow boxes of different rooms. Maybe even train some guides to impersonate various historical figures, like Nancy Cunard, Baudelaire, and that crazy Restif de la Bretonne, who went around at night and carved his diary on the walls with an ice pick—"

"Now, now, Amy. Don't get carried away."

"You know kids would love that sort of thing. I could even do one on famous women, like the scientist Marie Curie, the sculptor Camille Claudel, or was she a sculptress? And I mustn't forget the cosmetic queen Hélèna Rubinstein. Wow! Let me find some paper and write this down."

Jean-Michel frowned. He hadn't meant to get her off track. In her interview at the Préfecture, she had said that she hadn't noticed anything unusual. She had not been listening to Hortense Gallifet's report on the sanitation requirements for a canteen. She said she had been doodling. She would never admit she was making notes about different kinds of cups for her food column. The first thing she knew was Natalie's screeching that the general was ill. She looked at him and he was face down in his croissant. She saw him jerk around and drool. Félix and Marcel jumped up, went over to him, and put him on the floor to do CPR. The general turned bright pink, jerked around some more, and then went still. He stopped moving. Félix said it was too late to do any CPR because the general was already dead. Tristan went over, made the sign of the cross, and whispered a few words. Last rites, she guessed.

Amy's account of the events seemed to leave no stone unturned. Félix and Marcel said that they didn't think it was a heart attack, but poison, and Tristan agreed. Hortense then ordered everyone to remain seated and wait for the police to arrive. If the general had indeed been poisoned, then it was a crime scene and should not be disturbed. They had all sat there in total silence. Amy said she was literally paralyzed. She had been seated directly across from the general. All she really remembered was looking at that smashed half-eaten croissant. Then the police arrived and told them they had to go to a table at the other end of the room. She had had a hard time walking around the general's body. Amy finished the interview by saying it had been a horrible experience and that she had really liked the general.

Amy returned with a notepad of lined paper and started writing.

"I hate to interrupt you, *chérie*, but I really need to know why you told Mathieu and me at the Préfecture this morning that you hadn't been paying attention to Hortense."

"There's nothing strange about that. I was telling you the truth. Her reports are always dull, and they're so full of legal mumbo-jumbo that I don't understand most of what she's saying."

"Well, what were you thinking about? I mean besides cups. Had something happened in the café that morning that struck you as odd?"

From past experience, Jean-Michel knew that Amy was a keen observer and reliable witness if one asked the right question. The problem was her constant digression. Sometimes she purposefully omitted what she thought was insignificant, and on occasion she fudged. That was her word, *fudged*, meaning she didn't lie; *not exactly* was another of Amy's preferred expressions. She merely glossed over a given fact or observation because it might be embarrassing, so she *shaded*—another Amy word—what she reported. At other times she gave information that had nothing to do with the case at hand, misleading him and the police.

"Yes, I guess so. There was a really odd moment. I think it was the sweetener. No one on the committee uses a sugar substitute. The general always liked to put a cube of brown sugar in his café au lait. That morning, he told us that he was going to have to cut down on sweets, so he was giving up jam and real sugar. There wasn't any dish with packets of artificial sweetener on the table. He looked around and saw a dish on the table next to us. The one where that strange man who always wears a glove on his left hand and drags one leg sits. Just like a pirate. He even wears a black eye patch. You know who I mean. He owns that peculiar map shop on the Rue des Deux-Ponts. I've never been in there, but I did once peer in the window, but I couldn't see a thing. It's so dirty. I don't think the shop is open more than two days a week, and I've never seen anyone go in or out. I don't know how he stays in business. I've heard that his wife is some sort of doll doctor, but I don't know that for a fact."

Inwardly, Jean-Michel moaned.

"His name, Amy, is François Lacour. He's really quite good at what he does. Someone on the committee should talk to him. He could probably locate some old maps of the Ile for the museum and for planning tours. And, yes, his wife Maryse does repair dolls."

"Really? I'll tell Natalie. Still, he's an odd duck, but then, so is she."

"Let's get back to the dish with artificial sweetener. Where was it exactly?"

"It was on that man's table. He got up to leave and the general asked him to give him the dish with the packets. And he did. Then he left. That's all there was to it."

The packet of artificial sweetener. That could easily have been the source for the cyanide. Everything on the table where the committee had been sitting had been packed up for examination by the lab, but that item probably didn't have a high priority. Now it seemed that François Lacour was involved. And that made sense.

Earlier, Amy had asked him if he thought the general had been the intended target or if it was just one of those random poisonings that happened from time to time when someone with a grudge against society put poison in ordinary products and killed for the sake of killing and not with a specific victim in mind. Jean-Michel knew that the police were considering that theory, but now he thought differently, thanks to Amy. Lacour could have been the intended victim. Given his past, it made sense.

"I have an idea, Amy. It's Friday. Let's go to Le Singe Vert for bouillabaisse. You've not been for a long time and you know how popular you are with Clotilde and Clovis."

"I'd love to go. I called Claude and Aline and told them not to bother with a meal tonight because I would probably be too tired to cook anything more than an omelet. I had to spend all morning with the police, then I had to go over the plans for the reception next weekend, spend an hour on the phone with Léonore, who was having one of her meltdowns over her wedding, e-mail Foster that I would miss my deadline, again, and so on. I think Foster has some of my articles as backup, but I've lost track. It's just been a crazy day. I'll go change my clothes. I even have time to take a shower and wash today away."

Amy stood up and started to leave. Suddenly, she stopped in the doorway.

"By the way, *mon amour*, do you realize that I didn't know that this mansion has a ballroom? There are all sorts of rooms for entertaining on the second floor or what you call *le premier étage*. You know that's a crazy system. Your first floor is my second floor. Anyway, it'll be a grand party and since it's here, Caroline will be forced to attend. Or at least make an appearance. Why didn't anyone ever tell me that the Hôtel de Rochefort was once a center for glamorous soirées and balls and all that? Oh, I know. You're going to say that I should have known. And you're right. I knew it and didn't realize I knew it. I mean it just didn't register, but, of course, that grand staircase had to lead somewhere special. It does in Julien's mansion, so it should here. I guess I just got into the habit of taking the elevator and so I didn't think about skipping a whole floor. I'm going to do an article on cafés, but I think I'll put off the one on cups and instead do one on the floor system and grand stairways, the landings, the stonework, all that. There are lots of them on the Ile, and those I can visit and even photograph. Foster says he'd like to have pictures with my cultural articles. The café will be easy. Then a grand staircase. The one right here! That reminds me, Jean-Michel. I have a big problem and it's beginning to drive me crazy."

"What is it, *chérie*? Can I help?"

"I hope so because it's all your fault."

"My fault? What did I do?"

"It's the name. You were there. Philippe Jammet referred to me as the Countess of Bourdonville."

"Well, you are. The wives of counts are countesses. That's simply the way it's always been and that's the way it is. Surely you know that."

"Of course, I know that. I just don't think of myself as a countess. I still think of myself as Amy Page. Amy Lucile Page, to be exact."

"I guess we never discussed the name business. You are Amy Lucile Page. Marrying me didn't change who you are. I think you should continue to publish your articles under the name Amy Page. If you don't want to take the name Jolivet, it's fine by me. You don't ever have to be Madame Jolivet, but you do have to be the Countess of Bourdonville."

"I'm going to have to think about it some more. I was just shocked to be called a countess. Mathieu still thinks of me as Amy Page. Sometimes he calls me Amy and sometimes Madame Page. It gets so that I don't know how I'm going to be addressed. Now there's this countess business. I hadn't even thought about Jolivet. I wonder what Caroline would say."

"Knowing my aunt, I'd guess she'd say that names don't really matter, but manners and titles do. Go get ready. I'll call Clovis and tell him we're coming."

As soon as Amy left his study, Jean-Michel picked up the phone and made a series of calls.

"Priority, Uriel. Check the artificial sweetener packets. They are probably the source of the poison."

"Hello, old chap. Come tomorrow on an early train. You know you enjoy the full-course breakfast. I think our map friend is in trouble."

"Gabriel, set up a meeting with your gang of four. Yes, it's connected to the general's death. No, I don't know how, but I have a gut feeling about it. Say on Sunday in your bookshop. Yes, I've called him and told him to get on the early train. Tell Raphaël to send Achille to meet him. And I want watchers on the Ile as soon as possible. No, no specific reason, just a precaution. They're to look for anything out of the ordinary. Yes, twenty-four hours. Amy and I will be at Le Singe Vert this evening."

"Ah, Hervé. I'm glad I caught you before you left. Yes, I reinterviewed Amy. It looks as though General Reboursier was not the real victim. I'd rather not say, but wait for some more evidence. Give me the weekend to gather some more information. What? Still no trace of the waiter Fernand Douchet or his cousin Oscar? Does Oscar have a last name? No? Well, even if he did, it's probably false. Just so you know, I'm going to set the Angels in motion. Yes, we'll talk on Monday."

"René, guess what? I think the death of General Reboursier this morning was an accident. I think that the intended victim was our old friend Lacour. Had he been poisoned, the case would have been on your desk since he's not a French citizen. Just keep your eyes and ears open. I've spoken with Mathieu. Yes, the Angels are at work. Yes, I called London. Yes, Sunday at Gabriel's. Two o'clock."

"Who are you talking to, Jean-Michel? I'm all ready. It's the perfect night for that wonderful rustic bread and bouillabaisse. Suddenly, I'm very hungry. I just remembered. I didn't eat lunch today. Let's go! It'll be our first visit to Le Singe Vert as . . . um, the Count and Countess of Bourdonville!"

Amy was still laughing when they walked out the door.

"Look, Jean-Michel, there's that old man with the nice little dog. I haven't seen them for ages."

"Amy, I think I'll drive instead of our taking the Métro."

Jean-Michel put his arm around her and led her back into the courtyard of the Hôtel de Rochefort and over to the dark blue BMW. He could now relax. Everything was in motion and at least one watcher was already in place. They would spend an enjoyable evening at Le Singe Vert, and when they got home that night and were in bed, they would do what newlyweds all over the world do. Piaf had been right. With the right person, one discovered "la vie en rose."

III

Seated in a large leather chair in the back of Gabriel's bookstore, Jean-Michel looked at the three Archangels and Rémy Legrand. The so-called gang of four had met earlier with the Archangels and they hadn't learned anything new. Pip, a retired British intelligence officer, had come to Paris the day before and spoken privately with François Lacour. He hadn't learned anything either, just that Lacour was convinced he was not the target. He'd been out of the game more than five years. Yes, he still had contacts. All agents did, but he wasn't active and he didn't think any of the rest of the retired members of the gang of four were either.

For a few minutes, no one spoke.

"Let's review everything we know so far," Jean-Michel suggested. "I did tell Mathieu that I was going to involve the Archangels and keep him informed of anything we learned, but I'm not quite ready to bring him fully into our confidence. He has to walk a fine line between established procedure, several overly ambitious underlings, and us. Even though the Archangels are now legitimate French citizens, we all still have to be careful. One never knows when their checkered pasts could compromise an investigation. By the way, I did put in a call to that rascal Brooks Fairfield in Hawaii. He's the one who originally recruited Lacour, but he wasn't helpful. I then called our Irish friend, who admits that he did work once with Lacour, but that was a long time ago. He's positive that the IRA is not involved."

"And I contacted Interpol in Lyons," added Rémy Legrand. "Not one of the gang of four is involved in any current operation. They met with their Interpol liaison in early March and reported that everything was quiet. Not one of them had heard from anyone in their old life."

"Do you believe them?" Raphaël asked. "I mean, we're all accomplished liars, skilled in verbal evasion. When Jean-Michel formed the Archangels as his private investigative unit, it was because we had a certain experience and had acquired skills that a life outside the law had given us. We were survivors, thanks to our wits and to our established contacts, who operated in the shadow world of criminal activity. I know how to beat a polygraph test, and I'll put my money on the fact that this gang of four is equally adept, maybe even more so, since each one is a former highly placed government spy."

Again, the group fell silent.

"Well, Gabriel," Jean-Michel said, "you're the one who works with them the most. What did you think of their professions of innocence, non-involvement, outright ignorance, and complete surprise?"

"Well, of course, each one is a consummate actor. But, they're an aging group. Personally, I think that all four of them have really found peace at last. It's not easy for a spy with a heavy price on his head to retire. It's not even easy for people like me, Uriel, and Raphaël to live in the open without fear. I still marvel that Uriel is now paid by the police for his forensic skills, Raphaël works in the theater, and I have this bookstore. From time to time, Raphaël uses the gang as watchers, but that's about it."

Raphaël laughed.

"That's true. And they're excellent. They automatically keep an eye out and quickly report anyone suspicious, and they like to be involved from time to time, but the one who enjoys being a watcher the most is Jacob Poncet. His dog-walking act is a classic. No one pays any attention to him and his muttering to the dog. And that dog never misses a tree or blade of grass for that matter. They appear completely normal. Amy, for example, has never suspected them and she's been under their surveillance a lot. Before Jean-Michel started his car Friday night to go to Le Singe Vert, I had a call from Jacob that he was on his way and that there was no one suspicious on the Quai de Bourbon."

It was Jean-Michel's turn to laugh.

"How true. At first, I thought we would take the Métro so that I could see if we were being followed, but when I saw that Jacob was already on the job, I nixed that idea and decided to drive instead. What I'd like to know is how Poncet got there so quickly. I thought they changed their cell phones every other week."

"That used to be the case," answered Gabriel, "but I was finally able to convince them that it wasn't practical for us. We compromised. They now change every three months. Tiago Luiz was the hardest one to convince, probably because of his KGB background. They didn't even trust each other in that organization. Of course, Poncet as a former Mossad agent doesn't trust anyone either, not even yours truly."

"Don't you think they trust us a little? We've gone to extreme pains to provide them with safe havens," Jean-Michel confided. "Tiago Luiz has been here the longest and he has the best cover. I don't think anyone would suspect that he's actually Russian because of his Portuguese mother. He's totally fluent in the language. I think he's finally happy, teaching and playing chess, not to mention his involvement with a certain widow. Jacob Poncet's age protects him. And that dog! Paul Champion seems to be adjusting well, but then he's not been here very long. Still, he is somewhat enigmatic. Lacour plays the eccentric shopkeeper to the hilt and that has worked well so far. He's the most paranoid of the group, but then he's the one who paid the highest personal price."

"Isn't he the one who was tortured?" Legrand asked.

"Yes, he was," Gabriel responded. "It was one of our first cases. Actually, it was Pip's case. I know you think that he was a Canadian agent, but his cover there became shaky early on, so Brooks Fairfield relocated him to London and eventually to Pip, who supervised his work for the British. We never knew all the details, but Pip asked us to get him out. It was a dicey job all around. Somehow he had made it to a small coastal town in Brazil. Anyway, we managed to set it up, but it was Jean-Michel who physically went in and brought him out. Uriel patched him up enough for us to fly him to a safe house in Luxembourg and our involvement ended. I don't think we were really surprised that he turned up here five years later."

Jean-Michel shifted in his seat and picked up the story.

"The Brits got him back to England, where he had a long recovery and a long rehab, first in a clinic and then as an outpatient. For a while, they put him to work at a desk, doing what, I don't know. Codes probably. Maybe some planning operations. Pip thought he wasn't progressing as he should, so he contacted me about rehab facilities in France, and I asked my cousin Laurent. He recommended the sanitarium in the Jura Mountains outside Besançon. One thing led to another. He went, met Maryse, who worked there, they got married, he improved a great deal, and he decided not to return to London but to retire. He also met Nikki Raymonnet, who took a great interest in him. At the time Nikki was still a wanted man, so he contacted Clovis at Le Singe Vert and he in turn called me, and I called Pip. Pip and I decided to set him up on the Ile. The four of us had already dealt with Tiago Luiz and so we were keenly aware of the need to handle old spies. Regardless of debriefings, they still have to find somewhere safe for their retirement and old age. Now we have four of them on our doorstep. End of story."

"And you think Lacour was the intended murder victim, not the general."

"Yes, Gabriel, I do. Think about it. He was the only one in the café who might be on a hit list and the only regular customer who used artificial sweetener. It was a fluke that he wasn't feeling well that morning and ordered a pot of tea instead. Who would have guessed that he would put real sugar in his tea when he usually put artificial sweetener in his coffee? He had to be the target. And we mustn't forget that the packets were originally on his table. He's the one who gave them to the general. Another fluke. The general habitually put two brown sugar cubes in his morning coffee, but just that morning he decided to use artificial sweetener instead."

"I see your point, Jean-Michel," Legrand agreed. "It's the only reasonable explanation. Still, it doesn't make any sense if Lacour's been out of the game for a long time. Why now? Unless he's not out of the game."

"That's what I suspect."

Gabriel nodded. "Come now. You know that he still plays from time to time. Even you still have dealings with him, Jean-Michel. Admit it! You know I'm right."

Jean-Michel smiled at Gabriel, but said nothing.

"Fine, have it your way," Gabriel concluded. "*Alors*, let's begin with the premise that Lacour is still a player in games not run by Jean-Michel. That's the only possible reason for the attempt on his life. When I met with the four of them this morning, I was struck by a certain lack of curiosity. When a murder occurs close to home and targets a member of your group, you usually want all the details. Their questions were perfunctory. They feigned astonishment, but somehow I didn't think their collective surprise was genuine. Pip called me before he returned to London and said more or less the same thing. His meeting with Lacour was, in his words, 'too textbook to be true.'"

Legrand shifted in his seat.

"Textbook! Then the question becomes whose book? KGB? MI-6? Mossad? And just who is the new one? The Vietnamese? What's his name? I know. It's Paul Champion. What's his book? We refer to them as the gang of four, but is there any chance that they were an actual gang of four in a previous life? Did these four know each other before they wound up on the Ile Saint-Louis?"

"Good questions," Jean-Michel replied. "Honestly, we don't really know and we'd like to. We like to think they met here for the first time, and, of course, that's exactly what they would want us to think if indeed they knew each other before. Since they were all top agents, they certainly knew of each other and could have met several times. Spies tend to know spies, or rather who is spying for whom and why. So yes, they most definitely knew of each other. The unknown is if they ever actually met and worked together."

Everyone spoke at once.

"Can't Pascal use his computer expertise to hack into all those spy agencies and see if the paths of our gang of four ever crossed? Have we thoroughly investigated their backgrounds? Their covers? Do we know for a fact that they have really retired? How did they really get here of all places?"

Jean-Michel rapped on the table, calling for silence.

"Maybe we should redo the background search, but we have to remember that they and the agencies they worked for are pros in covering tracks and planting false information. I doubt that a new in-depth background search will yield any new data. But to answer one of your questions, here's the history of their arrival on the Ile Saint-Louis. Lacour and Luiz were the first to arrive, and I had Gabriel introduce them to one another. The staff at the Besançon sanitarium had said that Lacour needed contact with someone he could talk shop with, so to speak. Gabriel seemed the natural conduit and Luiz the obvious first acquaintance. Then Poncet arrived after ten years in the south of France; I had worked with him on several occasions, so he didn't hesitate to ask me for relocation help when he feared that his retirement cover in Arles had been blown."

"And the Vietnamese? When and how did he wind up here?" Legrand asked.

"First of all," Gabriel answered, "there are a lot of Vietnamese in Paris, as you well know, Rémy. Second, he has several cousins here and one of them is in the restaurant business. When that cousin learned that Champion needed a lawyer, he called his restaurant friend, Adèle Jolivet of Chez Ma Tante, for a recommendation, and she naturally recommended her nephew, Jean-Michel. There's nothing strange about it."

"You don't think there's something too pat about the arrival of the four of them on our doorstep?" Raphaël asked.

"No, I don't, but I understand why you think their relocation here might be a setup. But if so, then by whom? Certainly, Lacour's physical and emotional situation at the time could not have preplanned or even programmed it."

"I see your reasoning, Jean-Michel, but Lacour's move here might have been the catalyst necessary to keep Luiz here and get the other two to come. It might be worth some investigation."

"You have a point, Raphaël," Jean-Michel replied. "I'll ask Pascal to dig into it. But to go back to Rémy's question about Paul Champion. When I first met him through his restaurant connection, I realized immediately that he had been some sort of undercover agent. All he would admit was that he had done investigative work for a private security firm located in Singapore, but that was good enough for me to add him to the group already here. Besides, with such a large Asian population in Paris, I thought the police and IBS could use a trained insider should the occasion arise. Setting him up on the Ile with a French name seemed like the obvious thing to do. After all, he grew up under French rule. I was simply waiting until he was better adjusted to living here before telling you, Rémy."

"So, he's actually one of mine! Wonders never cease. I just had a case involving the murder of an Asian girl, who, we think, may be a North Korean national. No one will talk to us, so I could use someone like this Paul Champion to help me. How do I get hold of him?"

Jean-Michel laughed.

"He's the fisherman you see almost every day on one of the quays around the Ile de la Cité. The best cover is the one that doesn't seem like a cover."

Raphaël nodded in agreement.

"Exactly. Here we have a dog walker, a peculiar shopkeeper, a chess teacher, and a fisherman. Who would ever suspect that they are four retired spies, who literally wrote the book on covert operations? It would be useless to put watchers on them. Do we have anyone totally unknown to them, yet someone who might be able to give us some sort of lead? At the moment, we really don't know that Lacour was the intended target. If he was, then knowing more about him might tell us why. Can you tell us, Jean-Michel, what exactly Lacour's specific area was?"

"Pharmaceuticals. He nearly completed a PhD in chemistry and started a dissertation on counter-opioid receptor antagonists."

"What?"

"Antidotes, especially in biotechnology. As I understand it, he started out working on neurotoxins, what you know as nerve agents or gases. Uriel, this is more your field than mine. Just remember that you're talking to non-scientists."

"No problem. As you know, chemical warfare consists of the development of weapons of mass destruction. During World War I, everyone became familiar with mustard gas. That's a good example of a nerve agent. Just before and during World War II, the Nazis worked on what we commonly call the G-Series: tabun, sarin, soman, and ultimately cyclosarin. Next, after the war, the UK gave us the V-Series, which is much more toxic than anything in the G-Series. Lately, there are the Russian Novichok compounds, which are brand-new nerve agents for which there is no known protection. Okay so far?"

"Yes, go on," everyone answered.

"When Lacour joined the intelligence service, his primary responsibility was to monitor the destruction of stockpiles of chemical weapons. He found it boring. He began to focus more and more on therapeutic drugs, hoping to discover new chemicals in natural products, especially those that can block the effects of opiates. As you know, the illegal drug trade is a multi-billion dollar industry that operates worldwide, so any active drug that could produce immediate withdrawal would be seen as a threat to the drug lords."

No one said anything. They were all familiar with the illicit drug trade, but the idea of a threat from therapeutic drugs was new to them.

Uriel took up where he had left off.

"Lacour's youngest brother was a heroin addict. Detox program after detox program failed; the urge to use always remained, and he died of a heroin overdose shortly after completing his third rehabilitation program. Lacour became increasingly convinced that a counter-drug—not just an inhibitor, but an actual antagonist—was needed and could be found. He persuaded the British government to let him use his resources for monitoring chemical weapons in a study of bioprospecting and phytochemicals. The Brits agreed because phytomedicine was already emerging as a billion-dollar industry and Lacour had the necessary training. Besides, he was already on the payroll."

Legrand shook his head. "Stop! I'm lost. What on earth is bioprospecting? I've never heard of phytomedicine either."

Uriel chuckled and then went on.

"Think about this, Rémy. Right now laboratories in Malaya are working on lichens to combat malaria. Just as some people prospect for gold, scientists prospect for plants to use in medical research. Through bioassays, plants are collected and catalogued; then they are screened for certain compounds and various extracts are isolated. It's always hoped that the screening process will lead to a new chemical agent that has therapeutic properties. The plant kingdom is the primary resource, but, as you can see, this kind of undertaking is capital-intensive."

Gabriel nodded knowingly.

"I suppose this is where Nikki Raymonnet comes into play. That kind of research also requires a large database and highly sophisticated computers."

"Yes," Uriel confirmed. "It's also dependent on worldwide collaboration, and Lacour had global contacts. Once he retired and tapped into his Swiss bank account—"

"Surely, Uriel," Jean-Michel interrupted, "you of all people don't subscribe to the myths put forth in popular spy novels. Lacour wasn't at all like James Bond, a super agent with a license to kill. He couldn't have amassed a fortune and had it hidden away in Switzerland."

"Well," Uriel countered, "you can't prove it. Pip might not even know. I'm sure he was trained to kill. All those agents like the gang of four were, and you know it. He was certainly a danger to someone since he was captured by somebody and tortured. I've always thought he was extremely well paid for his services. Highly trained agents usually are. I remember that the Archangels were paid a hefty amount to get him out of Brazil. Who paid for all that rehab? Not just in England, but here? The sanitarium outside Besançon is quite expensive and he was there for some time. Then he bought that shop on the Rue des Deux-Ponts and he works hard at not doing any business. There's a pot of gold somewhere, Jean-Michel. Probably several pots."

"I agree with Uriel," Gabriel said. "Lacour didn't just buy that shop; he bought the whole building. What's more, his inventory is impressive. He really has some rare maps and charts. I don't know where he found them, but I can assure you that he paid dearly for them. I think that our friend Pip is also suspicious of Lacour's retirement income. His comment, 'too textbook,' is a giveaway."

Raphaël gave everyone a chuckle. "Maybe we should turn to old mystery novels for help. You know, *Cherchez la femme*. And if there's no woman in the case and you know for sure that the butler didn't do it, then a good sleuth will follow the money."

"Not to change the subject," Uriel interjected, "but I will have the full toxicology report sometime tomorrow, Tuesday at the latest. There's no doubt that General Reboursier died of cyanide poison. I'm hoping that the report will tell us the nature of the cyanide compound. That information could provide us with a place of origin if nothing else."

"I've been wondering," Raphaël added, "if I shouldn't put out some watchers for Amy's protection. She's been a target before, and she's an eye witness to the general's death. Could we put it about that she saw someone out the window?"

"That's a great idea," Legrand replied. "Maybe not that she saw someone through the window because she couldn't possibly have seen passersby from where she was sitting at the end of the table. But, we could build a rationale around her cell phone. I know she has one, and I'm pretty sure it's a camera-phone. Am I right, Jean-Michel?"

Jean-Michel didn't want to answer. He didn't want to put Amy in any danger, but he grasped quickly the script that was being proposed. Amy was the ideal one for them to use. No one would suspect her. In fact, it was a stroke of genius to think she might have taken a picture of Oscar, the waiter who had vanished. She was known for walking around with a notebook and sometimes she carried a disposable camera. It would be in keeping for her to have been taking pictures during the committee meeting. She had been sitting directly across from the general when he died, and she had been making notes to describe the café. Her interview at the Préfecture had been quite short. Too short for Amy, now that he thought about it. He would have to go over her statement and then get her to fill in the missing pieces. She probably hadn't told the police everything she knew during the interview. Experience had taught him that often Amy didn't know what she knew or that she didn't know that what she knew was important.

"Yes," Jean-Michel confirmed slowly, "of course, she has a cell phone with the capability of taking pictures. In fact, she's just acquired a new one. I see where you're going with this idea and it is plausible. You're right, she could have taken a picture of Oscar. So what is her cover for contacting Lacour? I assume he's the one you want her to approach."

"How's this?" Gabriel offered. "We know that Lacour's wife, Maryse, doctors dolls. Let's ask Amy to take an old doll to be repaired and get into a conversation. Surely, somewhere in the Hôtel de Rochefort, there's a doll in need of a fresh wig or eyes that blink or a new voice box that says 'Mama.'"

"That'll work," Raphaël exclaimed. "Amy can go back several times to check on the doll, discuss a proper dress for it, and so on. It would be natural for her to mention seeing Lacour in the café and chat about how she had witnessed the general's death. Jean-Michel can go with her one day . . . what might you want an old chart of? Think of a special gift for Sylvestre or Julien or someone. That would open a different conversation with Lacour. How about going into the shop with Amy to ask about old maps of the Ile Saint-Louis for the new museum? That would work. You could even say you'd like to buy one or two to donate to the center."

Gabriel clapped his hands. "That's the perfect scenario. We need to put some pressure on Lacour and force him into action. He'd never suspect that Amy was now a spy."

Jean-Michel threw up his hands in mock surrender and ended the meeting on a jocular note.

"I wish it weren't the best idea we have at the moment, so I'll try it. Amy will be thrilled to have an excuse to go into Lacour's shop, especially if she thinks she's part of an official investigation. I'll talk to her. It might take us a while to find the right doll, but we'll come up with something. If I wind up buying an antique map for the Ile museum, I'm going to send you the bill, Raphaël!"

As Legrand and Jean-Michel left Gabriel's bookstore, they didn't notice an old lady watching them from the café across the street.

IV

Amy's note told him she was in the dining room and he should join her there. When he opened the large double doors to the elegant Hôtel de Rochefort dining room, he saw that Amy had set the large kitchen breadboard on one end of the table that could easily seat thirty-four guests.

Jean-Michel was amused. It was one of Amy's French picnic dinners. He didn't know where she got the idea, but once a month, usually a Sunday night, it was her idea of supper: two to three cheeses, two different pâtés, a fruit, a baguette, and invariably some dates. He had once asked her why she always included dates, and she had replied, "Because the offering needed something sweet." He supposed it was as good a reason as any. Nuts, she had once declared, were a nice addition to a cheese course, but they just weren't right for a picnic.

Tonight he saw that she had chosen a very ripe Brie, what looked to him like an English Stilton, an herbed goat cheese, a rustic pork pâté that was balanced by what looked like a very smooth mushroom pâté, and a bunch of green grapes, which he knew were seedless. She only bought seedless ones, and she rarely bought peaches for any cheese board.

According to Amy, an American picnic usually featured watermelon, while an English one had a decided preference for berries, but neither of those was appropriate for a French one. Bananas and pineapple were also taboo. The best choices were green grapes, pears, plums, apples, nectarines on occasion, and figs whenever she could find them. However, when it was a matter of figs or dates, for reasons known only to her, she invariably added nuts.

He had given up trying to figure out the logic behind her choices because invariably her French picnic meal was enjoyable and, as she declared solemnly every time, very romantic. Yes, it was most definitely romantic.

"Why are we eating in the dining room?" he asked.

"It's a celebration, *chéri*. I've even chilled a wonderful bottle of champagne for us and I found the most delightful cake called 'Le Puits d'amour.'"

"I don't think I've ever had such a cake, but then I'm not a chef. Just what is this marvel that you've found?"

"Well, actually, it's not a cake in the usual sense of cake. Rather, it's the name of an individual little cake that is round and has a crown filled with pastry cream or sometimes jelly, and then it has a glazed sugar icing. It's shaped like a well and then filled with something special, and so I guess it gets its name from its shape. I'd never heard of it until I started this project about the names of different foods. In the research that Serge has done for me, I learned it was created in 1843 for a comic opera by that name, 'The Well of Love.'"

"That's really interesting, Amy. Tell me, what are we celebrating?"

"Well, silly, us! We're celebrating us! Your surprise is behind that enormous silver étagère. Look! All our pictures! They're now all here! The last batch arrived yesterday from the States. I've spent this whole day putting them in chronological order. Tomorrow, I'll put them in that large album in the middle of the table. You have to help me do a triage. We can't possibly use them all. We'll just keep the best ones."

Jean-Michel was awestruck. Most of the Hôtel de Rochefort dining room table was filled with piles of memorabilia and photographs, each one with a tent card label in front of it: leaving Paris, flight, Bermuda, ship, cruise, ceremony, Florida arrival, visit to Savannah, Charleston homecoming, family reunions, Edward's party, Dory's party, beach cookout, sightseeing, departure, return flight. He'd had no idea their wedding and honeymoon had been so well documented. Even their baggage tags were there, along with some dried flowers, a monogrammed cocktail napkin, several menus, and a piece of a burst white balloon.

"We really did pull it off and surprise everyone, didn't we, *chéri*? I had such a hard time trying to decide whether we should do it here on the Ile or at my brother Carter's in Alexandria or in Bourdonville or at my sister's in Savannah or at my daughter's in Charleston. No matter the choice I was bound to hurt someone. There was no way I could include everyone. Then I learned that it's impossible to elope in France. You have to do all that legal stuff, provide all sorts of documents, such as death certificates if one has a deceased spouse, proof of domicile, medical documents, list of witnesses with copies of their official identity cards or passports, and everything must be in French, and that would require in my case a translator. Then if there is to be a religious ceremony, banns must be posted two weeks in advance. On and on and on. There's twice as much red tape in France when one of the two is a foreigner."

Jean-Michel smiled, as he remembered the struggle to get Amy to set a wedding date and decide on a place. By the end of February, it seemed that they would never marry. In France, there had to be a civil ceremony in order for the marriage to be legal. Usually, one had the civil ceremony and right afterwards, that very afternoon or evening if possible, the religious one. In the States, they could marry either way, civilly or religiously, but each state had different requirements.

Amy couldn't decide what she wanted. One day it was a traditional wedding in the Eglise Saint-Louis-en-l'Ile after a civil ceremony at the Hôtel de Ville. By the next morning, it would be in Alexandria, Virginia, in her brother Carter's living room with a judge of Carter's choosing; her son Jack would give her away and her daughter Mary E. would be the matron-of-honor; Carter could then be Jean-Michel's best man.

Two to three days later she talked about the Episcopal Church in Charleston, with all of her family and friends, and a reception at the country club.

One time she even considered a wedding chapel in Reno, Nevada.

Another week she talked about Bourdonville and the church that Jean-Michel's family had attended for several centuries. After all, he was the Count of Bourdonville, so it was probably best to marry there than anywhere else, but Bourdonville was in France and France insisted on all that paperwork!

As the weeks passed, Amy jumped from one plan to another. If the wedding were on the Ile, would his reclusive aunt Caroline attend? If in the States, would Sylvestre, his best friend, be free to stand up for him? What would his mother think? What about Julien? Charles? Laurent? If in Bourdonville, could Mary E. arrange her schedule to be there? What about Jack? Her brother Carter? Her sister Anne? There were so many people that she wanted there. Her editor, Foster, for example. And Margot from the Hôtel de l'Ile. Two different continents. Two very different worlds.

At one point, the differences threatened to take over their relationship. They became increasingly more aware of what they didn't have in common than what they shared. Their values and outlook on life were the same, but their formations and ties to the past were radically different.

He was European, she was not. She was Protestant, he was not. He was disciplined and orderly, she was not. She was an extrovert, he was not. He was worldly and urbane, she was not. She was a parent, he was not. He knew the dark side of human behavior, she did not. She was passionate about food and its role in culture, he was not. He prided himself on logic and reason, she did not. She enjoyed shopping, he did not. He was extremely wealthy and from the nobility, she was not. Where he found the absurd in the world around him to be a source of angst and concern, she reveled in it as a source of wonder. What was an item of curiosity to her was innocuous to him. What he took for granted, she considered deserving of special attention. While she frequently mistook the forest for the trees, he was certain that he never did.

The more Amy dithered and changed her mind, the more irritated Jean-Michel became. At their monthly lunch in early March, Sylvestre commented on Jean-Michel's mood. "If I didn't know better, *mon vieux*, I'd say that since you and your beloved Amy decided to get married, you aren't romping in bed as you used to do. Nothing else can explain your testiness. You're wound tight as a spring. What is going on? Do you want me to call the fair Artemis and find out if there's a new sex toy on the market that might help?"

"No, dammit, Sylvestre. It's not sex. Of course, we still romp, as you choose to put it. It's just that we can't seem to get married. Whoever thought it would be this difficult. I thought getting her to commit to me would be hard, but it wasn't. It wasn't at all. We are committed, body and soul. We just can't bring it all about. Make it legal. Do what we want to do. It's always on her mind. Shall we get married here? Shall we get married there? Civil? Religious? As soon as we agree on a plan, the complications arise. In a sense, we're already married. Maybe we should leave it at that and just go on living together."

"And what would the gossips of the Ile say to that? Your aunt Caroline would be on the phone to me morning, noon, and night. I'm your best friend. You owe it to me to take pity on me and get married right away. I'll even get down on bended knee and beg if that will get you and Amy down the aisle."

"Be serious, Sylvestre. We just can't work it out. Maybe in time, but—"

"Nonsense! Listen to me. I'm the one who is up the creek without a paddle, as Americans like to put it. I can deal with all sorts of business problems, but I can't deal with your aunt and her cronies. Then there's your mother, not to mention my wife; you know that Véronique would get involved, and that would mean Laurent's wife, Marianne, then your cousin Mireille. Hell, all of Paris would be on my doorstep, blaming me for not having seen to it that you got married. They all picked Amy out for you a long time ago. Actually, they've been pretty patient about it. That ring of commitment was a *tour de force*, and then, of course, Amy's move to the Hôtel de Rochefort. Both events bought you a lot of time, but now she's wearing that ring on her left hand and you both admit that you're engaged. Engaged to be married. Not engaged to go on as before. Engaged to move forward. To a wedding of some sort. It's all been decreed, Jean-Michel. In fact, it was decided before you and Amy fell in love. I'd even say it was decided before you two went to bed together. It's your destiny. You can't escape it."

"I do want it to be my destiny. I want to spend the rest of my life in married bliss with Amy," Jean-Michel said, "but that's just it. A wedding of what sort? Amy has planned at least a dozen different ones, but each one is unsatisfactory because of who it excludes. She wants to include everyone. Everyone here, everyone in Bourdonville, everyone she knows in the States, her family, my family, her friends, my friends, etcetera. Her list is endless. If we do it here, we offend more than one group and vice versa. Should it be civil and religious? Or just civil? Or just religious, which you can do in the States? If we do it there, we slight another group. There's no solution."

"Yes, there is. Forget all of us. Why not get married . . . I've got it! Get married at sea! By a sea captain! Yes, that's it! No civil servant, no priest. Do it in the middle of the Atlantic Ocean so that you aren't in France and you aren't in the United States. And with no one from here or from there present, so you will offend everyone but favor no one. It's the perfect solution. The hens will love it! I will be spared. Everyone will forgive you. After all, they'll all be relieved that you finally tied the knot. Then everyone will forget that you got married without them because they'll be concentrating on parties. We'll all spend months going to bashes to celebrate your wedded state. Artemis will get over not giving you a bachelor send-off if we invite her to one of the galas. If you wish, you can have Father Moreau bless your union on the Ile, and whoever bless it in Bourdonville to make your mother happy and reaffirm that sacred cow, your title."

For the first time in several days, Jean-Michel laughed out loud.

"You know what? That actually would work. In fact, I even know a sea captain I can call to help me find the right ship. *Mille mercis*, Sylvestre. Let's have a glass of cognac to salute your wisdom. I'm going to call Amy and tell her to buy a new dress for a special night on the town. I really think she'll go for this idea."

As predicted, Amy was enthusiastic about getting married at sea. Jean-Michel contacted a sea captain he had known since his time in London as a maritime lawyer. It turned out that he had a contact who had a brother who was the captain of a small cruise ship that sailed regularly between the island of Bermuda and Jacksonville, Florida. He was positive his brother would even arrange for Jean-Michel and Amy to use his luxurious stateroom for the trip, while he took one of the cabins usually reserved for passengers. The date was set for late March. The plans were made and no one was the wiser when Amy and Jean-Michel left Paris on Sylvestre's private jet for a flight to Bermuda, where they boarded the *Sarah Bernhardt*, a 694-passenger cruise ship.

Only Sylvestre was in the couple's confidence. No one even suspected that a wedding was being planned in secret. Amy told everyone that she and Jean-Michel were going to Charleston to celebrate her editor's fiftieth birthday party and everyone agreed that she should be there. The trip would also give Jean-Michel the opportunity to meet all her friends. No one thought that her search for a special dress for the occasion was out of the ordinary. Fortunately, Amy and Jean-Michel had already selected and bought their wedding rings. Since there was no paperwork involved, Caroline's contact at the mayor's office could only confirm the fact that the couple had not asked for any of the required forms.

The night before they left, Julien hosted a gala bon voyage dinner at Chez Ma Tante and toasted Amy and Jean-Michel with champagne. Sylvestre, who was passionate about American cowboys, made a show of asking Amy to bring back everything she needed to make a big pot of chili and a large pan of cornbread. Not to be outdone, Charles said that he too had a request: a wedding date. After much good-natured teasing, Amy finally stood up and said that she promised they would all be given a definite wedding date when she and Jean-Michel returned. No one suspected that it would be an announcement after the fact.

It was a very simple ceremony. Amy and Jean-Michel had written it themselves. The captain was resplendent in full dress uniform. The witnesses were two ship officers: the chief engineer and the purser, who was a woman. Jean-Michel wore his tuxedo with a white brocade vest, while Amy was dressed in a pale blue silk gown with long sleeves and a beaded bodice. She wore long diamond teardrop earrings and had tucked a daisy-shaped diamond broach in her hair. On her right wrist, she wore a garnet bracelet, the first gift that Jean-Michel had given her, and on her left she wore her mother's watch with the platinum band set with diamonds. Instead of a bouquet, she carried several white flowers, which she had taken from the large floral arrangement that had been waiting for them in their stateroom. It had no note, but they were both sure that the flowers came from Sylvestre and he would be pleased to know that his gift had played a role in their wedding.

Afterwards, they joined the other passengers in the ballroom, where they ordered champagne and danced until the orchestra leader announced the last number.

Back in their stateroom, they were surprised to find a small three-tiered wedding cake in the center of the coffee table, a bottle of vintage champagne cooling in ice, and a small tray of canapés and dainty sandwiches. They laughed as they remembered that they had forgotten to eat dinner.

"I'm really hungry. I can't believe we skipped dinner. The time went by so quickly. All of a sudden, we were there, in front of the captain and then we were dancing and now we're here and I'm not sure what to do. It's really different, isn't it, Jean-Michel?"

Her question caught him off guard. Yes, it was different. It was supposed to be different. Maybe not different, but, well, yes, different. For once in his life, Jean-Michel couldn't think of a thing to say. He seemed rooted in place, unable to act or speak.

"I don't want any more champagne, so we should put this bottle in the refrigerator for tomorrow, but I do think we should cut the cake now."

Amy didn't wait for an answer.

"How thoughtful! Look! Someone has even furnished us with a proper cake knife. Let's do this right, Jean-Michel. Come here. I'll put my hand on yours and we'll do the honors on the first piece. Wow! It's a white cake with a raspberry filling and a buttercream icing. It's the perfect wedding cake. Here. Take a bite. Is it as good as it looks? Give me a bite. Mmm! That is delicious cake! I'm really starved and I'll bet you are too. Here, unzip me. I don't want to spill anything on this dress. I'm going to have to wear it to Foster's birthday party."

Amy walked over to Jean-Michel and turned her back to him. He unzipped her dress and then unhooked her bra. As her clothes fell softly on the carpet, she leaned back against him. With her head on his shoulder, his hands began to move over her body and desire overtook them. Food was no longer important.

"It really was the most perfect wedding and most perfect honeymoon ever," Amy declared, as she and Jean-Michel examined the pictures assembled on the dining room table.

"And the wedding celebration is still going on. We went to all those parties in Charleston. Everyone was so surprised when we made those phone calls from the ship. Carter and Jack met us in Jacksonville and drove us to Savannah, where Anne had arranged a cookout on the beach at Tybee Island. It was the first time you ever tried to pick a crab. You should have seen your face when you looked at all those hard-boiled crabs and ears of corn! Here's a picture of me trying to teach you. I've always been a pretty good crab picker!" she exclaimed.

"I have to admit it's a talent I didn't know you had."

"I told you that a long time ago. I also know how to tong oysters and dig for clams. We'll have to do that another time. Let's see. From there, we all went to Charleston and you met everyone I've ever known. Didn't you just love my carriage house? Here we are in front of it. You can see why I gave the big house to Mary E. and Mark, but kept the carriage house for Jack, and we can use it whenever we're in Charleston. He wanted the hunting cabin and all the land that goes with it, so it was a fair deal for the kids."

Amy picked up another picture on the other side of the table.

"Look! Here's one of me on top of that elephant! Only Dory would theme Foster's birthday party as a three-ring circus, complete with animals and clowns. I wonder if Mireille has ever thought of a circus for one of her Bastille Day extravaganzas. Oh, look at this picture. It's a gathering of the entire Page family at Edward's. I wasn't too sure how John's brother and sister would take to the idea that I've married outside the fold, so to speak, but I actually think that the Pages are glad to be rid of me."

"Amy, what a thing to say! Your late husband's family couldn't have been more gracious. It was obvious that they are very fond of you."

"I know. And I'm fond of them too. Edward has really been a brick. It's just that I think I was somewhat of a problem. Not a problem, so much as a concern. Certainly, a complication. Edward and his wife tried hard to fix me up with different men, but they were all . . . well, they were all very nice, but I just knew them all too well, knew their first wives, knew their children, and they just weren't right. One or two were even gay and they turned out to be the ideal escorts."

Amy laughed.

"No problems with them! Then when I would go to Savannah to visit Anne, she would trot out all the eligible men she knew and it was just a repeat of Charleston. I really didn't want to be fixed up. I just wanted to be . . . I didn't know what. I guess in retrospect I wanted to be me and not be put in a mold and go on doing the same thing I'd been doing for decades."

"So you came to Paris and there I was, your prince charming."

"Yes, that's it exactly! You saved me from all that! Now get serious and help me decide which pictures to put in the book. You know that this album will be the feature at one of Caroline's teas, and we'll have to take it to Bourdonville for your mother to see. Damn! I'm going to have to wear that blue dress there too, aren't I? It's not enough that I wore it in Savannah and again in Charleston, I'm going to have to wear it to the next party here in the Hôtel de Rochefort."

"But, Amy, it's a beautiful dress."

"I know. I did get something really fabulous for the party Sylvestre is giving next month."

"Who is this?" Jean-Michel asked, as he picked up a photo.

"How in the world did this picture get in with our wedding trip? You know who it is. It's Florian Renan. He's going to be in the first play performed at the Ile Theater this summer. Something about a Bedouin and goats. He's in costume. Maybe he's a goatherd. I don't remember the role, but he called one day and asked me if I minded taking some pictures so he could decide on the look he was trying to achieve. I took quite a few pictures with his Polaroid."

"But this photo wasn't taken with a Polaroid."

"I see that. No, it wasn't. Oh, I know. I was experimenting with my new cell phone camera. That's the only one that turned out. Actually, it's fun to have a camera on a cell phone. I've started taking pictures all around the Ile and most people have no idea that they are being photographed. I'll bet undercover policemen and spies love those gadgets."

"Yes, I'm sure they do, Amy."

It would be useless to tell her that technology had such miniaturized cameras that they could place them undetected in buttons, earrings, cuff links, even rings.

"Tell me, you didn't by chance take some pictures with your cell phone in the café on Friday, did you?"

"Of course I did. I told you. I decided to write an article on cafés, so while I was sitting there, making detailed notes as to what the interior of a café is really like, I took several pictures. I'd forgotten all about them."

"I'd like to see them, if I may."

"I don't know why, but I'll go get my cell phone for you. Honestly, Jean-Michel, you surely don't think I photographed the murderer," Amy humphed as she left the dining room.

It was possible, Jean-Michel thought. It would not be the first time that Amy was involved by chance in the solution of a major crime. It had happened before and it could happen again. Maybe her photos would reveal a clue.

V

The pictures on Amy's cell phone turned out to be useless to the investigation.

Jean-Michel spread them out on his large desk in front of the window of his new office in Amy's former studio apartment on the Quai de Béthune. He saw that he could easily discount half of them. He smiled at the shots of different doorways along the quays, probably places where famous people once lived. He chuckled over two of the displays in the cheese shop, three from inside the wine shop, one of people lined up at the take-out window of the Berthillon ice cream store, a curious one of just a crate of oranges that she must have taken at the grocery store on the Rue des Deux-Ponts. She had said that she had been practicing with the new cell phone and enjoyed taking pictures in secret. Four photos from one of Caroline's teas made him laugh out loud. Amy as an undercover spy had caught Caroline, Agnès, Charles, and Julien completely off guard.

He looked at her notes on the café and arranged them with the pictures she had taken. Side door. Side windows. Tables for six, tables for four, two tables for two. Display cabinet with pastries and shelves with extra glasses, tableware rolled up in paper napkins, stack of burgundy paper place mats, pile of burgundy cloth napkins. Condiment caddy. Door to the unisex toilet.

Three photos were quite lopsided, indicating that Amy had held the cell phone sideways several times and once upside-down in order to get a picture of the bar in the entry room. One picture of Corinne. Pictures of the committee huddled at the table in one corner of the room and engrossed in writing down for the police what they had witnessed. A shot of Mathieu giving directions. Several of the backs of policemen. Two of the ceiling.

There was even one of him, looking exasperated. It had been too much to hope that she would have gotten a picture of the missing waiter, Oscar.

In contrast to the pictures that were actually boring, Amy's notes describing the café were excellent. She had meticulously written down every detail. Her written statement had been somewhat terse and lacking in detail.

On the other hand, the interview that Mathieu conducted and had recorded by a police stenographer had been typical of her rambling style.

"You already know all this, but here goes. I am a U.S. citizen with a permanent resident visa. I reside in the Hôtel de Rochefort on the Quai de Bourbon. The name on my passport and on my carte d'identité is Amy Lucile Taylor Page, and I am married to Jean-Michel Jolivet You know him. In fact, you've known him longer than I have. Isn't that funny?"

She barely paused before continuing.

"Well, the committee to establish an interactive cultural center on the Ile Saint-Louis meets every Friday morning at 9:30 in the Café du Coin, and I am a member. The very first thing one does at the café is give the waiter an order. I usually get a grand café crème. All committee members order coffee of some sort, and a few add juice and croissants or petits pains or tartines. There is no assigned order of seating. This morning, I happened to sit directly across from the general. Jammet had suggested that he sit in the middle, but the general said that he really preferred to be at the head. He chairs the meetings and they always begin with reports. I remember clearly that the lawyer, Madame Gallifet, was giving a report on health regulations for canteens, and I really wasn't interested. Please, don't tell her I wasn't paying attention. I was doodling. Well, not exactly. I was thinking about what to take to Margot when I visited her in the hospital that afternoon. I'd already taken her a really beautiful bed jacket, flowers, and some magazines. She's not supposed to have chocolates. I thought maybe a small spa basket with lavender soap. She loves lavender."

Jean-Michel smiled as he imagined Mathieu trying to be patient. She invariably rambled and digressed when she was interviewed. She gave more details than necessary and inadvertently skipped one or two salient ones. He continued listening to her testimony.

"The next thing I knew was that Pierre Richard was shouting that the general was face down on his croissant. I looked at him and he was! Immediately, Marcel de Montvalont and Félix Dubois jumped up, shouting that he must have had a heart attack. They rushed over to him, picked him up, and stretched him out on the floor. I was right there. The general was drooling a lot, twitching around, gasping for breath, and then he started to turn pink. Actually, a bright cherry red! I was next to him and I could see his skin turn red. Tristan—oops. I should say Father Moreau—yelled that Marcel and Félix should not try CPR because he didn't think the general had had a coronary. He was more likely poisoned. Poisoned by cyanide because the general had turned bright pink and that is a sign of cyanide poisoning. I'm really curious about that. In mystery novels, cyanide poisoning is always detected by the smell of bitter almonds. I never read about the skin turning pink."

"In lots of cases," Mathieu confided, "there is no bitter almond odor. If the skin turns bright pink, it is definitely a case of cyanide poison, although we in the police always wait for the toxicology report to be certain. Please continue."

"That's it. It was really all very confusing because everyone was talking at once and it happened very fast. Maybe in just two minutes. We were all stunned. Someone yelled in the background—Madame Gallifet, maybe Philippe Jammet, I don't really know who—to call the Préfecture and let them know that there had been a murder in the café. Anyway someone said that. I know that Madame Gallifet, she's a lawyer, said that no one was to move because it was a crime scene and we would just have to sit there and wait for the police."

Amy let out a sigh and realized she was expected to continue.

"The next thing that happened was really dreadful. All of a sudden, the general's body functions were released. I was right there, next to the general. You just can't imagine how horrible it was. If I were the fainting type, I would have fainted. Or swooned like the heroines do in Victorian novels."

"What happened next?" Mathieu asked. It was clear to Jean-Michel that Mathieu was exasperated.

"Next? Well, you arrived and we all had to keep on sitting there, next to the dead man and those awful odors until the physician on the ambulance said he was indeed dead and it looked like poison to him. Someone threw a sheet over the general. Finally the police made everyone on the committee move to another table. And we sat there for a very long time. Jean-Michel arrived and told all the other patrons they could leave the café after giving their statements, but we on the committee had to march to the Préfecture. And here I am. I've already given you a written statement. I didn't see anyone put cyanide in the general's coffee or on his croissant."

Under further questioning, Amy swore that she hadn't had a good look at the waiter at all because her back was to the main part of the café. The general had been sitting with his back to the wall and she was directly across from him. She hadn't really looked at the waiter at all when he took their orders. She thought he was very tall, but then she was seated and people look tall when they're standing and one is seated.

Jean-Michel marveled at Mathieu's patience, but then both of them had interviewed Amy on previous occasions and knew that she sidetracked easily and often provided irrelevant information.

Oscar's hair color? A very pale blonde, that she remembered. Sort of like a blonde who is graying. That color. A yellowish white. Sort of sandy, she supposed. His hair was thin, she remembered that. Oh, a tattoo on his hand. Left hand. It was a number. Yes, a number. A Roman numeral. IX. It was at the base of his thumb. He was standing at the end of the table, between her and the general, taking orders. He wrote on the order pad with his right hand and held the pad with his left. She looked up and noticed the tattoo, but when he served them, he didn't have the tattoo. It had disappeared.

"Disappeared?" Mathieu asked.

"Yes, gone. It wasn't there. I know it was there when he took the orders, but I didn't see it when he brought them. You know that there are all sorts of fake tattoos that either peel off or wash off. He probably had one of those, although personally I think he was a bit old to be playing around with fake tattoos."

"When the waiter served you and you noticed that the tattoo had vanished, was it because it had a Band-Aid over it or had it truly disappeared?"

"I don't know. I didn't look that closely. It was there and then it wasn't. Why, do you think it's important? I don't see how a fake tattoo could be a clue."

"Every piece of information helps," Mathieu commented. "Was there anything else? Anything at all out of the ordinary? Anything that didn't happen every time the committee met in the café?"

Amy sighed.

"Well, the only little thing I can think of is that business of the artificial sweetener. The general and I were the last two committee members to arrive. That's why we were on the end. We ran into each other on the Rue Jean du Bellay and walked together to the café. He told me that his doctor wanted him to lose a few pounds, so he was going to give up sugar in café au lait, order just one croissant, and not put any marmalade on it either. I told him that was a good way to start. Sometimes it's really just the little things in one's diet that add up to additional pounds. I suggested that he buy diet drinks and just have dessert twice a week as a reward instead of every day. I also told him about—"

"Please, I'd like you to go back to the artificial sweetener in the general's coffee. How did he get it? Is it usually on the café tables in the morning?"

Even though Mathieu and Jean-Michel already knew the answer to the question, they wanted to hear Amy's version.

"No, it's never there. Corinne really doesn't approve of substitute things. I'm surprised she serves decaf and Diet Cokes, but then she depends on tourists a lot. I've never seen packets of artificial sweetener on the table. I guess one has to make a special request."

"Did the general make such a request?"

"Yes, he did. He told Corinne when we went in the café and he said something about his new diet to the committee as a whole. Come to think of it, he didn't mention it to the waiter when he gave him his order. I guess he thought that Corinne would automatically take care of it. I guess she forgot because there were a lot of men standing at the bar when we went in."

"So how did he get the sweetener?"

"You know how. That odd man who owns the map shop gave him a small white dish with sugar packets. White for real sugar, yellow for artificial. He was seated at the table across from us. Usually it's two small tables pushed together for four persons, but because the committee needed a table for ten, we took two four-person tables to make a longer one and then someone took one of the two-person tables from the map man's table, leaving him at a two-person table. Here, I'll give you a diagram:

X X X X A
X X X X G Z

See? I am A, Amy, G is the general, and the other committee members are X and the map man is Z. I don't know why Z; it just popped in my mind. Anyway, he's in the corner across from the general. He always sits there, with his back against the wall and his foot propped up on a chair. I can tell you that he reads several different newspapers, and not just in French."

Mathieu prodded.

"Just how did he give the general the sweetener? Did you actually see him give the dish with the sweetener in it?"

"Yes. I was facing the general, who complained that he needed sweetener in his coffee. The map man must have overheard him. He was already standing up and folding his newspapers. He picked up the dish from his table and said something like, '*Pardon, Monsieur*, I couldn't help but overhear. I didn't use any sweeteners this morning.' And he left. I remember that there were exactly just two yellow packets of sweetener in the dish. The general smiled, muttered thank you, opened both packets, and stirred them into his coffee."

Jean-Michel reshuffled the papers on his desk. No matter how many times he reviewed Amy's written statement, looked at her pictures, studied the crude diagram, went through the police stenographer's transcript of the official interview with her, and listened to the recording of her testimony, he was increasingly convinced that there was a vital clue that kept slipping through his fingers. He reread all the statements and interview transcripts.

One of the problems was that the case had too many credible witnesses. What was more frustrating was that all the witness accounts agreed, and that was highly unusual. The witnesses may have used different words, but basically they all said the same thing.

He had never before encountered a case with so many witnesses of such impeccable backgrounds. The two priests had sat across from each other at the far end next to the window. The new priest, Father Camille Maréchal, had his back to the wall, so it was Father Tristan Moreau who had a good view of the general; his position enabled him to recognize immediately the change of color in the general and assert that the general was a victim of cyanide poison. Recognizing the probability of cyanide prevented another death from mouth-to-mouth resuscitation.

Next to Father Moreau was Pierre Richard, the retired concierge, whose testimony repeated almost word for word Father Moreau's, with one addition. He thought that the new waiter was Alsatian. Then came Marcel de Montvalont and Félix Dubois, who were also across from the general and saw him choke and convulse. It was natural that they rushed to his aid. Amy was on the end.

Next to the general was Natalie Darcet, the historian and curator, who had not really seen anything until the general collapsed. She was apparently the one who had screamed. Her testimony was useless. She saw nothing. She had a terrible migraine and really hadn't paid much attention to the proceedings. She had asked Amy for some aspirin and had been waiting for it to take effect. She didn't remember the waiter at all because she had ordered nothing, having brought with her a thermos of vegetable bouillon,

On the other side of Natalie Darcet was Philippe Jammet, who was in the middle seat that morning. There was no regular seating arrangement, although he had tried to convince the general to sit in the middle instead of at the end. He was aware that the usual waiter, Fernand, was not there. The substitute man, who said his name was Oscar, seemed quite professional and efficient. Between him and the new priest was the actor Bernard Gourdon, who echoed Pierre Richard's observation that the new waiter seemed to be Alsatian.

All the patrons in the café, the committee members, and the café owner described the waiter as tall, medium frame, light hair (white, pale blonde, sandy), no scars. No one recalled his eye color. Only Amy thought she had seen a tattoo on his left hand, but then she said it had disappeared. Mathieu said there was no tattoo, that what Amy thought she saw as a tattoo, the Roman numeral IX, was in reality something the waiter had jotted on his hand as a reminder and had then washed it off.

There was no getting around it. The general was poisoned by accident and the intended target had to have been François Lacour. The packets of sweetener were on his table. He was the only one who habitually used artificial sugar. In her statement, Corinne swore that every Tuesday and Friday morning, she put a small sign that read 'reserved' and a small dish with two yellow packets of sweetener on that table for him. It was an unvarying routine. She had been surprised that he had picked up a small dish of sugar cubes from the bar on his way to his table. No, she hadn't known that he had ordered a pot of tea instead of his usual coffee.

Mathieu had agreed with Jean-Michel. Oscar would have thought that there would be both a dish of artificial sweetener packets and one of sugar cubes on Lacour's table. He wouldn't have known that usually there was no sugar there. Therefore, to Oscar, it wouldn't have mattered if Lacour ordered coffee or tea. He wouldn't have realized that Lacour had completely changed his order from coffee with sweetener to tea with sugar.

Jean-Michel looked at the dossier on General Reboursier. There was nothing in his background to indicate that he had made dangerous enemies. He had been primarily a desk general, who taught military history at Saint-Cyr. At his death, he had been working on a biography of Blaise de Montluc, who was the primary army general during the Italian Wars when King François I was taken prisoner. In contrast, as Jean-Michel knew all too well, there was every reason for Lacour to be targeted. The problem was by whom? Lacour had crossed and double-crossed several powerful organizations. While he might have been officially out of action for some years, he was probably involved somewhere with a scheme that was perceived as a major threat by someone very powerful.

A tapping on the window interrupted his thoughts. He turned around and saw that François Lacour was outside and had come to pay him a visit. He was expecting him. Lacour had given him enough time to talk with Pip, meet with the Archangels, study all the reports from the various witnesses, revisit the crime scene and establish who had been sitting where, who did what and when and why, and last, but not least, review his dossier. Their meeting would be like an intricate ballet, each following a well-choreographed set of steps. There would be no major surprises, but Jean-Michel anticipated that Lacour would nudge him in a new direction. In return, Jean-Michel would provide him with whatever document, information, or resource he wanted. Both sides would profit. Such had been the nature of their relationship for years. It was how they did business.

VI

Jean-Michel stood up and stretched. It had been a profitable meeting with Lacour, but it had also been a demanding one, and Jean-Michel wasn't sure he could deliver what was requested. Only Lacour knew about the secret safe that was in the corner of the fireplace mantling in his study in the Hôtel de Rochefort and now the new one that the two of them had created in the molding of the kitchen doorway in the studio. They had installed them together, and they alone knew not only the locations, but also the combinations. A third one was in a bank in Basil, Switzerland, along with a secret bank account to which only the two of them had access.

Their association dated back decades. They were the same age, give or take a few months, and they were related by family.

Jean-Michel recalled clearly the first day they had met. A chilly, rainy, foggy London day in late September. They had literally collided at the hospital door and both had uttered at the same time, "Pardon, Monsieur." Both had been surprised to encounter a French-speaking person. They had immediately shaken hands and fallen into a conversation. It turned out that they were at the hospital to meet a friend who worked there and both were early, so they quite naturally went to the hospital cafeteria for a cup of coffee, laughing in their shared disdain of the English love of a *cuppa*, meaning tea.

In an even more remarkable coincidence, it turned out that the two of them were meeting the same people: Jean-Michel's sister Emilie and Lacour's cousin, Joseph Longuet. Lacour had explained that their grandmothers had been sisters. Both Emilie and Joseph were medical interns who had opted to spend one term in London in a special program in neo-natal oncology. They had quickly connected because of the language factor, just as Jean-Michel and François Lacour had so quickly hit it off.

The four of them met fairly often in the same quiet pub where they were able to commandeer a table in an alcove and spend the evening undisturbed, speaking French. Jean-Michel's wife, Pamela, had joined them on occasion, but she really didn't enjoy speaking French. However, she didn't object to Jean-Michel's evenings out with the group.

Soon it became obvious to Jean-Michel that his sister Emilie was in love with both men and that both men were in love with her. In a way, he had gotten a kick out of his brilliant sister's double courtship. She had been so single-minded in her pursuit of a medical degree that she had given up the dating game, much to her parents' despair. While her mother in particular didn't understand why she couldn't be content with being a nurse, the family supported her medical ambition and aspirations whole-heartedly.

Only Jean-Michel knew that her ultimate goal was to take over the hospital in their hometown, Bourdonville, and turn it into a first-class facility. Rightly or wrongly, she was convinced that her best friend had died at age fifteen because the local hospital didn't have the appropriate resources.

Around Christmas, Lacour disappeared. Jean-Michel suspected that he was involved somehow with British Intelligence. He later learned that he had been trained in covert operations by the Canadian government. When his brother died of a drug overdose, his cover was blown and he quickly relocated to London. He immediately landed a job as a government translator, a position that Jean-Michel thought at the time was a cover for something clandestine.

Lacour had no sooner left London than Emilie told Jean-Michel that she was pregnant and asked him if he and Pamela would go with her and Joseph Longuet to Gretna Green to act as witnesses to their marriage. Jean-Michel immediately agreed, knowing that his presence at the elopement would somehow cushion their parents' disappointment that their eldest daughter had married someone they didn't know and that there would be no elegant wedding extravaganza in Bourdonville. That responsibility would now pass to his sister Denise.

Shaking his head, Jean-Michel started to laugh.

How Amy would love to know the real details of his relationship with the man she considered "really odd, even weird, certainly out of place on the Ile." Of course, Amy, his aunt Caroline, and her coterie had their own definition of who was appropriate, but he'd never figured out what the criteria were, much less how this one was "in," that one was "acceptable," but another was "one of those."

The group itself was certainly eclectic in terms of social background, economic status, educational level, professional training, artistic talent, nationality, personal philosophy, political view, cultural attitude, even sexual preference. Somehow the term *snob* didn't apply to them because of the make-up of the group: a gay art critic, a free-thinking parish priest, a gossipy antique dealer, an urbane industrial tycoon, an unattractive dwarf who ran a three-star hotel, an elegant recluse, a highly self-disciplined somewhat aloof retired history professor, and a mercurial American food writer. But that was just the inner core of the group, for also "in" were a flashy theater director, a fussy retired concierge, a rather flighty florist, a grim-faced popular seamstress, and—

Jean-Michel paused.

"*Mon Dieu!*" he almost shouted, "Amy is right in her corkscrew thinking when she says in all seriousness that everyone who isn't 'out' is 'in,' that is, everyone fits in except the ones who don't and the few whom no one seems to know, and so they aren't in or out because they just are."

When he asked her to explain how one could be neither in nor out, she had scowled and then spoken to him as though he were a recalcitrant child.

"Really, Jean-Michel. You do know. They are just like Sartrian mushrooms: they are, they exist, nothing else. I mean they breathe and move, like a bunch of carrots that poke their heads above ground but don't do anything about tending the garden they're in. They simply don't think. They're really dull. They aren't anymore interesting than a . . . an old radish or turnip, so they are 'out.' Others just blend into the woodwork, so to speak. I mean they simply are, like park benches. We see them, we know they are around, we expect to see them, you might say we take them for granted, but for some reason we don't know them. Oh, enough of this discussion, Jean-Michel. It makes me sound like a nitwit and a persnickety snob, and you know perfectly well that I'm not."

Apparently, in the eyes of the Ile inner circle, Lacour was an "out," and the rest of the gang of four was simply taken for granted as part of the Ile population, which was, of course, the way he and the Archangels wanted them.

The worst scenario would be for any one of his aunt's circle to become curious about the four retired spies. Lacour had capitalized on his difference and intentionally become an "out," but an acceptable "out" because he ran his business in what the Ile "ins" considered a non-business-like manner, but one that caused no problems, so in a sense his shop-keeping fit in with the mythology of the Ile.

By avoiding attention, Lacour practiced the unspoken motto of the Ile. Besides, his wife doctored dolls and, according to the Ile, that meant that they were bound to be "good people." One couldn't think otherwise of people who liked maps and dolls.

The self-appointed guardians of Ile behavior and attitudes had quite naturally noted the dog walker and the chess master, but neither piqued their curiosity. The dog walker had quickly become part of the daily routine, an old radish in Amy parlance. The chess master who played and taught chess elsewhere in Paris might have generated some curiosity, but his presence only served to reinforce a long-held view that there was the Ile, where one lived, and there was Paris, where one worked. By living in two known worlds and having the added stature of belonging to the arcane world of chess, he was automatically an acceptable "out."

On the other hand, the fisherman hadn't been noticed by either Caroline's group or by the police, whose headquarters were next door on the Ile de la Cité. It was as though he had become one more park bench, dismissed as a subject of interest and relegated to being an object of no import. He was just part of the landscape. If one could fool the hens who ruled the roost of the Ile, then the gang of four had indeed found a safe refuge from their former worlds.

Or were they using this new planet as a base of operations for . . . what? Why the attack on Lacour? Why the so-called textbook, well-scripted behavior with the Archangels? Had the recent arrival of the Vietnamese Paul Champion been somehow arranged by Lacour, Tiago Luiz, and Jacob Poncet? Had Lacour and Luiz earlier convinced Poncet to move to the Ile? Even earlier, had Lacour chosen the Ile because Luiz was already there?

Or had the gang of four planned all along to wind up on the Ile because they knew that Jean-Michel was there? Was it possible that a fifth one was on the way or was the group now complete? Or would just those four suffice for whatever game they were playing?

Had they in turn kept any contacts from their former lives as undercover agents? If they were the nucleus of a group in charge of a certain project, it stood to reason that they had a considerable network at their disposal, a stateless network undefined by specific agency or known organization. If so, then there wouldn't be any paper trail whatsoever, no proof of prior or present existence, no files or even database for Pascal Machaut to access. Everything would have been wiped clean.

Everything? Jean-Michel wondered. Maybe not.

Jean-Michel quickly picked up his phone and called Pascal. "*Allô, mon vieux.* Here's what I want you to try. Go back into the dossiers of our gang of four and see if you can find any trace of their having been in contact in their previous lives. *Oui, oui, d'accord, je comprends,* I know you've already done it, but you need to get back into their government files, their pasts, find out what operations might have created opportunities for communication. Fortunately, all governments do keep complete records. *Oui,* go back to the beginnings, records that everyone has forgotten exist. While agencies might create all sorts of codes to hide the names of those involved, they never hide well the contacts and the operation itself. Every erasure leaves a trace of some sort and all webs can be untangled. It's a matter of finding the right blank space or thread. Take a new look at what they did, where they did it, and when. In particular, look for any connection with phytomedicine . . . p, h, y, t, o, medicine. Got it? Also, look for anything connected with bioprospecting. Yes, you heard me correctly. And instead of starting with Lacour and coming forward in time, go backward and start with Paul Champion. His real name is Boc-Ninh and Lacour's was originally LaFlèche."

Jean-Michel smiled. Pascal's computer expertise was invaluable. He had never failed to hack his way through every firewall encountered to date without leaving a trace of his ever having been there. The world of technology had radically changed the world of espionage.

"*Comment?* Good idea! I'll call Nikki to contact you with what he has. I had forgotten that Nikki had set up some programs for Lacour before he left the sanitarium outside Besançon. You're right. If you can set up a grid with those programs and the dates that our gang of four members were in a given place, even if on different jobs, then we just might come up with the lead we need. It's quite clear that Lacour was the target of the cyanide attack. It's also obvious that whatever game he's playing includes the other three members of the gang of four, which in an of itself would be all right, but, Pascal, in the words of my aunt Caroline, involving the Ile St-Louis is simply not acceptable. *Voilà.*"

Jean-Michel then called Nikki Raymonnet with his request. He then punched in his uncle Roger's number and was visibly relieved that his uncle Roger promptly answered. As Jean-Michel had predicted, yes, he would be delighted to take Amy to Lacour's map shop. What? *Mais si.* An old doll to take for the wife to repair. Yes, a very old one would be best, but certainly any doll would do. Yes, that was better. A group of dolls dressed in clothing through the centuries. As luck would have it, Roger just happened to know the right person to design the outfits and use the appropriate fabrics. His friend Patrice had retired just last year from the *Dernier Cri* House of Fashion and was beginning to get a bit bored. Well, Roger went on, it was really the break-up with Gilbert that was the problem.

Aware that his uncle was getting ready to launch into the details of the Patrice-Gilbert affair, Jean-Michel interrupted him: "I'm sorry that I don't have time for a long chat, but I'm working on the investigation into the general's death and this request is part of it. I need your help."

Jean-Michel smiled, as Roger took the bait. He could envision his uncle preening at the thought of being given an official mission.

"You must promise to be discreet. You cannot tell anyone, not Amy, not Alain, and most certainly not Caroline. It's not just that I want Amy to have a reason to go to that shop, but you too. I want you to look at maps. Ask for some early ones of the Ile. Lacour knows that you're on the committee, so it will seem completely natural if you ask to see early ones of the Ile. And who knows? You just might find one."

Roger was so flattered to be given what he called a mission that he readily agreed to serve as Amy's escort and act as Jean-Michel's personal undercover agent. Once before he had been a consultant and had actually been invaluable to the solution of a very difficult case.

"But, Jean-Michel, I really think that all the early maps of the Ile were located a long time ago. I might find a rare decent copy of an original, but that's about it. If I'm going to be a proper agent, I need a proper reason. What am I really looking for? I doubt that it's something to do with the Ile. You can't possibly want to know just what kinds of maps Lacour has. I realize that many old maps are distinctive for the artwork on them, but that's not my field."

"Of course, you're right, *mon oncle*. I'm looking for geographical maps of mountainous areas, specifically the Andes and the Urals, as well as the Himalayas. You know, the sort of thing done by the first explorers of those regions."

"You're not making a whole lot of sense, Jean-Michel. Level with me. Why mountains? Surely not for the geography itself. I think they're all done and all known. That won't work. Are you talking about animals that live in those regions? Or maybe the vegetation?

"The plants, Roger. Surely, there are maps that tell one how to find . . . I don't know . . . Venus fly traps and that sort of exotic plant."

"Aha! Flora! Botany! There are collectors who are passionate about illustrations of all sorts of plants, especially the leaves, and even better the fossils of leaves. Accurate drawings of specimens are always in demand. In fact, I just heard from a gallery owner in Nassau about his idea to do a showing on leaves. Yes, just leaves. He's really an odd character. I met him at an unusual show in Tenerife—"

Jean-Michel groaned inwardly and quickly interrupted what he knew would be a long-winded description of the gallery owner and the show in the Canary Islands.

"Leaves, Roger? That sounds a bit far-fetched to me."

"No, no. Doing just leaves can be quite legitimate. I mean, I wouldn't do anything like that, but think about it. Leaves are everywhere in the broader world of art and an intricate part of the human creative endeavor. We find them in prominent position in prints, wallpaper, rugs, fabric, still life paintings, scrollwork, china patterns, embroidery, special cheese plates, wooden trays, and serving dishes. Depicting leaves in art is as old as man."

Roger was on a roll and Jean-Michel knew there was no way to stop him now.

"There's primitive art and tribal carvings, Arabic decoration with all those vines, laurel wreaths of Greece and Rome, tropical place mats, and today leaves are quite popular in sponge painting and salad bowls. Then there's cooking and all those herbs. Remember, Jean-Michel, the fig leaf is of prime importance in portraying the expulsion of Adam and Eve from the Garden of Eden. In fact, when one looks at all those paintings and sculptures, the thing one really notices is the position of the fig leaf. Why, one could do a showing of the fig leaf in art through the ages!"

Jean-Michel laughed.

"I'm convinced. Would someone who is in the map business like Lacour have that sort of thing?"

"Oh, I doubt if he has any botanical artwork, but I should think he might have an early map with some interesting leaves or even an accompanying botanical chart. If he doesn't have any on the premises, I'll see if he would agree to locate some for me. By the way, I do happen to know someone who would buy a really old botanical chart. I think you may have met him—"

Again, Jean-Michel interrupted.

"I knew you were the right one to send on a scouting foray into that shop. Here's your cover. At one of Caroline's teas, Amy happened to mention the fact that she was going to take an old or broken doll there and you decided to go along for the Ile and to see if by chance he had anything for that leaf show in Nassau."

Jean-Michel smiled. Roger's babble and knowledge along with Amy's chatter would get a rise out of Lacour.

"Maybe you'll even get a nice commission out of this adventure."

"Well, it'll certainly give me reason to visit Lacour's shop. But, tell me, Jean-Michel, if I happen to run across a map appropriate for the Ile museum, will you pay for it? As a donation, of course."

Jean-Michel chuckled. Before he hung up, he reminded Roger of the need for discretion. He didn't tell him that he expected Lacour to see through Roger's ruse, but not Amy's. How else was Jean-Michel going to force Lacour to take the next step in whatever game he was playing?

There were two more phone calls to make before going home to Amy. In a sense, he really didn't want to involve her and his uncle, but he also knew that they would enjoy playing their respective roles. After all, both were skilled snoops and indulged in similar corkscrew thinking, going from point A to point F with no regard for points B, C, D, and E and then leaping to N, by way of Q and T. Maybe it was a shared penchant for art, as well as polished social skills that enabled them to adapt quickly to any situation and have instant meaningful conversations with strangers. It was very rare that either of them was at a loss for words.

Lacour wouldn't know what hit him when those two appeared in his shop, but their visit would put him on guard. And, of course, the map shop would then become a subject of conversation among his aunt Caroline's cackling hens and the focal point of discussion at her teas. The Archangels would have no problem with a team of watchers, for the map shop was about to become popular. Jean-Michel was certain that several members of the committee, such as the retired concierge Pierre Richard, would visit the shop and actually buy items or request that Lacour find certain maps or charts. The gang of four would not be pleased with all the attention that the map shop was going to attract, but if they were going to play games, so was Jean-Michel.

"*Salut*, Serge," Jean-Michel said when his nephew answered his cell. "I need you in Paris. In fact, I need you here on a permanent basis. It's time for you to quit your job in Bourdonville and relocate to Paris. I'll explain when you are here. And, before you ask, yes, Justine too if she can work it out with Interpol. *A plus tard.*"

Jean-Michel stood up and walked over to the kitchen. He pressed on a section of the molding around the archway. The secret panel opened, revealing a small compartment. He picked up a small dark brown leather notebook and peeled back the cover to read a series of numbers. Back at his desk, he unlocked the bottom drawer and took out a cell phone. The number he dialed was routed through several servers before he was finally connected to a small convent high up in the Alps in the German part of Switzerland. After identifying himself to the abbess on the other end, he was given another phone number. "Time to pay the piper," he muttered under his breath. Soon he heard the raspy voice of the man known to Jean-Michel and François Lacour as the Pirate. "*Oui, c'est moi.* Here's the situation . . ."

VII

"Which one would you pick, Jean-Michel?"

He looked at the pile of dolls that covered Amy's bed in the blue and white Provençal suite at the end of the apartment. He'd had no idea there were so many kinds of dolls. Big ones, small ones, even tiny ones. Some were babies, others were brides. He saw dolls that represented historical figures, a few old ones with porcelain faces, and even a couple of boys. Several were rag dolls, one looked as though it were made out of straw, three were obviously souvenirs from different countries, one was a witch, another a clown, and there was even one that he guessed was supposed to be an educational toy since it was anatomically correct with the skeletal system and internal organs visible.

"Where did they all come from?"

"That's not all, Jean-Michel. There are more. A whole lot more. They're just wonderful! Léon brought me all these boxes. See? I haven't yet opened them all. I'm really surprised."

"I thought you were just going to look around the Hôtel to see if there was one doll in a box somewhere from the days when there was a nursery and a large playroom on the fifth floor."

"That's right. And I did. Léon took me up there. Did you know that there are tons of boxes up there, marked *jouets, livres, jeux, chemins de fer, camions, casseroles, animaux, costumes, meubles,* not just *poupées*. Who knows what's packed away up there. Do you realize that I am forever uncovering rooms and things in this mansion? I'll bet some of those toys should be in museums. Just look at that copy of Marie-Antoinette. It's really perfect. And one of those baby dolls is life-size and dressed in someone's real clothes. There's a doll trunk full of doll clothes for a teenaged doll, sort of a precursor to Barbie. It even has a genuine mink coat, an umbrella that opens and closes, and a pair of real leather boots!"

Jean-Michel didn't quite know what to say. While he wasn't surprised to learn that the playroom had been carefully packed up in neatly labeled cartons, he never thought there were that many dolls. Unfortunately, all the dolls on the bed appeared to be in perfect condition and not in need of the services of a doll doctor. He leaned over and picked up one that was a sailor.

"I remember him, Amy. I don't know who he belonged to, but when I was here for my grandmother's funeral, Emilie and I spent most of the time in that suite that included the playroom. It was the first time I'd ever seen a boy doll. I was six years old and thought that dolls were strictly for girls."

"Isn't it silly how gender-specific the world was? Dolls for girls and trucks for boys. Cooking and sewing for girls; sawing and hammering for boys. Look at your uncle Victor with his trains, and his wife with her dollhouses, yet neither one thinks it odd that he makes doll-sized buildings for his trains and she rigs all sorts of lighting effects for her dollhouses. I once said that it was wonderful that their hobbies complimented each other. She could help Victor with his towns and he could help her with some of the more intricate technical projects. Oh, no, she said. Victor did his thing and she did hers. And that's why they work on different floors of the house! She had learned all she needed about electrifying her houses by reading a book."

Jean-Michel laughed.

"I don't doubt that she read a book, but what she didn't tell you is that her brother is an electrical engineer who probably wrote the book and who I'm sure continues to help her."

"I swear, living on the Ile Saint-Louis and meeting all the people connected to it is like peeling a whole mountain of onions. Layer after layer after layer. I don't see why she couldn't tell me the truth."

"Well, she did, Amy. I'm sure she read a book. Probably several. She just omitted the detail about her brother. It's important to Victor and Isabelle that you think that they pursue their beloved hobbies by themselves, without help from others. Here's a thought. You should try to involve them in the center. Their eye for detail and knowledge of display could be invaluable. Don't forget Isabelle's expertise in dollhouses. She could easily do the shadow boxes of various rooms that you think would be of interest. And, you mustn't forget either that their daughter-in-law is Marcel de Montvalont's sister and that Victor is a Rochefort."

"I'm going to have to set up a chart of who's related to whom. Everywhere I turn, I'm bumping into someone's relative. You know that I still can't get over the fact that Julien Turenne and Charles Pichon are half-brothers and that Marcel de Montvalont is your first cousin's wife's brother. Then there's the business of the old school tie. I mean Charles and your uncle Roger have been best friends since their earliest school days. It's far worse here than where I come from."

"I suppose so, but I really think that family ties and long-standing friendships from one's school days operate all over the world. You too have a wide network of relatives, friends, and acquaintances."

"That's true, Jean-Michel, but they're not all here within the three miles that define the Ile."

"Point taken, *chérie*. What about using Victor and Isabelle?"

"I'll see what I can do. You always have such good ideas. Do you think I could convince Isabelle to serve on the planning committee? We've lost the general and should replace him. I think that Philippe Jammet will take over as committee chair and maybe even be put on the permanent board. Isabelle would be an excellent addition and could probably be useful to Natalie Darcet, who needs direction as curator."

Jean-Michel was delighted. His cousins had been looking for a way to get their parents out of their mansion more often and involved in something other than model trains and dollhouses. Where Isabelle went, Victor would follow. But the request would have to come from Roger, not Amy and not Caroline. Roger would know how to flatter them and bully them at the same time. It would please everyone.

"Dolls aren't my only problem this evening, Jean-Michel. Just look at this."

Amy stooped down and lifted up the bed skirt. She pulled out two long black velvet cases.

"I'm sure you know what's in here. What possessed you, Caroline, and Roger, and for all I know everyone else in the greater Gramont-Rochefort-Jolivet tribe. It's really not me. And none of it will go with that blue dress I'm beginning to hate. Don't look at me that way. You know my dander is up. You knew how I'd feel. I'm really put out."

"No, I didn't think it would upset you. After all, you had no problem wearing any when you helped host that grand gallery opening for Roger. This reception is the same. Surely you understand that it's just as much about the Gramont-Rochefort family as it is about the two of us. The *soirée* has to be an event. And it will be. There hasn't been such an evening at the Hôtel de Rochefort since I don't know when. Certainly, not in my lifetime."

"It's not just these things. It's the whole affair. Caroline sent me a copy of the guest list with a note about my needing to learn names and who is who and who is related to who, excuse me, to whom. Whatever. Jean-Michel, there are over 1,000 names on that list. It's not a party. It's a spectacle. A light and sound show with food!"

"Come now, Amy. You do know most of the people on the list. By the way, it's not 1,000, but a little over 700. You've met most of them at various parties and events. It's just that you've never seen them all at the same time in the same place. It's to be an extravagant coming-out party for the entire family. Yes, you married me and that must be celebrated in high style. That's what the Gramont-Rochefort family does. High style in this case means the Hôtel de Rochefort itself with the hope that even Caroline will make an appearance after all these years. Ergo, the diamonds. They must be brought out of the vault. It's expected. And it's not showing off, Amy. There hasn't been a proper *soirée* held in the Hôtel de Rochefort in decades, since before World War II, actually."

"What about your parents?"

"No, not even when my parents were married because that took place so soon after the war. I've been told that their wedding was a rather modest affair. I'll see if there are some pictures of it in the library. I think my mother wore her mother's wedding gown. I'm sure it too has been packed away somewhere. The Rochefort family trait is to keep everything, Caroline and Roger being self-appointed guardians of it all. That's why so many toys are there and who knows what else. It's going to be maddening to the next generation, but then again it's why there's so much here that you enjoy, like the antique furniture, the china, the silver, and so on."

"And the diamonds."

"Always and above all, forever and a day, the diamonds."

"So I have to wear a tiara?"

"Think about Queen Elizabeth. She normally wears a diamond tiara instead of a jeweled crown to important events. This party that Caroline and Roger are hosting in our honor is for them a royal function, so all the tiaras and diamond whatnots must come out. Every woman who is a Gramont-Rochefort by birth or marriage will wear something from the collection: Isabelle because she's married to Victor, and of course their daughter Mireille, even if she is married to the comte d'Aubois. They're like a social i.d. bracelet, announcing that you belong. Think about it, Amy. It's a compliment. The Countess of Bourdonville is most fortunate to have married into the Gramont-Rochefort line."

Amy laughed. "I know when I'm defeated. You know I do love everyone I know in the Gramont-Rochefort family, so of course I'll do what pleases them. Still, my blue wedding dress isn't quite right. I need to wear something more dramatic. Not light blue, but maybe a royal blue. Hmm. Better yet, a bright peacock blue! Then I could wear the garnet one we bought for Sylvestre's ball next month, but I think a really rich blue would be best for that Rochefort tiara because there are dark blue sapphires among the diamonds."

"Thanks, Amy. And to show my appreciation of your understanding, I'll take you shopping tomorrow."

"Oh, yes, you will, so wipe that grin off your face. I think I'll buy the most expensive dress I can find! In the meantime, Jean-Michel, tell me why no one from your family in Bourdonville is coming. Each one of them is certainly as much a Gramont-Rochefort as you, and your mother is actually an Ile native. I know that we don't have enough spare rooms here, but we could accommodate some. Frankly, I'm surprised that no one is coming. "

"If one came, all would have to come, and the focal point would be on the Jolivet branch. All of this was decided by my mother, Caroline, and Roger. Of course, Victor in his role as the family doctor would approve anything of a social nature that involved Caroline, and then in his other role as the family genealogist agreed that the event should be a Gramont-Rochefort show. Think about it. If the Jolivet clan gathered here, their presence would detract from the Gramont-Rochefort luster. Despite my brothers's protests, each Jolivet has a title."

"And no Gramont-Rochefort has one, except by marriage. I keep forgetting the importance of titles."

"And rightly so, Amy, but you know they are important to Caroline and Roger, and they still play a significant role in certain circles. It's one thing for Sylvestre and me to find them a bit anachronistic in the modern world, but quite another for all those who don't. There's no getting around the fact that every Frenchman will go to the barricades in the name of *liberté, fraternité, égalité*, but in his heart he's still a royalist."

Amy laughed.

"I guess you're right. Even I know that the comte de Paris visits the Chapelle Expiatoire every January 21 to honor Louis XVI and Marie-Antoinette, who were thrown into a common grave nearby after they were guillotined. I went there once, and it's an exquisite small chapel with large statues of that famous pair, each one holding a last will and testament. In fact, it's really quite moving."

"I never knew you went there. See, even Americans have a soft spot for monarchs."

"Well, the popular press certainly never lets us forget that there are lots of royals still around in Britain, Monaco, Spain, The Netherlands and—"

"And where there are royals, there are titles, one of them now being yours."

"Oh, I get it. Your mother is also the Countess of Bourdonville because she married your father. You inherited his title, so when I married you, I too became the Countess of Bourdonville. There are two of us, but since this is a Gramont-Rochefort show, there can only be one of them and that one must be the newest one, as well as the one who lives in the Hôtel de Rochefort. Come to think of it, Jean-Michel, that makes perfect sense to me."

Jean-Michel didn't say anything at first, but he was relieved that Amy had worked it all out in her own fashion, as his sister Emilie had predicted she would. He realized that she would now enjoy her role at the *soirée* instead of just going through the motions.

"Now you know why no one from Bourdonville is coming and why no one from here, except Sylvestre, is going there for that one."

"Only Sylvestre? Of course! I should have guessed. Caroline would never consider having a big party without the marquis de Granvelle and your mother would never exclude your best friend."

"Besides, Amy, it's business. Sylvestre sits on the board of directors of the Jolivet winery."

"I give up! I'll wear the tiara, but with a new dress that in its own way makes a statement. And I'll work on memorizing that list of guests and learning who's related to whom and who's connected by business. I haven't had to do that in years."

"No, but you know how to play the game. Besides, it really will be the social event of the decade. You can trust Roger to have attended to every detail."

"With Mireille's help, no doubt."

"Ah, yes. After all, she's the acknowledged queen of the Parisian social scene. But don't overlook Julien's input either."

"And probably Sylvestre's."

"Just have a good time, Amy, because when all is said and done, this gala is all about family, and you are now one of us."

"Tell me, Jean-Michel, do you think that Caroline will actually make an appearance? I mean, she's been a recluse for years, keeping up with everything that's going on by way of her major entertainment room and her teas, to which only a select few are invited. It must be over fifty years since she's been at a public gathering of any sort. I know she's had a new dress made for the occasion."

"Honestly, I don't know. As physicians, both Victor and Laurent are concerned. Laurent told me that either way, the *soirée* will have a dramatic effect on her. It will fill her with deep regret if she doesn't go to her own party, to which all the who's who in Paris have been invited. But if she does attend, it could cause a serious psychological relapse. It is too bad Margot can't be at her side. Her growth problems and misshapen body have always helped stabilize Caroline's view of the world, and, honestly, Caroline's fragile psyche has always given Margot a certain determination to be in the public eye. They are very much alike. She runs a three-star hotel and her husband, JoJo, is one of the leading artists of our day, while Caroline runs the Ile and keeps her former fiancé at her side."

"And now Margot's in the hospital, meaning Caroline has lost her crutch. I know that they talk every day on the phone. When I go to see Margot tomorrow, I'll take her one of these dolls. I'll take her the clown to make her laugh. And that one too. I think it's supposed to be Little Red Riding Hood."

"Ah, Le Petit Chaperon Rouge," Jean-Michel translated. "Margot will be delighted, but maybe instead of the clown, you might consider the one over there on the pillow. I think she's Alice, you know, *Alice au pays des Merveilles*."

"Alice in Wonderland. How perfect!"

Sometimes Jean-Michel thought that Amy wandered in her own wonderland. She got enthusiastic about things that most people would consider frivolous, if not downright silly. Still, her penchant for the oddity or the offbeat and then making sense out of it was part of her charm. Today, however, she was deliberately avoiding discussion of the murder, and he needed to get her to refocus.

"I need to change the subject, Amy. I've been wondering if the general had a cell phone?"

"Of course, he did. Everyone does. Why?"

"Was his phone also a camera phone?

"Yes. He had just gotten it. In fact, his phone was a very lah-de-dah hi-tech one and did lots of things besides making phone calls and taking pictures. His son was in Tokyo on business and sent it to him. He was quite proud of it. I borrowed it . . . I borrowed it that morning."

"You borrowed the general's cell phone?"

"Well, not exactly. He knew I was secretly photographing the Ile. He caught me one day and thought it was such a great idea that he offered to lend me his new one because it has higher resolution or capability or . . . well, to tell the truth, I don't know what it has higher of, just that it has more of whatever than mine. The general's camera phone does the same things as mine, but better. No, that's not right. It does more things."

"But did he indeed lend it to you that morning?" Jean-Michel prodded, in an attempt to get a clear answer out of the digressive Amy.

"No. He offered it and I accepted. He didn't actually give it to me, but I have it."

"You have it?"

"Yes, I already told you that I sort of borrowed it. You know, by default."

"By default."

"That's right."

"Well, then, how did this 'by default' borrowing take place? How did it come into your possession?"

"Is that really important? You sound so very official."

"*Chérie*, it is very important, so please tell me how you wound up with it."

"When we got to the café, the general put his cell phone on the table and told me not to forget to take it. So I took it. I mean I did it after he died and the police ordered the whole committee to move to another corner in the café. I picked up my pen, my notepad, my cell phone, and quite naturally the general's. He didn't give it to me, but he had told me to take it, so I did."

Jean-Michel was dumbstruck. Lacour had told him to look for the general's cell phone because he thought it might have recorded an image of interest. The police had thoroughly searched the café for it and not found it. No one on the committee had mentioned it, not even Amy. Cell phones had become so commonplace and ordinary that even a new highly sophisticated and very expensive version didn't generate any interest, except to a former spy such as Lacour. He had immediately recognized that the general's new phone was a Lotus, which was the latest tool for both communication and information gathering on an individual level. Gabriel had ordered a dozen of them for the Archangels and Raphäel's team of watchers. Jean-Michel had gasped when he was told the cost.

According to Gabriel, the Lotus had several features that no other cell phone had. One was the retouch button; by setting it, the camera would take a picture every time the air around it was disrupted, by so little as a scrap of paper or so much as a person. Another feature was that it didn't have to be manned. A watcher could just place the cell phone in a given spot and it would photograph whoever passed by; the spotter could then pick it up and quickly transmit everything to another site. The photographic process was automatic and the relay of voice information was instant.

"Where is the general's cell phone, Amy?" Jean-Michel asked.

"I think I put it in my desk. Once I got home, I really didn't know what to do with it. It was such an upsetting day, and then there's this upcoming *soirée*, and despite all its features, it's still just a cell phone with a camera. Everyone has one. I didn't think the general's son would want it back. I really didn't know what to do with it. I guess I just kept it. I certainly didn't steal it, Jean-Michel. He did offer it to me."

"I know you didn't steal it. I'd like to see it. All of the general's effects are important. It's quite possible that a picture or message on it could relate to his murder."

"I see. I hadn't thought about that, but I can't imagine that the general was involved in anything . . . you know, anything untoward."

Jean-Michel grimaced. *Untoward*, indeed! At times, Amy sounded just like his aunt Caroline or whatever novel she was currently reading. He was so glad that they had visited both Charleston and Savannah. Spending time where she had spent most of her adult years had given him some insight into her former world. It wasn't so very different from the Ile Saint-Louis or Bourdonville for that matter. No wonder she had adapted so quickly. In retrospect, her bit about the upcoming *soirée* and the wearing of a diamond tiara had been more about him than about her. She simply wanted reassurance about her role in his world—or maybe it was assurance about his role in hers.

"I've got it," Amy announced when she returned to the bedroom. "When I picked it up, I made sure I clicked it off. I knew how because the general had shown me how to turn it on and off, and what buttons to press for talking, for text messaging, and that sort of thing."

"I didn't know you were up on text messaging, Amy."

"I'm not. It's just that I know where the button is. Let's see what's on here."

Before Jean-Michel could stop her, she pressed the camera button.

"That's just the ceiling. That one is the order pad from the bottom. You can see the pencil stub. That's the bottom of a plate. That's one of a cup of coffee. Good garden peas! That's one of me. I've got a mustache from my café crème. How embarrassing! We must erase it immediately."

"No, Amy. Officially, whatever is on here belongs to the investigation. Is this one the waiter?"

"Let me see. Yes. I mean it's quite out of proportion because it's looking up at him, but that's Oscar. Yes, it is. That's the waiter! Is he the murderer?"

"I don't know, but he is a person of interest. I need to take this over to the police station immediately. Do you feel like walking over there with me?"

"No, *chéri*. I've got to put all these dolls back. None of them will do for a visit to the doll doctor, so I'll have to rummage through those unopened boxes. Maybe I'll just yank a wig and an arm off one. I'm so grimy already, I might as well get on with it and get even grimier. Did you know that to see Madame Map Man or the doll doctor, you have to make an appointment? I mean it's just like going to a real doctor?"

"Her name is Maryse Lacour. I think she works several days a week at the Musée de la Poupée."

"I had forgotten that there was a doll museum in Paris. I've never been! We'll have to go one day."

"I've never been either, but right now, I need to get this camera cell phone to the police station and you need to do something with all these dolls."

"You're right. Then I think I'll take a nice bubble bath and just maybe you'll be back by then."

Jean-Michel smiled, as he left the apartment. Indeed, he'd be back by the time Amy was ready for her bubble bath.

Out on the Quai de Bourbon, he nodded at the old man walking his dog.

As soon as he crossed the footbridge to the Ile de la Cité, he turned left and walked around the back of Notre-Dame Cathedral to the small park where he sat down on a bench.

He grinned as he remembered sharing sandwiches with Amy early in their relationship. She had a way of drawing him into her world, bubble baths especially.

Caroline's *soirée* would be the event of events and quickly enter Ile lore. Amy would probably become a fan of wearing tiaras.

Maybe later after they had played and made love in the large tub under a blanket of bubbles, he would give her the tiara he had had made for the party his mother was planning in their honor in Bourdonville.

While the Jolivet jewels were not quite as lavish as the Gramont-Rochefort collection, they were still considerable, but the only really good tiara in the lot would be worn by his mother. His sister Denise had advised him to take several pieces from the collection to the jeweler and have him fashion a tiara of garnets, pearls, and diamonds.

He planned on surprising Amy with her very own tiara and ask her to wear it first to the ball that Sylvestre was hosting in their honor next month. He knew she was planning to wear an elegant designer garnet-colored gown to it. He'd gone shopping with her to find it and had already received the bill. He'd encourage her to wear it again in Bourdonville. He too was getting tired of the blue dress.

"*Allô*, François. You were right. I have the general's cell phone right here. Amy had it all along. I'm going to turn it over to the police, but, as promised, I'm going to send you a copy of everything on it. Where am I? On a bench in the John XXIII park with a pleasant view of the left bank. Perfect security."

Jean-Michel frowned as he listened to François Lacour identify the waiter.

"Oscar is definitely Reinhardt Bader. A very nasty guy and a highly skilled assassin. I thought I recognized him that morning in the café, but he could have been there legitimately. All spies eventually get tired of the game and retire. We have to go somewhere with a new identity. He could easily have decided to reinvent himself as an Alsatian and emigrate to Paris. He didn't give me any sign of recognition, and I pretended not to know him. It's what we do when we quit. We protect each other's new lifestyle. Luiz, Poncet, and I enjoy the cover you've given us, and now Champion has been added, but no more old spies, Jean-Michel. Four in one place is quite enough."

"But you do agree that you were the target?"

"Yes, that's obvious. But I don't know why there was a contract out on me after all these years."

"You're not really retired, François, are you?"

"Don't be such a skeptic. For all intents and purposes, I'm out of the hired spy business."

"You may no longer be on the books as an agent, but you are most certainly involved in something dangerous to what has to be a large and well-funded group. In fact, something so risky that someone you describe as nasty is after you."

"Well, maybe it's just an old spy who's bored with civilian life, so he decides to play the game just for the sake of playing the game and goes after another old spy because that's who he knows."

"That's bull and you know it, François."

"It has happened, Jean-Michel. Surely you remember that incident in Budapest between a former policeman from the old Estonian regime and the retired director of the Romanian secret service."

"That was a grudge match. It had nothing to do with one old spy going after another out of boredom."

"You never know, Jean-Michel. You have your Archangels and that other group you call the Relics: you, Pip, Sean, and my first handler, Brooks Fairfield. While Pip may enjoy growing roses, he's not completely on the shelf. You see, the problem with old spies is that they can never get totally out because they know too much. Not everything in this business is committed to paper, so memory has an important role. There are always those operations that are so secret and so . . . well, let's say unsavory for lack of a better word, that the top echelon itself is purposefully kept in the dark. The fewer in the know and the least possible amount of paper to destroy or lose, the safer the agent. In particular, a record of the failures, and we all have failures. It's just that some are fatal and others are not and those are the ones most in need of protection."

"So you're retired but still in the system?"

"No, not at all. It's just that I was also a handler as well as a field agent. Did you ever hear that American country western song about being your own grandma? Well, that describes me. And before you ask, that also describes what you and your people call the gang of four. It's why we meet periodically with Interpol. We're the good guys, Jean-Michel, the ones who wear oversized white Stetson hats and get on snow white horses to ride off into the purple sunset. Only the sun never finishes setting behind those distant mountains. There's always an operation somewhere that just might have come to our attention and so we are contacted and questioned. Just like you, *mon vieux.* You retired from IBS, but you're still tied to it. You're not any freer from that life than I am from my past. But we're the lucky ones. I have my maps and charts, you have your security business, I have Maryse, you have Amy, who, by the way, really does compliment you. I never thought you'd have enough sense to marry your counterpart, but you did and I congratulate you for it. Bravo, Jean-Michel!"

Jean-Michel laughed in spite of himself. Leave it to François Lacour to tell him exactly what he wanted to know without actually saying so. He had picked up the key words, the ones repeated twice or repeated via a definition: *old, spy/agent, handler/director, memory/paper/maps/charts, America/ west/mountains, snow, sunset, game/ride, white, shelf, failure, retired/past/tied, protect/IBS.* Now he needed time to work out the code within the code.

Lacour had once told him that no system was truly secure, therefore one had to use several at the same time. Yet, Jean-Michel knew from Nikki Raymonnet that Lacour's building on the Rue des Deux-Ponts was a veritable fortress. At his request, Pascal had once tried to hack into his computer and had failed to breach the last firewall. Lacour had then e-mailed Jean-Michel a picture of a braying donkey

Now, on a chilly day, he was sitting on an uncomfortable bench in a nearly deserted park, talking on an untraceable cell phone to a man on an equally untraceable cell phone in a building that could be entered only by a highly specialized team of commandos. So why the conversation in a double, if not triple, code?

"Thanks for your good wishes on my marriage and for the information on the waiter. I'll be sure to tell the police who he was and that maybe indeed he was after the general for a grievance of some sort that happened a long time ago. I don't know that Mathieu will buy it completely, but it will get the case off his desk and onto Legrand's at IBS since he's the one who deals with criminal cases that involve foreign nationals. In turn, Legrand will notify other EU agencies as well as Interpol. And I think that's where you want it, which is fine by me. He's not our primary concern. By the way, Amy will be coming by to see Maryse about dolls and Roger is going to accompany her. They're on the committee for the Ile center, so be at your charming best."

"I aim to serve, old timer. *Au revoir.*"

Jean-Michel shut the cell phone and stretched. Then he slowly got up, stretched again, took several deep breaths, and began to walk along the path between the cathedral and the river. When he got to the Rue d'Arcole, he turned right and crossed the Place du Parvis in front of Notre-Dame. He stopped to look down at the small bronze plaque that marks the beginning of the point from which all the national highways of France are measured.

So much history and so many personal memories.

He smiled as he remembered Amy's discovery that the word *parvis* is a form of the word *paradis*. For her, it is no wonder that the spot marks the spiritual center of France. After all, there sits Charlemagne on his horse, proving that this square is indeed the historic center of Paris.

Of course, the presence of Charlemagne denies the role of Clovis as the first French king and overlooks the fact that Paris is not the geographic center of France, but not even a dogged unbeliever and realist at all cost can deny the power exerted over all who stand in the square and look at the lavish monumental edifice that is the Cathédrale de Notre-Dame. A spectacular architectural wonder at the very least.

At the entrance to the archeological dig in progress under the Parvis, Jean-Michel stopped and read the visiting hours posted on the wall. Yes, the woman was still there. François was right. He was being followed.

Over by the statue of Charlemagne he suddenly saw Poncet and his dog.

The words *old-timer, spy, game,* and *memory* came readily to mind, but he just didn't recall anyone who used an old woman. When he got to Mathieu's office in the Préfecture de Police, he'd call Raphäel about the old lady and then Pascal.

He was even more curious about the earliest beginnings of the gang of four, starting with Lacour. Jean-Michel suspected that part of the solution was in Lacour's past: *America, memory, handler, ride.*

As he crossed the Rue de la Cité to enter the police station, the old lady waved at a motorcyclist, who was idling around the corner on the Rue de Lutèce. He quickly drove to where she was standing and stopped just long enough for her to get on behind him.

Jean-Michel nodded at Jacob Poncet, who grinned, as he keyed in a number on his cell phone.

"Dark blue moto. Here's the license. They went across the Pont Saint-Michel and turned left. You should be able to pick them up easily on the Quai de Montebello. They'll never guess that they're being followed by such a disreputable noisy motorbike. Yes, I'll report this incident."

In a second call, he told Tiago Luiz that he could leave the corner of the Quai de la Corse and the Pont Notre-Dame, which led to the Rive Droite. Their quarry had chosen the Rive Gauche and Champion was tailing them. He would inform Lacour that he needed to go to Basil, Switzerland, with Jean-Michel. The time had come. Would Luiz please notify their contacts to start getting ready? In particular, they needed Isis.

VIII

Years later, Jean-Michel realized that he had been a part of one of those events that make their way into local legend. For him at the time, that particular reception was just one more social affair in a series of parties that spring. For him, the *soirée* to celebrate the marriage of one Jean-Michel Honoré Jolivet, comte de Bourdonville, to Madame Amy Lucile Taylor Page of Charleston, South Carolina, came and went, as all major events do, and life in the Hôtel de Rochefort quickly returned to normal. The ballroom and its adjoining public rooms, or what Caroline referred to as the antechambers, were once again empty. The famous Gramont-Rochefort diamonds went back in the vault in the wine cellar, its several keys once more divided between the small safe in Caroline's bedroom and the one behind a bookshelf in Victor's study in Neuilly.

Jean-Michel had long given up trying to convince his aunt and uncle that their security methods were rather antiquated and that they should place the collection in a bank. Since the construction of the mansion in the seventeenth century, the family had kept its jewels there. They claimed that while a clever thief might know to look in the wine cellar, he really would never guess the exact location of that vault. After all, it was a very large basement and just one section was given over to the safekeeping of bottles of wine. The vault could be anywhere.

Those familiar with the old mansions on the Ile knew that the Hôtel de Rochefort housed a very large basement, where they stored over 1,000 bottles of fine wine and assumed that was where they kept fur coats, stoles, and other pelts, along with the diamonds that remained in the Gramont-Rochefort collection. What only a few knew was that the section given over to wine had within it three different secret vaults. It was Jean-Michel's great-grandfather who had had them installed. He had reasoned that all mansions were expected to have a vault hidden in its basement recesses; therefore, his would have one that was only partially hidden and it would contain the paste or copies of the family jewels. The location of the other two would require special knowledge.

According to family lore, the use of three vaults had been particularly useful during World War II. During the Nazi Occupation of Paris, a highly decorated colonel was sent to take possession of the Gramont-Rochefort diamonds. It so happened that this colonel was a descendant of a noble Prussian family known to the Rochefort elders from two or three marriages among cousins. Being a noble, he recognized paste when he saw it, but because he also was a distant relative, he readily accepted the family tale that they had had to sell them off in order to cover substantial business losses. They had sorrowfully taken him down to the basement and shown him a vault that held just one necklace, two bracelets, a pair of shoe buckles, and one lone earring. No tiaras, no diadems, no rings, no matched pairs of earrings. The colonel had left without the diamonds, but with a case of rare wine.

Naturally, the genuine diamonds remained untouched, being kept in a different vault. The third vault in the basement was empty and no one remembered why it was there. Roger had speculated that perhaps it was for the safekeeping of gold coins in decades past, which made sense to Caroline and Amy. However, when asked why he was skeptical of Roger's explanation, Jean-Michel found that he couldn't come up with a better reason. Sometimes it was useless to argue.

With the diamonds back in their hiding place, routine quickly reasserted itself. On the Quai de Bourbon, normalcy meant that before sunup, Claude and Léon, whose wives had given them lists of what to buy, were among the early shoppers at various markets, buying for their respective households. As they selected different foods from the vendors, their wives, Yvette and Aline, bustled in different kitchens with breakfast preparations for the households they managed, and each wrote out a schedule of chores to be done that day.

Every morning, Caroline rose at the same time, had the same breakfast in the small sitting room off her bedroom while listening to a news program on a small portable television and simultaneously reading the morning newspaper. Before bathing and dressing for the day, she began her series of phone calls. If her brother Roger had spent the night at home in his apartment, chances were he would sleep late. By the time he was ready to face the day, she would already be well informed on political and cultural events, as well as any tidbits involving life on the Ile Saint-Louis. Behind closed doors, Amy and Jean-Michel often made love before rising and going to their Tuscany-style kitchen for breakfast. As the residents went about their morning routine, Chantal discreetly left Pascal's ground-floor apartment to go to her beauty shop to prepare for the clients who insisted on early morning appointments and were willing to pay extra for being accommodated.

Other than the hotels, two pastry shops, one grocery store, the only newsstand, and the Café du Coin and the Café du Pélican, shops on the Ile Saint-Louis were usually closed until 10:00 a.m. and most restaurants were open only for dinner. While there was a steady stream of traffic on the Rue des Deux-Ponts, there was hardly any movement on the long transversal street, the Rue Saint-Louis-en-l'Ile. In fact, most of the cars parked along the side streets and those along the quays remained parked. Traffic in Paris was such that automobile owners rarely drove to work, but chose instead the Métro or bus. Those who could, like Jean-Michel, walked.

The walk, he declared, gave him the opportunity to switch gears from life with Amy and all that surrounded the Hôtel de Rochefort to his security business. He enjoyed the morning quiet, exercising both his body and his mind, as he thought about the problems needing both his attention and his expertise. He frequently took the long way to his new office on the Quai de Béthune, walking along the Quai de Bourbon, past the Rue Le Regrattier and the Rue des Deux-Ponts to the Quai d'Anjou, which was the quietest quay on the Ile and the one that boasted the largest and wealthiest mansions still in existence. He was always grateful that very few people chose to walk along this part of the island. He didn't know why, except perhaps because it was so very residential and because it was on the non-sunny side. He would then turn right and stroll along the Rue Poulletier, one of the three cross streets that lead from one side to the other. He would pass the church on the corner of the Rue Saint-Louis-en-l'Ile and then reach the Quai de Béthune with a view of the Rive Gauche, the Pont de la Tournelle to the right and the Pont Sully to the left.

When he opened the large door to the building in which he now had his office, he invariably thought about Amy and wondered why she never took the route that he preferred. Instead, she immediately left the Quai de Bourbon by the Rue Le Regrattier and then ambled slowly down the Rue Saint-Louis-en-l'Ile, window-shopping along the way and stopping to read all the menus posted in the restaurants. Then she would turn right on the Rue des Deux-Ponts so as to visit her favorite grocery store, even if she didn't need to buy anything. Next, she always stopped on the corner of that street and the Quai de Béthune to look far right to see the Eiffel Tower, then across the Seine to make sure that the large French flag was still flying over the famous restaurant, La Tour d'Argent. Invariably she would count the barges tied up on the other side of the river and try to identify the different flags flying from their sterns.

Finally, she would take note of any homeless living under the Pont Sully and count the floors of the Arab Institute on the other side of the bridge. Only then would Amy walk down the Quai de Béthune, cross the Rue Poulletier, and arrive at her former studio apartment, now Jean-Michel's office.

One of Raphaël's watchers had once timed Amy. It took her nearly an hour to cover the six blocks. It took longer when she decided to continue down the Rue Saint-Louis-en-l'Ile to the Rue de Bretonvilliers so that she could admire the archway over the street. Amy knew that the historian Hippolyte Taine had once lived there, but when asked why that was important to her, she confessed that she hadn't yet gotten around to reading any of his work. Still, she asserted, he was famous and Amy made it her business to know the location of every place on the Ile that had been the home of a famous person: Baudelaire, Camille Claudel, Marie Curie.

On the Monday morning after what the family considered the social event of the year, Jean-Michel left the Hôtel de Rochefort earlier than usual and began to take his usual route to his office. However, he didn't turn right on the Rue Poulletier. Instead, in accordance with the message he had received, he turned left, toward the river, and walked down the steps from the street to the small wharf below.

He knew he was early for the rendezvous, but he welcomed the opportunity to be alone in a place where he would not be interrupted. During the *soirée*, he had suddenly become aware of an important piece of the puzzle involving the gang of four, but he couldn't quite pin it down and he had quickly forgotten it. Now, this morning, during his walk, he remembered being struck by something someone said, but it remained elusive. Mentally, he began a review of the celebration in his honor.

In a nutshell, the *soirée* had even exceeded Roger's expectations. There were no glitches worth noting. It had not rained as predicted, and Mireille's husband had managed to keep the paparazzi at bay with the promise of full coverage by his having set up a select group to cover the event: a photographer, a videographer, a society reporter, and even one gossip columnist from a well-known tabloid.

The reporting had indeed been complete. Even Artemis's surprise appearance on the arm of a genuine duke escaped notice by the press representatives. Jean-Michel didn't know how Sylvestre had managed that particular coup, but he rather enjoyed seeing recognition on the faces of many men at the party. She had been the queen of Pigalle sex shows for decades and had become one of the wealthiest women in France through investments made possible by her many contacts.

Elegantly dressed in a pink silk gown exquisitely embroidered with tiny seed pearls, Caroline had entered the ballroom on the stroke of midnight on the arm of Father Tristan Moreau. It was the first time in over fifty years that she attended a public social event, but Caroline knew that protocol and good manners demanded that she be seen at a party she was hosting; to do otherwise would have been unacceptable, if not disgraceful. Caroline being Caroline, she had timed and staged her appearance for maximum effect.

The first one to approach her was Julien Turenne, her former fiancé. A hush fell over the gathering, spellbound at seeing the star-crossed lovers begin to dance.

Everyone knew the story. During the Occupation, the Gestapo had mistaken Caroline for a courier and taken her to their headquarters, where they had repeatedly raped her and then thrown her naked into the streets. After several years of therapy and various stays in a private rehabilitation facility in Switzerland, she seemed cured and accepted Julien Turenne's proposal of marriage. As the wedding date approached, Caroline began to relive the rape and had a complete breakdown. Once again she spent considerable time back in the Swiss sanitarium. When she returned to Paris, she announced that she could never marry. From that day to the *soirée* in honor of Amy and Jean-Michel, she had lived behind the walls of the Hôtel de Rochefort, creating her own dominion where she was in complete control. As for Julien, he respected her decision, never married, and belonged to her inner circle. No one doubted his deep love for her and this belief had quickly found its way into the Ile legend.

Tears welled up in Amy's eyes as she watched Caroline and Julien perform a stately waltz around the ballroom.

"I must look a mess. Do you have a handkerchief, Jean-Michel? I'm sure that my make-up is ruined. Well, I don't care. I'm so happy to see Caroline and Julien dancing. I really can't believe what I'm seeing. Wait until your mother finds out! Won't she be thrilled? Imagine! After all these years, Caroline is dancing in front of . . . what did you tell me? Seven hundred people?"

"Here's a handkerchief, Amy."

He too found himself in disbelief at the sight of his aunt and godfather. It was a moment worthy of one of his nephew Serge's gothic romance novels. While he was a true believer in the love unfulfilled between Caroline and Julien and always shared with the rest of the Ile the hope that one day they would marry and be together, somehow he knew that this particular event was staged. They were thoroughly enjoying this particular moment, not as lovers but as conspirators. They knew that this waltz would be the talk of the Ile and all of Paris for weeks to come. Secretly, he saluted them both. It took courage and nerve, but this performance—and he never doubted for a moment that it was anything but a performance—would be worth a small fortune in donations to the Ile center. Nothing less than that expectation would have gotten his aunt to appear, although staging her grand entrance on the arm of the local parish priest came within a hair of overdoing it. Julien's quick move to take her onto the dance floor was so natural and so expected—from the blessings of the church to the honorable arms of one of the most important men in France in one fell swoop! And the orchestra knew to play a particular waltz at just that moment!

Amy blew her nose.

"Oh, Jean-Michel, it's pure magic! Just look at them! You know that they belong together. It's so sad that circumstances have kept them apart. Do you think that maybe they'll marry after all these years? Wouldn't that be something? Just think—"

Jean-Michel let Amy ramble. He wondered who had helped Caroline and Julien work out this scenario. He had never questioned the guest list, but now in retrospect he understood just how it had been put together. He had thought nearly 700 guests was going overboard, but he had kept quiet on the matter because he was sure his aunt and uncle wanted to make a statement in celebrating his marriage to Amy. He'd never guessed that the event would be a statement about the Ile center. What a clever receiving line: he, a count, and his bride Amy, now a countess; Roger, a mover in art circles; Victor, a respected retired medical specialist and his wife Isabelle, whose family built most of the nuclear power plants in France; Laurent, a highly regarded physician, and his wife Marianne, who was from one of the very oldest and most respectable Ile families; last but by no means least, the very social Mireille and her husband, the media magnate and the comte d'Aubois. The Rochefort family with its important connections, wearing the famous Gramont-Rochefort diamonds, welcomed the guests who were then immediately aware of the absent Caroline and therefore led to remember the story of ill-fated love. Indeed the stage had been set from the outset. The only thing missing was a trumpet fanfare when Caroline made her grand appearance.

"Look! Now Sylvestre is dancing with Caroline! You're going to have to dance the next dance with her, Jean-Michel. It's a party in your honor and she is the hostess, so you must. You know you must."

Sylvestre! Of course! He had to be the one to work this out, Jean-Michel thought. He convinced Caroline to double her money. She could honor her favorite nephew with the *soirée* and without saying so bring attention to the Ile and its center. By not mentioning the need for financial contributions, everyone at the ball would be impressed, first, by being invited to such an affair at the Hôtel de Rochefort, which had not sponsored such a gala since before most of them were born.

Second, the guests would be aware that the general had been poisoned on the Ile, so recalling that event lent another dimension to the occasion. The

Rochefort mansion was located around the corner from the scene of the crime, enabling the guests to walk past the café in question if they wished.

Third, when Caroline made her appearance on Tristan's arm, they would all be impressed that a priest was among them as one of the invited elite, making it a blessed affair.

Sad but true, Jean-Michel mused, the whole affair had been designed to appeal to the snob within each one. And four, the waltz with Julien would create the sentimentalism desired in future donors, further realized by the follow-up dance with the marquis de Granvelle, and then, of course, the comte de Bourdonville—nostalgia, money, titles, connections to all the movers and shakers in the social, business, and even political worlds—a winning combination in anyone's book. Sylvestre even had that wealthy Pigalle sex queen Artemis on board.

"Excuse me, Amy, but I think it's my turn to dance with my aunt."

"Yes, yes, Jean-Michel. Go ahead. I've got to go repair my make-up. I'm convinced that Cupid knew what he was doing when he shot his fatal dart at Caroline and Julien. It was meant to be and it will be. Just you wait and see. Look what that love child did to us!"

Jean-Michel walked over to where his aunt and best friend were standing.

"My turn, *ma tante*. And by the way, congratulations you two, you really pulled it off."

Sylvestre merely grinned, bowed to Caroline, and left the two together.

Caroline laughed.

"We wondered if you would figure it out, Jean-Michel. Amy doesn't suspect, does she?"

"No, she doesn't. She's a true believer, and I promise to keep the secret. I gather that I'm the only one besides her who wasn't let in on the plan."

"Well, dear boy, it was important that you be surprised. And I knew you wouldn't mind if I took advantage of your marriage to garner support for my center. If it makes you feel any better, Victor didn't know either. It was just me, Roger, Julien, Tristan, and Sylvestre. And, of course, your mother was in on it. That's really why no one from Bourdonville came."

"Sylvestre was the mastermind, wasn't he?"

"In a way. He's been very helpful to the whole project. You know that he's going to be on the board when we get it going. It always helps to have a marquis."

"Especially a very wealthy one."

Caroline didn't even blush at the comment.

"You know, Jean-Michel. I may not live my life in the public eye, out in the world, but I do know what's going on. I keep up in my way. I'm really quite content, and this center is going to be my legacy to the Ile for having permitted me to live my life as I have. The wonderful thing about being a *ludivicienne* is that we know where we are from, who we are, and what we are all about. We don't really need anything more."

Jean-Michel smiled. Indeed, Caroline was right. That had been the Ile mystique since its beginnings. It viewed itself as self-sufficient and self-sustaining; therefore, those who lived there were self-satisfied. While this sense of self-importance might seem arrogant to some and even be ridiculed by a few, it remained part and parcel of its ability to survive in a changing world.

It was no wonder that the four retired spies had found refuge there. The Ile fit their need to be impregnable, unassailable, literally invulnerable. François Lacour had once said that life on the Ile was "unexposed." Caroline had lived most of her life protected by the Ile. She had chosen to emerge from behind the walls of the mansion in order to preserve the glorious past of the Ile, and, that achieved, she was now free again to withdraw into the inner sanctum of her mansion on the Ile.

Footsteps on the stone stairs interrupted his thoughts.

"*Bonjour*, Jean-Michel. I see that you got here well ahead of time."

"Oh, *bonjour*, Tiago," he replied, as the two men shook hands. "Surely, you're not the one I'm supposed to meet here this morning."

"No, I'm merely here, shall we say, as a witness. I usually come here every morning to do my exercises. There's not enough room in my apartment, and I generally have this little wharf all to myself."

"So how are things? Are you still seeing a certain ballerina?"

"Indeed, I am. Dancers are so limber; they bring a new dimension to joys of being, shall we say, consociational?"

"*Consociational*? That's not the right word, Tiago, but I catch your meaning. So, tell me, just why am I on this quay this morning?"

"It's not for me to tell you. Look! Here comes the reason for our meeting."

Jean-Michel saw a small boat approach, expertly steered by the fisherman, Paul Champion. He threw a rope to Tiago Luiz, who fastened it to one of the docking rings, and the passenger stepped onto the stone wharf.

Had he been given to flights of fancy, Jean-Michel would have sworn that she was an Amazon: over six feet tall, statuesque, long jet black hair, she was dressed completely in skintight black leather and wore expensive black leather boots. Her only adornment was a small gold ankh, that magic Egyptian looped tau cross that was considered the key of life. When she took off her goggles, he saw that she had violet eyes, enhanced by the use of Egyptian kohl, but no other make-up. She carried no weapon, or at least not one that he could detect at first glance.

"Jean-Michel, meet Isis," Tiago said.

Isis! The queen of trackers. Her exploits were well-known in certain circles. Jean-Michel had never met her, but he knew her by reputation. Once in Rabat, he had just missed her, but the information she had left for him had proven to be the key to a particularly difficult problem.

"Madame, it's a pleasure to meet you at long last. Your fame has preceded you, and, as one of your many admirers, I have to say that I'm delighted to know that you're still among the living. There have been many rumors about your retirement from the profession, chief among them a debilitating illness."

"Meeting you face to face is also a pleasure for me, Monsieur. Yes, I am retired. And I do have a serious health issue, but, as you can see, I'm still quite mobile, although not as physically able as I used to be. Still, like you, I have not entirely left the business; I do take on consulting work from time to time. This is one of those occasions."

"Do I assume that the Pirate has sent you?"

"Yes. Tiago here put out the first request. I suspect that it was Jacob Poncet who actually told him to contact me. You will note that I am using the new names that you have given this group you call your . . . what is it you call them? Oh, yes. The gang of four. Indeed, I'm quite *au courant* of their retirement to this tiny island in the Seine. It's actually quite clever of you to put four of the world's most successful and most dangerous spies in one small space in the center of a large city. But then you've always been considered extremely talented by the members of our profession. I'm sorry I couldn't meet you and François Lacour when you went to see the Pirate, but I was occupied elsewhere at the time. After hearing you out, he contacted me and said that you were agreeable to our financial terms and that the present situation could also benefit me personally, so here I am."

Jean-Michel shifted his weight. He wished he had brought his cane. Standing for a long period of time on such a hard surface was uncomfortable. Then again, he suspected that was a planned part of this strange meeting.

"I see that you dislike standing still, Monsieur. You're quite right to think that I have intentionally made you ill at ease. Well, I'm not as fast as I used to be. I find it maddening to have a neurological disease that weakens the muscles, so I find myself having to resort to all sorts of ploys in order to maintain control, and I rarely go out in the field anymore. It's too tiring and therefore dangerous. There's still a price on my head."

"It seems to me, Madame, that there's a price on a great many heads of my acquaintance."

"Ah, yes. Not just your gang of four but also your Archangels, and I daresay on the four of you who call yourselves the Relics after the Blue Coral affair. I could get a pretty penny for your head, Monsieur, and even more for Tiago's."

Isis fingered the ankh on the chain around her neck.

Jean-Michel realized that Isis was telling him that she had purposefully elected to be called Isis, naming herself after the most powerful ancient Egyptian goddess. The use of the ankh symbolized her power over life and death. As the world's foremost tracker or huntress of men, she wielded that authority: who was found and punished, and in some cases, who remained hidden. It dawned on him that she had long ago decided that he, the other three Relics, which included the English agent Pip, the Archangels, and now the gang of four were in elite groups, those whom Isis had determined were to be left alone. She was exceptionally well-informed, and in their world, all-powerful.

"I rather like your island fortress, Monsieur. I now understand why you continue to live here and why you brought Lacour here and he in turn managed quite cleverly to get the others of the gang of four here. The Ile Saint-Louis is literally the command center of Paris with both the Préfecture de Police and IBS next door. What's more, you're just a few hours away from Lyons, where Interpol has its headquarters. Just amazing. I should have thought of the Ile Saint-Louis years ago."

"You're still welcome, Madame."

Isis laughed.

"Always the perfect gentleman, Monsieur le comte. Well, let's get down to business. I know you're tired of standing. I have located your murderer, the missing waiter, but the Pirate and I think we'll let him stay in place for a while. When the time comes, we can easily eradicate him. He's really just a bit player in the present game and is no longer important. He made a major mistake, killing the general instead of Lacour, the real target, so maybe his employers will eliminate him for us. In the meantime, we can only assume that someone else will come after Lacour."

"Have you any idea of who might have hired the waiter?"

"No. And it doesn't look as though he knows either. Right now, it's best that he think he got away and has only his employer to face. On the other hand, the little old lady is new. We've not encountered her before. The Pirate thinks she is probably a young woman, but she could also be a young man. As you know, Champion there followed her one day, but she disappeared in traffic. I think she didn't disappear but was able to change her appearance rapidly and so throw Champion off course. Basic tailing procedures involve quick disguises: turning a jacket inside out, switching from a hat to a scarf, shedding a coat, and so on. The Pirate contacted the Magician, who was the master of disguise, and he swore that he'd not trained anyone since the Great Wizard, and he died five years ago."

"So you think Lacour is in danger?"

"Not just Lacour, but also your bride."

Jean-Michel gasped. Amy! How could Amy be involved? Why Amy?

"My wife? That's not possible. She's never been in the business. She's not a threat to anyone. Surely, Madame, you're mistaken."

"You're right. It's quite strange. Nevertheless, her name has popped up several times. She may actually be the next target. Tell me, does the Countess know Lacour? I mean, know him well? Enough to be some sort of carrier or conduit or messenger?"

Jean-Michel shook his head.

"No, not at all. In fact, she's only recently met him. She's been having Lacour's wife restore some dolls for the new interpretive cultural center. *Mon Dieu*! She just started visiting his shop several times a week, but not to see him. I can see how someone watching the map shop might think that she's going there for different reasons. And there's also the fact that they are both in the Café du Coin for breakfast at the same time once a week. In fact, she usually sits at a table across from him. Of course, to an observer, it could easily look as though they are in some sort of secret communication."

"Communication for you, Monsieur. They don't dare go after you directly. That move could backfire. You're too well connected to legal and not-so-legal operations. They tried for Lacour and lost; that failure alerted the gang of four and Interpol. Now they'll change tactics and perhaps try for your wife as a way of neutralizing you and thereby crippling Lacour's project. It makes sense."

"Yes, I see your reasoning. But I already have watchers on Amy. For a different reason."

"That's all very well and good, but you don't know what game Lacour and his cohorts are playing."

"No, I don't. Not at all. I have my suspicions, but so far I've not been able to confirm them."

"That's the nature of the hunt. That's where I come in."

"But it's more than that, isn't it? I detect that you have a personal stake in this matter."

"I see Champion signaling to me. Let's meet tomorrow night at Le Singe Vert. I hear that they serve the best bouillabaisse in all of Paris. Besides, it's been years since I last saw that old reprobate Clovis and his wife Clothilde."

Isis turned, got in the boat, turned, and waved. As the boat left the small wharf, Jean-Michel turned to Tiago Luiz.

"I'm glad you were here with me. Otherwise, I wouldn't believe what I just heard. Do you think she's right? She and her brother, the Pirate? I'm sure that what we heard is his interpretation of events. Do you think Amy is in danger?"

"I don't think we can afford not to believe Isis. We should learn more tomorrow night. We did send for her because she is still the best, and, she didn't let us down. It took her no time to locate that ex-Stossi murderer. By the way, Jean-Michel, you asked me earlier if I'm still dating that lovely ballerina. Yes. She's beautiful, charming, witty, and so very, shall we say, eager, but at the end of the day, or night in this case, there's still only one Isis."

Luiz turned and quickly jogged up the steps to the Quai d'Anjou, leaving Jean-Michel to climb up laboriously. He felt like Sisyphus, eternally rolling a heavy boulder up a mountainside, only to have it roll back down each time he got to the top.

IX

"Dammit all! I'm sick and tired of being bullied and treated like a . . . a dumb blonde. For the record, I am not a ditz! Need I remind you that we are now married? And that means that we are partners who share. Two in one. A couple. Don't look at me like that. I'm not talking about sex. I'm talking about . . . well, you should know, not just respect, but . . . damn, damn, damn! I can't even think straight. I thought we agreed to share, to share every single thing. Not just the car and the bed, but the whole damn thing. Well, maybe not all your spy stuff, but that's supposed to be over. You're supposed to be retired from all that. But you aren't, are you? And here I am, in the middle of something I don't understand. I don't think I've ever been so angry! How dare you and all the rest, including Foster, your aunt, and my son, the entire Ile and the police and your Archangels and heaven knows who else think of me as a . . . a ditz!"

Jean-Michel was stunned.

"Amy, *chérie*—"

"Don't you *chérie* me! Honestly, Jean-Michel, just where is your head? What were you thinking? What are you and all the rest thinking?"

"Amy, I don't know what you're talking about. What is it that you think I did?"

"You know damn well! And it's not just one thing. It's a whole . . . whole wheelbarrow full!"

"Amy, you know I love you and not for one minute do I think that you are a . . . what was your word? Ah, yes, a ditz. You're not just my wife. You're my everything. You make me complete. I'm nothing without you. I'd give you the sun and the moon and the stars if I could."

"I don't want the sun and the moon and the stars. I just want to be me and not be treated by one and all as some sort of floor mat to be walked on. I'm not dumb and I'm certainly not a ninny."

Jean-Michel took a deep breath.

"Amy, I don't think anyone thinks you're a floor mat or a ninny. Everyone adores you. I'm not the only one who has put you up on a pedestal. Your children love you. Foster truly admires you and thinks you're a gifted food writer. You have lots of fans who use your cookbook and enjoy your articles. My family thinks you're perfect in every way. *Mon Dieu*, Amy, you've conquered not just my difficult aunt, but the entire Ile and the police and the Archangels. Everyone you know admires you and adores you. Especially me."

"Huh!" Amy snorted. "That's just not true. Look at what's happening to me! And you haven't done a thing about it! You don't even realize what's going on. You haven't a clue and that proves my point."

Jean-Michel watched Amy walk around in circles, fuming.

"Amy, why don't you sit down and tell me just what it is I've done and what I haven't done. Whatever it is, I'm sorry, and I certainly didn't do it because I think you're some sort of numbskull. You know good and well that I don't think that way. Deep down you know that you mean the world to me and that I love you better than life itself."

"Well, if that's really so, you can start with this mess!" she yelled as she threw a pile of papers at him. "See if you can fix this! It's just one example of my screwed up life. I'm out of here. I need my own space."

Amy turned abruptly, walked over to the door, yanked it open, and stamped loudly down the long hall to the suite on the end of the apartment, went in, and slammed the door shut.

Jean-Michel didn't move. He didn't quite know what to think about her outburst. It was their first quarrel and he didn't know what he had done to cause it.

He got up, went over to his desk, and leafed through his calendar and journal. There was nothing there that could have possibly offended.

He had taken her shopping and bought her another expensive designer-original ball gown, and he had given her the magnificent garnet and pearl tiara he had had designed especially for her.

Since their return to Paris as a married couple, he had faithfully accompanied her to his aunt Caroline's teas; he'd written another large check for the interpretive cultural center that had become her pet project; he'd helped her translate several recipes from French to English for her column in the South Carolina *County Chronicle*. He knew that she enjoyed their lovemaking; they were more than equal partners in that domain.

He picked up the papers that Amy had thrown at him. She must be really upset, and not just over the general's death. He looked at what she had written. One page consisted of a rather pedantic lecture on salt: table salt, different sea salts, Kosher salt, herbed salts, rock salt, uses of salt for seasoning versus salt for preserving, omission of salt for crab, mussels, and scallops, adding a pinch of salt when working with chocolate, praise for salt-free beef and chicken stocks, and salt lore: to be seated above the salt meant one was an honored guest while being below the salt meant one had no social distinction. The last line consisted of two incomplete sentences; one dealt with how at one time cakes of salt were used as money, while the other noted that because salt was so expensive, spilling was considered unlucky.

Jean-Michel smiled at the two questions on light blue sticky notes at the bottom of the page: round table? left shoulder? Obviously, Amy didn't know how to work that information into the article on salt and wondered how one sat above or below the salt at a round table and why one threw spilled salt over the left shoulder and not the right. Of course, what he read were just notes, but it was enough for him to see immediately that it was going to be boring to the general reader of food columns.

The next few pages dealt with the names of popular dishes and how they came about, such as *Tarte Tatin* for the Tatin sisters, the round *Paris-Brest* for the 1891 bicycle race, Saint-Honoré cake for the patron saint of pastry chefs, *poire Hélène* for the main character in the 1864 operetta by Offenbach, *millefeuilles* in the nineteenth-century because it had 1,000 leaves of pastry, *Baba* for Ali Baba, the tiered *Napoléon*, said to be the general's favorite pastry, and, of course, the crescent-shaped *croissant* named for the symbol on the Turkish flag in honor of the bakers who saved Vienna from an invasion. Intermixed with dishes named for a specific event were dishes that got their names because of their shape or circumstance: the very rich butter cake known as the *Financière*, the irregular loaf of white bread called *Bâtarde*, the long thin cookie known as a *langue de chat* or cat's tongue, *Quatre Quarts* for the four ingredients (sugar, eggs, flour, butter) that go into a pound cake.

Indeed, he thought, an *île flottante* does look like a floating island, and it was only reasonable that petits fours were named for the fact that those small fancy cakes are baked in a very slow (*petit*) oven (*four*).

He chuckled over the notation that sugar snap peas are called *mange-tout* because one eats the peas and the pods, the whole thing!

He had always known that the English teacakes Maids-of-Honor were *Demoiselles d'honneur* in French, but it was new to him that they were named by King Henry VIII for Anne Boleyn.

Another page consisted of just a listing of items, with a note attached to some. Jean-Michel immediately identified them as other dishes to discuss: Charlotte (British), Anna, Macaroon cookie (sisters in Nancy), *Opéra*, meringue (Swiss town), Suzette, *bombe*, Melba (opera singer), *tulipe* (shape of a cookie), *Jalousie, Oublie, timbale* (drum mold), *parfait* (no need for decoration vs. US version), *Manqué* (invented by mistake), *boule de neige, Nonpareil, Le Marquis* (chocolate cake), *béchamel* (finance minister). Scribbled in were *palmier* (palm tree), *pain perdu, chausson* (slipper), *religieuse* (nun's habit), and *Madeleine.*

In Amy's handwriting was a large index card with a list of definitions of French cooking terms. Jean-Michel looked at the list and burst out laughing.

She had made a list of French culinary words that she thought would amuse American readers: *fatiguer* = to tire out greens by mixing them in a salad; *purée* = from Old French *purer*, to cleanse; *compote* = from *composte*, composed or a dish on a stand; *ratatouille* = mix; *canapé* = couch or divan, something to sit upon; *sourire* = to simmer gently; *ragoût* = from *ragoûter*, to stimulate the senses; *consommé* = broth from the verb to boil down; *au naturel* = on the half shell, meaning uncovered. And so on. The last was *au gratin* = from *gratiner*, to take to, i.e., to put on, convey, meaning to add crumbs.

Jean-Michel put the papers down, stood up, and stretched. His leg was bothering him more than it usually did. "*Merde!*" he exclaimed out loud.

Talking to himself, he walked over to the fireplace and began a series of exercises to try to ease the tautness in his leg. "Of course, she's upset. She's done a lot of work, but nothing here is anywhere near ready for publication, and I know she's under pressure from Foster to send articles. He's used up her backlog. I see now that Foster's publication needs are competing with those of the interpretive center, while I've been focused on the general's murder, Lacour's involvement in some scheme, and the warning delivered by Isis. *Ma pauvre Amy!*"

He walked over to the small refrigerator in the bar in a corner of the room.

"*Bien sûr,*" he said to himself, "the damn thing is full of Amy's Diet Cokes. Aha! There's a bottle of Chardonnay on the bottom and a nice wedge of Port Salut cheese too. I know I have glasses and a corkscrew in the bar. Now if I can just find some crackers."

He quickly assembled a tray and carried it down to the French Provençal suite.

"Amy, *c'est moi*, please let me in. I've brought a peace offering. We need to talk."

Jean-Michel pleaded, as he turned the doorknob. To his great surprise, the door was locked.

"Open up, please."

"Just go away, Jean-Michel. I mean it. Leave me alone."

He put the tray on the floor and strode quickly back to his study, where he unlocked a drawer in his filing cabinet. He pulled out a small leather case and went back to Amy's suite. He quickly picked the lock, opened the door, picked up the tray of wine and cheese, and walked in.

Amy was sitting on the floor in the middle of the rose Aubusson carpet, surrounded by crumpled tissues. Her face was blotched, her eyes and nose were red, and she looked like a waif who had been abandoned on the streets, forlorn, unwanted, and lost. Jean-Michel immediately dropped down beside her and pulled her into his arms.

"I'm all cried out," she sniffled. "Not a tear left. Did you really pick the lock?"

"Surely you don't think that a mere thing like a locked door can keep me away from the woman I love and married."

"I'm glad. I missed you. I'm sorry about my temper tantrum, but I've really just had it. I'm totally done in."

"I know, *chérie*, I know. We've both been under a strain. We need to step back and reassess what we're doing. I think our personal priorities have become a bit skewed by the outside world. Here, let's turn a new leaf with a glass of wine. I even brought some cheese, and I found a box of crackers in the top drawer of my filing cabinet of all places. I wonder how it got there."

Amy smiled.

"I am hungry. You must be the only cat burglar in the world who arrives with food and drink!"

Jean-Michel handed her a glass of wine.

"Now, tell me about the straw that broke the elephant's back."

Amy laughed.

"It's not an elephant. It's a camel! And that's it! There's an old joke about the committee that set out to make a horse. It wound up by making a camel."

"One hump or two?" Jean-Michel bantered.

"In this case, I'd say at least three. You heard the committee that dreadful day in the café. They really do think I'm the spokesperson, the one in charge. Well, I most assuredly am not. And what's more, I don't want to be. I've always known that I was Caroline's spy. You see, you're not the only one in the family who's a spy! Everyone knows that Caroline is the driving force behind the center and that I'm her eyes and ears."

"But, Amy, several committee members are in Caroline's network: Tristan, Roger, Margot before her heart attack."

"Maybe so, but I'm the one they think is in charge. Everyone is calling me about this and that. I had no idea that the general was doing such an excellent job."

"Yes, I see," Jean-Michel said, nodding his head. "I'm sure we can convince Caroline or whoever to announce formally a committee chair and let you off the hook. I'll talk to her and you can then just go on being a committee member. I suspect that it'll be Jammet. He's planning to retire from the banking business soon and probably knows he's the obvious choice. There's no reason he can't start now. I imagine he's just waiting to be asked. He's a gentleman of the old school and a stickler for protocol, so he won't jump until Caroline tells him to jump."

"That would really be a big help. One hump down. What can I do about Foster? I'm simply not going to do another article on a food ingredient. I did one on cream and I thought it was boring. Interesting in a way, but boring. It was information overload. I have lots of notes on flour, which is an even more boring subject. And I have a stack of cards on salt, which is maybe less boring because my readers probably don't realize that the sea salt known as *fleur de sel* is actually grey, not white—"

"Yes," Jean-Michel interrupted. "I get the picture. I don't think you should do any more on ingredients. Stick to what you really enjoy writing about. I looked at the pages you so graciously gave me—"

"I'm sorry I threw them at you. Where are they? They're my working outlines. Don't tell me you actually read them?"

"Well, yes, I did, and here's what I think. You and Serge are working on the origins of certain dishes. That's an interesting subject, but don't go at it in a scholarly way. Keep up the research, but at the same time, remember your readership. Think of Foster's wife, Dory. Do one per issue as an offset paragraph, sort of like an index card and just give the facts. The history of the croissant merits a paragraph all its own. Then the next issue can have a paragraph on, say, the *Tarte Tatin*, which came about by mistake, and that's why it's actually just an upside down apple tart."

"That's a great idea. I bet I have enough material for several years. But what about my articles? I was playing with funny cooking terms. Would that work?"

"Amy, I doubt that the readers of the *County Chronicle* would actually enjoy that. Instead, go back to what you do best. Take a food, such as, hell, I don't know. Maybe French regional cooking. Alsace, perhaps. Normandy has lots of great specialties. The café is a terrific subject and that could lead you to doing one on a bistro versus a brasserie versus a restaurant. And then there's wine. You've never written about wine."

"I don't know anything about making wine or grape-growing or even different kinds of grapes."

"True, so don't get technical. Take champagne. Did you know that it was invented by mistake?

"No. Tell me."

"In 1693, a monk named Dom Pierre Pérignon was making wine at the Abbey of Hautvillers. His batch was full of bubbles, which at the time were a sign of bad winemaking. He tried to get rid of the bubbles, but he couldn't, and in the process discovered that the bubbles in that particular wine made for an excellent drink."

Amy clapped her hands.

"What a delightful tale! My readers would enjoy that history and in the same article I can discuss why it's better to use a narrow flute glass for champagne than a saucer-shaped glass. It keeps the bubbles in. And, of course, champagne is the only all-purpose wine. It goes with any food course. I could give the recipe for a Kir Royal and also one for a champagne vinaigrette, which happens to be your very favorite salad dressing."

"Including those two recipes would please Foster, Dory, and your readers. You could then do the one on cups and include glasses. You know: red wine glasses are larger than those for white and they should be egg-shaped because red needs to breathe more, and so on."

Inwardly, Jean-Michel felt relieved. The center and food column problems had been solved. Amy was back on track.

"Yes, that would work. I could even say that vintners don't approve of colored wine glasses. I know you don't, but I don't know why."

Jean-Michel grinned. If this was the only remaining problem, maybe he could at last get off the floor.

"That's easy. We like to see the wine because the color is part of the wine experience. But, to set the record straight, I don't object to Venetian cordial glasses, which have deep rich colors."

"I'm glad to hear it. That crazy Maltese knight, Sir Devesset, has sent us twenty-four as a wedding present."

"And all this time I thought we only had nine left from the set my parents bought."

"Speaking of wine reminds me of Jack."

Jean-Michel was puzzled. He was certain he would never get used to Amy's corkscrew thinking, which tended to leap from subject to subject via associations that no one else detected, but he couldn't imagine how wine and Amy's son were connected.

"What about Jack?" he asked, trying to follow her train of thought.

"Well, I've just had an e-mail from him, telling me that he's quitting graduate school and wants to come over here to learn the wine business. That boy just flits from one thing to another. I don't see how he and Mary E. can be twins. She's so levelheaded, and he just flip-flops. Yet, it's Mary E. who's encouraging him to leave school and hop a plane for Paris. You know that he hasn't the foggiest notion of the wine business. I don't know what to tell him."

Jean-Michel relaxed. He wasn't really surprised. He suspected that Jack would turn up. When he and Mary E. were in Bourdonville for Christmas, it was obvious that he was fascinated by the vineyard and winery, as well as by a certain Jolivet young woman.

"Jack's not a problem. We'll just send him to my uncle Antoine and my brothers to learn the business from the rootstock up. He's intelligent. He'll either take to it or have enough sense to decide it's not for him and go back to the States to try something else. Who knows? Maybe he'll find his calling in the vine, just as I who was born to it did not."

"You're right. It hadn't even dawned on me that I now have a wine business connection. It's the perfect solution. I guess I've been too caught up in the whirl of parties, plus the center, and then Foster on my case. There really hasn't been time to just be married. I'd honestly forgotten that your family is in the wine business. How dumb is that?"

"Let's get off the floor, Amy. I need to stretch and find a more comfortable place to sit. Now that we've solved the three-hump camel problem, we might think about that big bed with the canopy cover back there."

"Honestly, Jean-Michel. Sometimes I think you have a one-track mind. And for your information, what you've helped me solve is just the tip of the iceberg."

Tears welled up in her eyes.

"It's your past. You've lied to me. It's that simple."

"How have I lied to you? You know that the security business means that I can't tell you everything I'm doing."

"It's not your spy stuff that bothers me. I've gotten used to it. It's that I don't understand why you thought it would be appropriate for you to invite your ex-mistress to the *soirée*. You must still be mixed up with her. Did you think I wouldn't find out? She's apparently very important to you."

"Just who are you talking about?"

"Stop playing games! It's Artemis, that's who. Obviously, that's not her real name. But why she needs a *nom de guerre* is beyond me. Really, Jean-Michel, even you must admit that choosing the name of an ancient Greek goddess is just too much! Aha! I caught you! That look on your face tells me that you never ever thought I'd catch on. Well, I did. How could you? I just don't understand."

Jean-Michel was taken aback. Artemis, the Pigalle sex goddess, had been at the *soirée*, but under yet another false name. She had worn a very expensive but discreet black gown in order to blend in with the guests and avoid making a statement or drawing attention. Arriving on the arm of a duke had provided her with a superb cover.

"Artemis is a code name. That's all I can tell you, except to assure you that I've never slept with her. She's not an ex-mistress. I've never had a mistress. I give you my word. Where did you hear her name?"

"When you were shot and then when you were so ill with pneumonia, you received an enormous flower arrangement from Artemis, and just this morning we received a beautiful medieval silver salt caddy. It's a rare piece and must have cost a fortune. I put the card on my desk. It's on very expensive paper and embossed in gold leaf, something one certainly doesn't see every day."

Jean-Michel chose his words carefully.

"Artemis is an extremely wealthy woman and a friend. A good friend who provides me with information from time to time and in the past I've helped her with some legal problems. Let's leave it at that."

"Does she live in Paris? Did you invite her to the *soirée* and then intentionally did not introduce me to her?"

"It doesn't matter where she lives. You will never meet her. And, no, of course, I did not invite her."

And that was the truth, Jean-Michel thought to himself; it was that rascal Sylvestre who had arranged for her to be there. There was no reason for Amy to know Artemis, although Amy would probably get a kick out of meeting someone like her. Artemis was likeable. She was also quick on the uptake, witty, charming, and as knowledgeable about fashion, jewelry, and art as his cousin Mireille, the Countess d'Aubois, and his uncle Roger.

Jean-Michel had known Artemis since his university days. He'd heard that at one time Charles Pichon had fallen head over heels for her, but he had always wondered if it had actually been his godfather, Julien Turenne, on the rebound from Caroline. After all, only Julien could have afforded to buy Artemis her own theater.

On the other hand, Roger had once let it slip that Artemis was originally from the Ile and that the payoff had been not to Artemis but to her mother. When pressed on the issue, Roger had said that the deal had been handled by Julien's father. He swore he knew nothing more.

Artemis's antecedents remained a secret. Someone had seen to it that there was no paper trail. Had that someone been his grandfather, Honoré Rochefort? Probably.

Jean-Michel was one of the few who knew that Artemis had bought the Café du Coin and given it to Corinne Avouche, her younger sister, and at one time one of Artemis's most talented erotic performers. An automobile accident had left too many scars for her to continue to dance and perform.

The pair might be a part of his life, but there was no need for them to be a part of Amy's.

"I see. It's been such a topsy-turvy time. First, there was the general's death right in front of me, then the *soirée*, arguments with Foster, Jack, on and on. I know I'm being tailed. I spotted Achille's girlfriend yesterday. There's no reason for her to be here except to watch me. When I went into the pastry shop, I stopped and waved at her and she ignored me. Then I know I saw her again at the BHV department store, and just this morning when I went to Monoprix in Saint-Germain."

"Well, maybe she was on a job, tailing someone else."

"Huh! What about that odd old man with the dog? They appear and disappear regularly. I know you're working on the general's murder, and that means the Archangels are too. Is that why you pretend to be so interested in having dolls repaired for the center and having Roger go with me so he can talk about botanical charts and stuff? I've been trying to find a pattern. You've always said that I'm an excellent observer, a first-class witness. Do you think the map man holds an important clue, or do you think I'm a target and in danger?

"What I think, Amy, is that François Lacour was the intended victim and the general was killed by mistake."

"Why, of course! That makes perfect sense. The packets of sweetener were on Monsieur Lacour's table and by fluke he didn't use them but gave them to the general."

Jean-Michel smiled. He noted that now that Amy saw Lacour as the probable victim, he was no longer the "weird map man," but a person with a name. Maybe it was time to let her in on at least part of the case. Her intuition could be invaluable, and he was still convinced that she somehow held an important clue.

He shifted in the large wing chair and re-crossed his legs on the multicolored ottoman she had bought one day at the flea market. It didn't go at all with the décor of her sitting room and study. She always said she bought it because it was a bit tacky and had its own personality.

Amy was a good listener. He hoped that some detail would trigger a memory and give the investigators a different lead. They had the killer's identity and they knew his mission. They didn't know who was behind the scheme. Now Isis had appeared and said in no uncertain terms that Amy was in danger because she could be used as leverage against Jean-Michel and force him to call off the investigation. But why ask Isis to come in person? What was the gang of four up to that required the services of such a skilled hunter?

"So you see, Amy, I think that you should stay close to home until we have some of this sorted out. After all, you're connected to Lacour by virtue of being married to me. Whoever planned the murder knows that I helped Lacour relocate to the Ile."

"And to finish your thought, I'm now patronizing his shop because of his wife's doll business, so I'm probably your errand boy . . . or girl. Do they think you're sending secret messages or money via the dolls? That wouldn't even fly in a B movie!"

"No, I think they see you as the means to an end. The one they want is Lacour. Think back. You know what's normal in the daily life of the Ile. You immediately grasp who or what is out of place in the everyday routine. You easily distinguish who is a tourist, who is a resident, who is a regular visitor or passerby. That's how you picked out Giselle. She's not watching you so much as she's looking for who might be watching you."

"Good garden peas! It's really complicated. I hope I didn't break her cover by waving."

"I don't think so. Anyway, put on your thinking cap and see if you can recall something out of the ordinary. Start with reviewing the photos you took in the café and the ones that were on the general's camera phone. Are there any others that you took earlier while walking around the Ile?"

"Yes, I still have the very first ones. I'll get them. They're in one of the secret drawers in my desk. I had forgotten I'd kept them. Surely, they're meaningless. I don't know why I didn't throw them away."

Jean-Michel had counted on the fact that Amy was a pack rat and kept everything. He looked at the first ones she had taken, and there it was! The killer, standing on the corner of the Rue des Deux-Ponts and the Quai d'Orléans. He was talking to someone on a bike. The rider had a ball cap pulled low over his forehead. Somewhere in Jean-Michel's mind the picture stirred a memory. The motorbike! He had been followed by an old lady who in turn was followed by Jacob Poncet and his dog and who then hopped on a motorbike and was followed by Paul Champion for several miles, only to lose them in the evening rush hour traffic. The photo was evidence that they were dealing with a large operation. Champion had reported that the motorbike had a souped-up engine, which made it possible for its riders to get away.

"Amy, where is your magnifying glass?"

"Here it is. What have you found? Surely there's nothing in those pictures. I was just snapping away, holding the camera in different positions."

"Look at the rider. What do you see?"

"I don't even remember taking that picture. I think I was trying to get that huge French flag that flies over the Tour d'Argent. See? It's standing straight out and I thought . . . well, I don't really know what I thought. It just struck me at the time. It's really not much of a picture, is it? Look! The person standing is writing something on his hand. Do you think it's the Roman numeral IX that I saw and no one else did?"

"Yes. It's not some mysterious gang sign. I'd say it's no more than a way of pointing out just where Lacour would be sitting. It's not the Roman numeral IX, but an X with a line drawn under it, X marking the chair and the line marking the back wall of the café. Just turn the numeral sideways and you'll see what I mean."

"How simple!" Amy exclaimed as she looked at the <u>X</u> she'd just written. "That makes sense. X marks the spot."

"Look more closely at the two figures in the picture. Tell me what you see."

Amy frowned and moved the magnifying glass up and down over the photo.

"The rider is a girl! That's it, isn't it? Not a girl exactly, but . . . I've seen that person before! Let me think. I've got it! In the café! The woman with the long red hair. She was there twice before. You know that I was sitting with my back to the wall and so I had a view of everyone in the café, including her. I remember being fascinated by her because of the hair and I wondered if she were wearing a wig. Don't laugh! Of course, she was. Her hair was just too . . . perfect, too in place."

A female. The Australian tourist. IX wasn't a number and the killer had never been in the café until that morning, but the so-called redheaded Australian had been several times. That was in her statement. She had been so open in her statement to the police, explaining how she had discovered that particular café by chance and begun having breakfast there. She was in Paris on business and said she was staying at a hotel on the Right Bank, not far from the Hôtel de Ville. Jean-Michel bet that no one had ever checked her story. If she was the old lady who had followed him that day, then who was on the bike that picked her up? Another female? Of course, those twins from Algeria. It couldn't be anyone else. Everyone thought they had died in their attempt to blow up the French embassy in Tunis. No wonder Isis had warned him about Amy's safety. That pair was ruthless and had to know that Amy had snapped that picture. They wouldn't take any chances. Amy just might put two and two together and connect the bike rider with the woman in the café. After all, she was visiting Lacour's shop fairly regularly and it was a given that he was the real target. If he knew about the twins, then it stood to reason that they knew about him.

Amy had once again proven herself invaluable to the case at hand and unwittingly put herself in danger. Before going late that night to a meeting at Le Singe Vert with the Archangels, he would call Lacour and agree to his price. Perhaps tonight's session should include the gang of four as well as

René Legrand and Hervé Mathieu from the police. He had quickly run out of options.

Standing up, Jean-Michel felt as though a heavy burden had been lifted from his shoulders. Identifying the twins was the first real break in the case, for now he knew that it was possible to discover who had hired them and ultimately who was after Lacour. Once he met Lacour's price and convinced him that Amy was at risk, Lacour would surely be willing to explain why he was a target. The one thing Jean-Michel knew was that Lacour and his cohorts would never do anything to jeopardize the Ile and its inhabitants. They were probably as concerned as he and that would explain the arrival of Isis in person on the scene. The Pirate was known for caution. He must have learned something that alarmed even him. Why else send his sister? Tonight would mark the beginning of the end to the problem.

Jean-Michel took Amy's hand and began to lead her to the bedroom. Amy laughed. "I don't think we've been in this bed since we got married. Now that I think of it, there are lots of places to rediscover, the living room sofa, the rug in your study . . ."

X

The next six weeks went by quickly. To the outside world, it seemed that no progress was being made on the murder of the general. In fact, life on the Ile Saint-Louis had so returned to normal that the murder was no longer a topic of conversation, a situation that was actually part of the master plan that had been put together when Isis visited. Jean-Michel made sure that Amy, his aunt Caroline, and by extension the Ile gossips, were lulled into a sense of peace and security. All was still right with the world.

To that end, he went with Amy, Caroline, Roger, and Alain, Roger's significant other, to Neuilly, where they celebrated Easter at the traditional Rochefort family lamb dinner that was held every Easter Sunday at Isabelle and Victor Rochefort's home. Amy was delighted with the group of shadow boxes that Isabelle had made for the cultural center as well as with Victor's painstakingly detailed model of the Ile Saint-Louis when it was still two small islands divided by a ditch dug in 1357.

To everyone's great surprise, Victor told the family that he and Isabelle were working together to recreate the famous Hôtel de Bretonvilliers. When it was finished in 1641, it was the largest and most elegant mansion ever built on the Ile; it actually occupied the entire southeast end. Unfortunately, it fell on hard times and underwent such radical changes that it was destroyed in the middle of the nineteenth century.

Amy couldn't help elaborate on its history.

"It really was a château. It was immense: four major sections, with all sorts of pavilions, grand apartments, huge courtyards, an extensive terrace, an orangery, three wells, and its own reservoir. The great hall alone measured 107 feet. Only traces remain today, and the Square Barye occupies a small part of what was once an extremely large garden. The model will be a big hit. I think they attract more interest than drawings and maps."

Laurent and his sister Mireille were totally taken aback. To their knowledge, their parents had never collaborated on a project, preferring to carry out their separate hobbies on separate floors.

Somehow, Jean-Michel was not surprised. Involvement with the cultural center was the first time that anyone in the family had acknowledged the talent and worthiness of what Isabelle and Victor did with their doll houses and elaborate train sets. Only Amy had always been enthusiastic about their creations and been instrumental in getting them to donate their time and creative endeavors to the museum.

Once they had agreed to Amy's request, Jean-Michel had suggested that she ask Caroline to invite Isabelle to serve on the committee and bring that number back to ten. Caroline had immediately telephoned Jean-Michel, who reminded her, as only he could, that she was the one who had involved Amy in the first place. Caroline had had her doubts about asking Isabelle, but she did it anyway to placate her favorite nephew.

She later told him that the family was fortunate to have added Amy to its tree. Of course, she never admitted that getting Isabelle on board lent another dimension to the project. She and Jean-Michel both knew that Isabelle was very well connected.

Not long after Easter, Sylvestre held his ball in honor of the newlyweds. It took place at the baroque mansion outside Paris where he usually held his famous New Year's Eve black-and-white gala. For Amy and Jean-Michel, he hired a famous chef to create and oversee a truly regal buffet that featured a magnificent twelve-tiered wedding cake adorned with red roses and topped with an ocean liner sculpted in sugar. He also had the large terrace turned into a ballroom, lit by Chinese lanterns and adorned by tubs of fragrant flowers with heaters interspersed discreetly among them. The city of Paris had even given him a permit to have a fireworks display.

Even Jean-Michel was impressed.

A week later, the couple drove to Bourdonville, where the marriage was blessed in the ancient church in which Jean-Michel had been baptized and confirmed. Afterwards, his mother hosted a large reception at the château. It seemed to Amy as though the entire town of 6,000 attended both the service and the party.

The previous evening his brothers had held a Jolivet dinner. Amy had forgotten just how many relatives Jean-Michel had: aunts, uncles, nephews, nieces, cousins. She was deeply touched to see that her son Jack had been included. Jean-Michel had told her that Jack was really taking to his training with the vineyard and Jack himself said that he truly enjoyed being out in the fields, working with the rootstocks.

Shortly after her return to Paris, Amy realized for the first time that she had turned an important chapter in her book of life. It wasn't just getting married. It was being the Countess of Bourdonville. No. It was more that that. It wasn't just having a title and a given social status; it was a responsibility. For the first time, she understood completely why Caroline had insisted that she be on the cultural center committee. She wasn't merely Caroline's spy. She had herself become a living part of the culture around her.

With this discovery, Amy decided that writing her food column and serving on the cultural center committee weren't enough. She needed to be more proactive. Suddenly, it dawned on her. Serge and Justine.

When they had arrived in Paris and moved into Jean-Michel's office on the Quai de Béthune, Jean-Michel had explained to her that he was going to take them into his security business. He could not expand his activities without adding personnel. Serge had completed some special training and often did odd jobs for him, so he was a natural for the business, and Justine had excellent credentials from her service with Interpol. Besides, the couple was tired of a long-distance romance.

Amy hadn't questioned the decision. Serge was an excellent researcher, and she guessed that his ability to dig out information and synthesize it was exactly what the job with Jean-Michel required.

At first, she didn't question their living in her old studio. It had a nice bedroom in the loft, a really large closet, a full kitchen, and a decent bathroom. She knew that what she referred to as the "top secret stuff" was across the vestibule in what had been a large storeroom. She hadn't thought that their living in the office would be permanent. However, the more she thought about their domestic arrangements, the more uncomfortable she became.

She argued with herself.

"What if I or Jean-Michel or Pascal or a client or someone else walked in on them while they were . . . oh, my goodness! That would be terrible. I've got to find them their own place to live, and something that they can afford."

As it turned out, the perfect place was under her nose and she found it by chance.

On the way back from a visit to the map and doll shop, Amy brought up the problem to Roger. He promptly suggested the unused studio on the ground floor of the Hôtel de Rochefort and took her on a full tour of the mansion.

Amy marveled at the amount of space it had, but she found the exterior to be both deceptive in size and unpretentious, to the point of being uninteresting. Roger was in his glory to have such an enthusiastic audience. He explained everything at great length. His descriptions were as grand and refined as the interior structure itself. He was particularly good on the various renovations over time. And when he finally showed her the small unoccupied rooms that had once been turned into a studio for a great-aunt who fancied herself an artist, Amy realized immediately that she was looking at the perfect studio apartment for Serge and Justine.

"We can put a kitchen there, a bathroom over there, and create a lovely one-bedroom apartment. Roger, you need to tell me names to call. I'll need an architect, a contractor, a plumber, certainly an electrician. I can't wait to tell Jean-Michel. He'll really be surprised."

Jean-Michel took the news in stride. He was far more interested in the waiting game that was going on. The plan had been drawn up and the pieces were in place. He was relieved that Amy had taken the warning about her safety to heart and was staying fairly close to the Ile. Now she had the apartment project in addition to the cultural center to keep her busy.

Jacob Poncet continued to walk his dog regularly, while Paul Champion started to fish more often from the various small piers around the island. Their presence on the Ile made it possible for Achille and Gisèle to limit their surveillance to those occasions when Amy left the Ile.

Because she was such a good sport about the need to be watched, she had even proposed to become a part of the surveillance by calling Achille before leaving the Ile so that he or Gisèle could be in place. She hadn't a clue that there was another surveillance team at work.

At least, Jean-Michel thought he detected one. He had always wondered about Paul Champion's background. While the police were using his services in cases involving Asians, Jean-Michel thought that Champion was playing a double game, if not two different ones. He suspected that Champion fished contraband out of the Seine because he once spotted a very small waterproof package left along one of the quaysides that lined the Ile Saint-Louis. He doubted that this was the only such packet, and he was certain it did not contain drugs. On the other hand, it was likely that he had discovered a form of letter-drop for passing on information. He had also detected a change in the group of lycée students who habitually cut through the Ile on their way home, stopping at Berthillon's for an ice cream cone. Suddenly, they seemed to include several Oriental students, who looked to him to be Vietnamese.

One day, Jean-Michel decided to take different routes back to the Hôtel de Rochefort, and, yes, there in the wine bar on the corner of the Rue des Deux-Ponts was an Asian couple, and another time he spotted the same pair getting off a motorcycle at the brasserie on the end of the Ile near the bridge to the Ile de la Cité. Yesterday, an Oriental photographer was taking pictures of models on the different bridges that linked the Ile Saint-Louis to the Right and Left Banks. He was beginning to think that Champion had established his own network in Paris, but he didn't dare confront him about it.

Champion was a survivor because of his attention to detail and ability to change abruptly. His history, or what Pascal had been able to learn, told repeatedly of his backdoor tactics. He was invariably one step ahead of his pursuers and known for his multilayered jobs. It could well be that he was more familiar with the present situation than any of them, including Lacour, so much so that he had created a second team of watchers. Not just watchers, but a ninja-like team that could probably protect Amy better than the Archangels. Or perhaps protecting Lacour was their assignment.

For the time being, Jean-Michel decided to let Champion do whatever he was doing, but he would see if Pip or Sean could send him a team that could in turn identify and keep an eye on Champion's group.

He began to understand that where the gang of four lived on the Ile belied a given strategy. Francois Lacour had settled in the middle of the Rue des Deux-Ponts, which had been commercial since its construction in 1617. It was the only street connected by bridges to both banks of the Seine. It literally divided the Ile in half, crossing the Rue de Saint-Louis-en-l'Ile, which was the main street, forming the longitudinal axis. Because it was heavily traveled, the Rue des Deux-Ponts gave Lacour several exit strategies, and no one would ever notice a slight increase in traffic. Lacour had chosen his location with great care.

Tiago Luiz lived in an expensive apartment on the end of the island that faced the Pont Saint-Louis and the Ile de la Cité. Obviously, from his living room window he could easily keep an eye on the crowd that flocked to the brasserie across the street. He too had more than one exit strategy: the pedestrian bridge, the ramp and stairway down to the river, and easy access to the Pont Louis-Philippe around the corner. Escape by water was also a real possibility.

Jacob Poncet had settled in a modest suite of rooms on the other end of the island on the Boulevard Henri IV. The two Sully bridges were no more than a stone's throw, and he had a perfect view of visitors from either the Left or Right Bank. The main bus stop for the Ile was directly across the street, and behind it was the Square Barye, the only green space on the island. Again, his comings and goings were protected by a busy traffic pattern and he had more than one escape route handy.

Lacour had both ends of the Ile covered, and he was at its center. So where did Paul Champion live? Lacour would leave the Quai de Bourbon and the Quai d'Anjou to Jean-Michel; there was no need to place an observer there. And he would probably not place anyone on the other quays, de Béthune and d'Orléans, because Amy's studio and now his office were on the Quai de

Béthune, and the Polish library was on the Quai d'Orléans. Undoubtedly, Lacour had made a friend there; after all, he was frequently asked by the librarian to help with certain maps and charts in the archives. So where?

Jean-Michel pulled out a map of the Ile. The immediate neighborhood would have to mirror someone who blended into his surroundings, accommodate someone with irregular hours, prefer someone who minded his own business and was somewhat of a loner, and, above all, provide easy entry and exit. A building without a concierge. A nondescript street. A quiet street. A street everyone ignored.

Of course! The Rue Poulletier, which crossed the Rue Saint-Louis-en-l'Ile and connected the Quai de Béthune to the Quai d'Anjou. No doubt, Champion lived on the block near the Quai d'Anjou because that side had stairways down to cobblestone wharves to which small boats could easily tie up.

Now that he thought about it, he recalled that Champion usually fished on the other side of the Ile, as well as along the quays on the Ile de la Cité away from his home base.

Of all the blocks on the Ile, that one part of the Rue Poulletier fit the bill. The other cross street, the Rue Le Regrattier, now had an ethnic bar and restaurant, which attracted a boisterous late-night clientele. Only this one block was dull, uninteresting, and completely boring. It used to house a small police force, but that had been closed. Now it housed two small schools, which didn't interfere with the philosophy of the residents because the students came and went at certain times. In a way, the schools served as a village clock by which the inhabitants could set their watches. It was a truism that the best hiding place was the one out in the open, so ordinary that it wasn't noticed. Who would think that Paul Champion would elect to live on a block with two schools?

The Quai d'Anjou was noted for its lack of sunshine, so in all probability that particular block was always deep in shadows. Jean-Michel couldn't recall the last time he had thought about that part of the Ile. It didn't even have a single building that had an inviting iron balcony or unusual sculpted medallion of interest to students and tourists.

He was positive that even Amy's passion for all things in, on, and of the Ile did not include that particular group of buildings. He knew that the residents did not use that block of the Rue Poulletier as a means of getting to the Quai d'Anjou in the same way that they used the other end to reach the Quai de Béthune.

Then again that part of the Rue Poulletier went alongside the church, and several buildings had interesting balconies. The Rue de Bretonvilliers always attracted visitors because of its famous archway, while the short Rues

Budé and Boutarel were not without architectural interest and the Rue Jean du Bellay was simply too busy to be considered. Yes, on the whole Ile Saint-Louis, it could only be that block.

While Amy worked on readying the old studio for Serge and Justine, that pair of lovers was in South America, hiking in the Andes, beginning with the Inca Trail. It was to be strictly a reconnaissance mission. They were to attempt to map out old smuggler routes and at the same time chart trails that seemed to be heavily traveled. It was fraught with danger, for one never knew just which groups were living there, out of the reach of the authorities, hiding from this and that army of rebels who embraced different leaders, or merely on the run for any number of reasons, that ranged from false accusations to criminal activity of the most heinous sort.

As all students of geography and tourists know, the Andes form the spinal column of South America and connect disparate countries along the west coast: Columbia, Ecuador, Peru, Bolivia, Chile, western Argentina and western Brazil. The mountains are tall and rugged, while the jungles with their virgin rainforests are dense and largely uncivilized in Western terms. They are also a treasure house of untapped riches, plagued by unscrupulous gangs motivated solely by greed. Isis had determined that the ruthless drug cartels in Columbia, government protected oil-rich private armies in Venezuela, and coca farmers in Bolivia were of no importance in the present situation. Besides, leaving them alone would in large measure permit their operation to focus on its actual goal, and not be sidetracked by security issues involving those groups.

Immediately after the group meeting with Isis at Le Singe Vert, Tiago Luiz had left for a chess tournament in Rio de Janeiro and had announced that he would stay there for a while, seeking out distant relatives.

Gabriel's departure had soon followed; he was to play his favorite role: a Jesuit priest who was visiting the *reducciones* or missions established by that order in colonial times. He had started in Asunción, Paraguay, and had already worked his way to the province of Misiones in Argentina. Ultimately, he would wind up in Buenos Aires, where Isis had a trusted contact and where he would meet up with Tiago Luiz.

Jean-Michel often wondered if in Gabriel's past he had been a priest. Whenever he accepted an assignment that called for some sort of role-playing, he invariably chose to be a priest: Jesuit, Servite, Oblate, Franciscan, Eastern orthodox, even once a defrocked parish priest. His knowledge of philosophy, church history, and classical languages tended to betray seminary training.

Surveillance in disguise was best carried out in roles that stayed as near reality as possible. It also made the creation of travel documents easier. It made sense for Tiago Luiz as a highly ranked chess player to travel to Rio de Janeiro via first Mexico City. No one would suspect that he was a former KGB agent and that the reason for the stopover in Mexico City was because the KGB's largest overseas headquarters had been in that city. A change in name did not necessarily mean a change in activity. While there, he contacted a former colleague, now retired and living in a large hacienda with his mistress and several children. For a price, he gladly provided Luiz with a list of possible contacts in Brazil, proving that there is a sense of honor among old spies and that their networks remain invaluable. His second stopover was in Nicaragua, another country on more than friendly terms with Russia.

Raphaël had been the first to arrive in Brazil, playing his former Basque self; his assignment was to seek support for the Basque rebels, not just money and weapons, but safe training camps as well. Because one of his brothers was still on the Spanish government's most wanted Basque terrorist list, his credentials were impeccable. Besides, as Uriel had noted, while Basques speak other languages, such as Spanish, French, Catalan, even Italian, without an accent, no one but a Basque can speak Basque. A further asset were his long-lobed ears, the true physical feature of Basques.

Jean-Michel had refused to go to Lima and take Amy with him. While he could probably find a reason to go and check on his newly installed port security system, it was actually too early for an on-site visit. He considered it too dangerous to take Amy. Not even when Isis pointed out to him that Lima is one of the world's most beautiful and most romantic cities. Surely, she said, it would greatly appeal to Amy: the Spanish colonial architecture, the elegant boutiques, the glamorous nightlife, the magnificent beaches, the world-class restaurants.

"I personally guarantee her safety," Isis had declared. It was that statement that considerably raised Jean-Michel's suspicions.

He was convinced that Isis had a hidden agenda. In fact, it seemed to him that this whole venture was marked by hidden agendas and that great pains were being taken to create false trails, red herrings, impasses, and dead ends. Deception seemed to be the rule.

Earlier, Lacour had told him about his efforts in bioprospecting and the search for therapeutic drugs. He and the other three members of the gang of four were on the verge of a major discovery when a rival group appeared on the scene. At first, it seemed to be merely a competition to find, process, and ultimately market an anti-opiate, but as the months passed, they had become increasingly aware that the group they considered the enemy wanted to prevent the development of any such drug. However, they had not suspected that their enemy was so well financed and organized that they could and did hire the ex-Stossi thug to assassinate Lacour on his home turf. Whoever it was had vast resources. The appearance of the Algerian twins reinforced this line of thought.

Another conversation with Lacour was needed. This time Jean-Michel had the one piece of information he knew Lacour would prize above all others. He fingered the envelope that had arrived yesterday from Edinburgh. Pip had located for him a discreet lab with the capability of DNA testing. He hadn't opened it because he really didn't want to know the results, but he knew that they were important to Lacour. At least, he had Lacour's promise that he would never share the lab report; he swore that he simply wanted it for personal reasons and it was no one else's business. And Jean-Michel believed him.

Jean-Michel rubbed his eyes. He wished he had a better sense of the different games being played. He would call Lacour and set a date. Then Clovis at Le Singe Vert. He needed a face completely unknown to Champion to stroll the Ile, taking especial note of that block on the Rue Poulletier. As he was scribbling his list of calls to make, his cell phone rang.

"*Allô!* Ah, Amy! Dishes cooked with wine? *Mon Dieu!* That's a major undertaking. It would probably be easier to come up with dishes that don't use wine."

He listened to Amy chatter about the meal they'd enjoyed last night at her favorite restaurant in the Latin Quarter. She always tasted whatever he ordered, and this time it had been duck breast in a port wine reduction with figs, while she had been entranced by the simple elegance of her dish of scallops seared in dry vermouth. For dessert, she had indulged in a magnificent flaming dish of *bananes au rhum* and had thought that the secret ingredient in the plum tart was Kirsch. The meal had started her thinking about the use of different kinds of wines in French cuisine, not just red and white wines, but also sherry, Madeira, brandy, as well as specific wines in certain dishes, such as Riesling and Calvados.

Jean-Michel easily grasped how such an article would appeal to her readers, but again it would be a matter of keeping Amy on target. She tended to overdo and give too much information.

"That's an excellent idea, Amy. I think Foster would really go for it, but it should be kept fairly simple. You could discuss the general use of different wines to create different dishes and perhaps give a recipe for something like *coq-au-vin*, which is traditionally made with red wine, but changes when it's made with an Alsatian white wine, such as Riesling. I've got it, *chérie!* Why not add some recipes, such as a bisque, which uses sherry, then one chicken dish, one meat dish, such as beef stew or braised lamb shanks, a salad dressing with either a white or red wine vinegar, certainly a sauce . . . Madeira comes to mind, and a dessert, the crêpes you like so much."

He smiled when he heard Amy laugh on the other end of the phone. In his mind's eye, he could see her making notes as they talked.

"Yes, you could then end with the story of how *crêpes Suzette* were created by accident for a sweet young girl on the arm of a famous prince."

"Yes, you're right. They were flamed by mistake! I've got to get started. Don't forget, *chéri*, to pick up a baguette on your way home."

"I won't. *A plus tard. Je t'aime.*"

He hung up and leaned back in his leather-padded desk chair. Quickly, he made two calls, got up, and left his office. On the way home, he walked up the Quai de Béthune to the Rue des Deux-Ponts and turned right toward the Rue de Saint-Louis-en-l'Ile. He stayed on the right side of the street and noted a different Oriental couple in the wine bar on the corner. As he walked down the street, he casually glanced at Lacour's shop. In the lower left-hand corner of a grimy window was a curly-headed doll in a pink dress and large pink bonnet, holding a scroll. Jean-Michel smiled. The date and time were set. This time he had the leverage necessary to get some answers.

A motorcycle roared past him and halted abruptly at the corner. He noted that the driver and his passenger were wearing bright green scarves. Sean's team of watchers was still in place and was obviously enjoying the assignment. No doubt, Sean also had a pair in the wine bar, watching that Oriental couple.

And there in the distance, he saw Jacob Poncet cross the Rue des Deux-Ponts from the Quai d'Anjou to the Quai de Bourbon. Watchers watching watchers. Jean-Michel suddenly felt better. He would turn onto the Rue Saint-Louis-en-l'Ile and pick up the requested baguette. Tonight, however, he would make several stops: a bottle of champagne, a wedge of Amy's favorite blue cheese, Bleu d'Auvergne, and finally two éclairs or maybe millefeuilles. He didn't know what she had planned for dinner, but he did know what he was planning for the evening.

XI

Lacour sat across from Jean-Michel in a back room of Le Singe Vert. "Thanks for getting this done for me. I deeply appreciate it and I'm sorry to have had to involve you, but I had no other choice. Thanks too for not asking me to share the lab results with you. You're that rarity in today's world, a true gentleman."

"Cut the crap, François. I know damn well that you wanted a DNA test because it's 99.99% accurate and shows definitively if one individual is directly derived from another. The old paternity test relied on blood tests and is not nearly as reliable."

"Yes, of course. I'm sure you've already guessed why the result is important to me. My injuries were so extensive that I'm now impotent. At least, they don't interfere with my sex life, just my genetic one."

"Does knowing that you are or are not Serge's biological father mean that much? It's a given on your family tree that you're cousins. Doesn't that knowledge suffice? I have no children and I've married a woman who can no longer bear children. I'm content with having just her children and my own nephews and nieces, not to mention lots of cousins on both sides."

"Point well taken. Maybe it's all come about because you want to take Serge into your security business, which means involvement with me, and now he's here, living in my backyard, so to speak. He hasn't a clue that I'm a relative. The whole family, including Joseph, thinks I'm dead. You know that we were closer than most brothers. I've purposefully kept my relatives, including Joseph, in the dark for their protection, and your sister Emilie too, of course."

"I had wondered why you avoided contact with Joseph. Perhaps it's time for you to come clean and see if I can help you. I know that you've turned that building you bought on the Rue des Deux-Ponts into a virtual fortress and that Nikki has helped you set up a communications system that not even Pascal can hack into. There's a reason you thought it necessary to bring an ex-Mossad agent and just recently one of Vietnam's most successful narcotics investigator. Looking back, it now seems clear that from your sick bed in the sanitarium you had Tiago Luiz settle on the Ile first. That was brilliant. Not until the attempt on your life in the café did I figure that out. You always had me and the Archangels convinced that it was by sheer chance that you and he wound up on the same little island in the middle of the Seine."

"Well, Jean-Michel, I was trained by the best."

"Yes, you were, and you have always had what most spies lack, a genuine passion for your particular area of activity. So, tell me, just what game is going on? Why is Isis so involved? It's obvious to me that she's playing both sides against the middle. I just don't know what the sides are. Then there's this new team of watchers, mainly Orientals, meaning that Champion is up to something. He also fishes more than fish out of the Seine."

François laughed.

"I thought you'd caught on to his games. But what about your team supplied by that old IRA hand who's always been in league with you and the unflappable Pip? That was clever of you to bring them here. Now that tourists are arriving in droves and some are paying outrageous prices to rent apartments on the Ile, we seem to have some very unsavory people among us. The situation is ripe for planting a sleeper cell despite the fact that the Ile is being taken over by overlapping teams of watchers. If it all weren't so deadly, it would be comical. I'm not so sure that young Serge and his delectable Justine should be caught up in this operation."

"So, you admit that there is an operation. Don't you think it's time to clue me in? At some point, we're going to have to bring in René Legrand, Hervé Mathieu, and the French police. Otherwise, one of their agents is going to misidentify one of our watchers as a terrorist and then we'll all be in the soup with covers blown."

"Is this where I'm supposed to say, *bien sûr, oui, oui, mon Capitaine*? You were a principal inspector in the Direction Régionale de Police Judiciaire de Paris, weren't you, Jean-Michel? I know that most of the world, including Amy, still thinks that the major criminal investigative division of the French police is called the Sûreté and that it's still located at number 36, Quai des Orfèvres, but you and I know that La Sûreté nationale was abolished in 1969 and replaced by the French National Police. The DRPJ is now at number 11, Rue des Saussaies, next door to the boss at the Minister of the Interior and near the Elysées Palace."

Lacour paused, but when Jean-Michel didn't say a word, he went on.

"Your IBS didn't even exist when those changes took place. When it came into existence, it was created as an entity separate from the criminal brigade over on the Rue des Saussaies. It had to be hidden out in the open. Presto! A special branch in the Quai des Orfèvres with the mystique of the old Sûreté! Your IBS was actually a cover within a cover. No longer the equivalent of the American FBI or British Scotland Yard, it was more like the American CIA or British MI-6. You're not the only one adept at laying false trails and working from hidden agendas. In many ways, *mon vieux*, we're alike, you and I, two peas in a pod."

Jean-Michel stroked his chin and leaned back in his chair.

"I don't deny the history you've just outlined. As you guessed, the Archangels came into existence the same way the Sûreté originally did in 1812. You of all people know that story."

"Yes, good old Eugène François Vidocq set it up with reformed criminals, not too unlike Sherlock Holmes's Baker Street Boys."

"And you took the name Lacour from the guy who succeeded Vidocq as chief, a member of that first bureau and a petty thief."

"Of course, but I stuck to my own name François. Did you know that Eugène is actually my first name? I didn't think so. Imagine my surprise when I discovered that I shared the same two given names with Vidocq! I just didn't think Coco was quite right for me."

Both men laughed.

"Why is it, Jean-Michel, that top-notch expert law enforcement always depends on knowing how to break the law?"

"I suppose it's because it takes a thief to catch a thief, the old Vidocq philosophy. Reform via the reformed. But let's get down to the matter at hand. Just what have you done to bring about so much interest from what I gather is a rather brutal international organization."

"Ah, the Titans. Well, that's the name Isis has given them. I don't think they really have a formal title. She's always been very much into mythology, hence her alias. You will recall that the Titans were elder gods expelled by Zeus and his Olympians. They really were an ugly lot. They ate their own children, freely intermarried, tried to de-throne Zeus, and are said to be responsible for introducing evil into the world by accepting that gift from Pandora."

"Spare me the schoolboy lesson, François. Who are they and what do they want?"

"In a word, Jean-Michel, they're after *nadamtha*."

"I never heard of it. Knowing you, it must somehow be related to the drug trade."

"Right on target, Jean-Michel. *Nadamtha* is the key to the drug I've been seeking for years. It really works in blocking cravings for opiates. All opiates. The Titans protect narcotic growers and producers throughout Mexico, Central America, and South America. They don't play favorites. Any drug trafficker in that region can hire them for military training, obtaining weapons, and in particular fostering anti-North American feelings, including Canada. In fact, part of their goal depends on keeping the US and Canada focused on Eurasian drug networks, which is, in a nutshell, the policy practiced by NATO in Europe. As a result, the US and Canada are not on the offensive south of the Rio Grande. Instead, they're being contained by the disruptions in Latin America in order to concentrate with NATO on the flow of narcotics from Eurasia to the West."

"So what you're saying without saying it is that these Titans are able to facilitate the drug trade by destabilizing the countries within its sphere of operation, which, if I understand you correctly, includes much of Latin America. Right now, opioids are the only known antidote, and they work by creating withdrawal symptoms and are commonly used in detox programs. I know the side effects of withdrawal are pretty miserable: chills, nausea, diarrhea, headaches. A drug that would effectively block the effect of opiates would be easier to administer and help avoid the horrors of present-day treatment. And, of course, such a pill would threaten not just the cartels in Mexico, Columbia, and Venezuela, but also the very existence of the Titans themselves."

"That's a good summary of the situation."

"So where is this *nadamtha* drug being made? Why hasn't anyone in law enforcement or the health care community heard of it?"

"Now we've come to it. *Nadamtha* is a plant. I did find it and I lost it. That's when you and your Archangels got me out of South America years ago. I was a prisoner of one of the drug cartels. As bad as that was, I was lucky that it was before the Titans were in control. Let's take a break and get a bottle of wine from Clovis's private stock and a couple of Clotilde's famous *pan bagne* sandwiches. I guess I should take you back to the beginning. It's quite a story. One of those tales that proves that truth is stranger than fiction. It all began during a particularly violent thunderstorm in London . . ."

For the next few hours, Jean-Michel listened. Seeking shelter from the sudden downpour, Lacour had dashed into a tea shop, which was actually a spice and herb shop. He was the only customer. As the storm raged outside, he became friendly with the owners, a young couple, Gwyn and Thomas Marshall. It turned out that they sold their spices and herbs not just for cooking purposes, but also for medicinal uses to treat all sorts of different ailments: indigestion, earache, toothaches, high blood pressure, diarrhea, gastrointestinal problems. They had one client who bought herbs to turn into dyes, another who made different soaps, and even one who specialized in jellies. Thomas had developed an effective lotion for sunburn and some rashes. As the afternoon wore on, the couple took François on a tour of their small greenhouse, where pots of thyme, rosemary, sage, parsley, basil, dill, oregano, mint, lavender, savory, marjoram, chives, chervil, and tarragon vied for space.

François had quickly realized that the couple's enthusiasm for their enterprise did not match their income. They were badly in the red. It was expensive to keep the greenhouse going, to import herbs, such as saffron from Spain and bay leaves from Turkey and just about all the spices: nutmeg from Granada, ginger from Asia, caraway from Germany, cardamom and cumin from India, cinnamon from Sri Lanka, star anise from China, black sesame seeds from Japan, paprika from Hungary, cloves from Madagascar, sea salts from France, black and green peppercorns from India but pink ones from the French island Réunion. They only made a few spice blends: Chinese five-spice powder, Indian garam masala, Mexican chili powder, and all the popular French ones: *bonnes herbes, fines herbes, herbes de Provence,* even *quatre épices.*

"I had no idea that those French blends were different combinations of herbs. I just thought they were different names for the same thing. I'll have to ask Amy if she knows."

"I'm sure she does. I looked it up and she's on the mailing list for the catalog for La Maison du Monde des Epices."

"What?"

"That's the whole point of telling you this story about my first afternoon with Gwyn and Thomas. You know that civil servants, like me, don't earn fantastic salaries, but still I had no expenses except my own daily living, so I had a nice nest egg sitting in a Swiss bank. I became the silent partner of that herb and spice shop. Today, it's an internationally known company with a shop in each major capital: Rome, Bonn, Paris, Tokyo, Washington, Ottawa, and so on. Most of the business is done over the internet."

"And I suppose it was one Nikki Raymonnet who set up this mail order business?"

François laughed and handed Jean-Michel one of his catalogs.

"You'll see that we're not into food stuffs, just herbs and spices; no oils, no sugars, no extracts, no chocolates, no vinegars And we haven't gone into all the trendy blends, such as Jamaican jerk seasoning, various rubs, etc. We prefer to tell our customers how to make their own poultry seasoning, pickling spice, mulling spice mix, Italian herb blend."

"If I'm following you correctly, young Thomas turned out to have a degree in chemistry and Gwyn's background was in botany. They continue to be the public face, but behind them is a lab where a team of scientists works on different plants discovered by another team or teams, also on your payroll. And you've concentrated your effort in South America because . . . governments there tend to be destabilized, especially in the hinterlands of the jungles, rainforests, and Andes. The indigenous peoples in those areas have passed their knowledge about plants unknown to the Western world from generation to generation, but these tribes are slowly being wiped out by so-called development and that medicinal lore is being wiped out with them. How am I doing so far?"

"Not bad at all. You're getting high marks so far."

"There's just one question left. How are you financing your bioprospecting enterprise and the subsequent combinational chemistry experiments? Where is the funding coming from? Surely not from an international catalog company."

"For your ears only, Jean-Michel. Agreed? And then we'll work out a story to tell the others. There are certain details that must be kept secret to . . . I think one says to protect the innocent."

As François explained the ins-and-outs of the funding for his billion-dollar industry, Jean-Michel's head spun. Not in a million years would he have guessed that the funding came about through Tiago Luiz and that damned vixen, Isis. While Baghdad was being bombed during the American-led Gulf War, Lacour and Luiz found themselves in the same hotel. Both were there, pretending to be newspaper correspondents, Luiz for the Russian news agency Tass and Lacour for the *London Times*. They not only knew each other from their respective files as covert government agents, they had also already met. The first time took place in Kabul, Afghanistan, when the Russians were being chased out, and a second time was in Cairo, where an Arab summit meeting was being held.

Their paths had continued to cross in various parts of the world, and, once the Cold War was over, their encounters usually found them on the same side. When they wound up together in Iraq, talk turned to Luiz's latest romantic interest, someone who shared his love of food and was considering beginning a catering business in Moscow, where millionaires were popping up with regularity under the new capitalistic regime. Lacour revealed that he had recently bought into a spice and herb shop. Luiz, who knew all about Lacour and the death of his younger brother from a drug overdose, as well as his background in biophysics, had immediately grasped the potential of the shop and its greenhouse. He was tired of his job and wanted to retire, but with his expensive tastes he needed a better source of income than what his pension would provide.

Jean-Michel couldn't help but laugh out loud at the thought of two of the world's best and most dangerous undercover agents worrying about their retirement. They were too old to be mercenaries; besides, military ops were not their specialties, and neither had the expertise needed for industrial espionage. Becoming trainers for future spies had no appeal and the pay was low. Both had seen enough to deplore the illegal drug trade. Luiz's only nephew had fallen prey to cocaine and caused his sister untold agony.

Moreover, the drug lords were no more than thugs, with no honor among themselves. They killed for the joy of killing. They had no code. True, many were trained in Russia, but that was the army, not his spy world. Luiz agreed to work with Lacour on his bioprospecting. The project was bound to earn enough to keep him in a certain style and perhaps do a good turn for the world as well. Regardless, it would be an amusing sideline that would relieve the inevitable boredom that usually comes with retirement.

Still, the venture required an immense outlay of money and they had nowhere near enough. However, they did have contacts on all five continents and their contacts had contacts. Along the way, they had taken the Israeli Mossad agent, Jacob Poncet, into their scheme. They had once helped him escape from a trap in Tripoli, and on one occasion in Beirut even saved his life.

The trio decided to buy into small businesses throughout the world and corner new markets. To that end, they financed a condom factory in Thailand, a microchip plant in Japan, a shoelace manufacturer in Indonesia, a gold mine in South Africa, a factory to make communion wafers for the Roman Catholic and Episcopal churches in Pennsylvania, a video game producer in California, and an exotic lingerie store in North Carolina.

Without informing anyone, Luiz contacted Isis about these business plans. While Jean-Michel knew that there had once been a romantic liaison between Luiz and Isis, he had no idea that the two had stayed in touch through the years. He now learned that Isis had innate business sense and, unknown to him and to most of the world except a chosen few, such as her brother the Pirate and her on-again, off-again lover Luiz, she had a master's degree in economics. A highly paid free-lance agent, she had invested her earnings wisely. Recently, she had been diagnosed with a rare neurological disorder, so getting into the development of therapeutic drugs had great appeal to her.

One day, she called Lacour and asked him to meet her at the original herb and spice shop. She was already there. He had met her once before, in Rio de Janeiro, and again marveled at her Junoesque form and Cleopatra hairstyle and heavy koal make-up. However, he assured Jean-Michel, she wasn't his type. She was holding a tube of suntan lotion in one hand and a small tin of red powder in the other; both had been early products created by Thomas and

Gwyn. Now that they were strictly in the herb and spice business, they were no longer experimenting with herbal byproducts, such as gums, ointments, diuretics, unguents, indigestion aids, poultices, even aphrodisiacs.

"Here are your winners, François," Isis declared. "A lotion guaranteed to soothe not just sunburn, but topical wounds, and an aphrodisiac that will have world-wide appeal. Have you any idea of how profitable a syndicate of sex shops could be?"

"The condom factory was a step in the right direction, don't you think?"

"Yes, but you and Tiago should have gotten into fetishes and kinky toys instead of shoelaces and communion wafers, of all things. Men! Here's the number of the Swiss bank account. It will more than enable you to get that lotion mass-produced and marketed worldwide. The aphrodisiac too. You should set up a string of sex shops that not only carry the usual toys, but the most erotic items found in various corners of the world. You'll make a killing and that will get you going in phytomedicine. Sometimes exploration has to begin with exploitation. This time, we'll exploit fantasies and fund your scientific research with the profits from crass commercialization. I'll be in touch."

Isis left as quickly as she had appeared. Lacour knew better than to try to follow her. He put her plan into operation immediately, and within six months the income from those two products far outpaced the earnings from the other business enterprises. A year later, they were well on their way to setting up a state-of-the-art lab and plans for sex shops under the name Le Jardin du Plaisir were in the works.

Soon the lotion became a best seller on the international scene, and their sex shops became instant hits everywhere, especially in the Far East. Lacour was able to begin sending small teams of researchers into the jungles and mountains of South America. His early friendship with Jacob Poncet paid off by providing him with several reliable contacts among the large European population in Argentina. Luiz then brought Paul Champion into the group on the theory that they could benefit from the experience of an expert narcotics investigator, who was totally unknown to the Latin American scene.

"One of the problems in this kind of field research, Jean-Michel, is dealing with the various tribes, especially their shamans, who are experts in the local flora. Their health care program is based partly on superstition and partly on their ability to draw benefits from the world of nature. The ethical problem lies in determining ownership of the products: the tribes who live on those lands or the people who develop them for legitimate medical purposes. The best example I can give you is that of the yucca plant; Native Americans long used it for food, clothing, medicine, and drink. Now it's in the hands of several private enterprises. Your friend Sylvestre, who is so enamored of the American Southwest, would be surprised to learn that the tequila that goes into his margaritas comes from the blue agave plant."

"I'll be sure to tell him. I do know that therapeutic drugs are being developed from living plants, animals, and organisms. My cousin Laurent told me that the drug taxol that was used successfully in treating a friend's breast cancer is surprisingly derived from a yew tree. He's hopeful that this sort of research will lead to a drug that is resistant to bacteria, such as *staph aureus*, which is so common in hospitals."

"You're well informed, Jean-Michel, but the average person doesn't know that there are over 250,000 tropical plants alone. We have no idea what the exploration of coral reefs and marine organisms will yield. New antibiotics are desperately needed to combat the spread of disease, treat pain, fight cancer, halt fungal infections, improve brain function, manage depression, handle toxic waste, and outwit viruses."

"You don't need to convince me. But tell me, where are we with the problem at hand: *nadamtha*, the Titans, and Isis? You found the plant and lost it and now want to relocate it. How did you lose a plant and do you now know where you can find it again? I understand that this group you call the Titans opposes your operation because they profit from the drug trade in Latin America. And you tell me that Isis is behind funding the project, yet I suspect that she's playing a double game, and I need to know what it is."

"Isis once worked for the Titans. The truth is that their success is due largely to her. However, of late she's been out of the game. Physically, her illness is taking its toll. My cohorts on the Ile agreed with me about asking her to come because she has the best knowledge of that group. At the same time, it put her at risk. It's obvious that the Titans have identified me as the ringleader of the effort to develop *nadamtha* and so they went for what they consider the head of the snake. There could be a traitor somewhere. I haven't yet figured out how they have learned where I'm now living. As they consolidated their control of South America, they probably set out to prove or disprove my death. They don't know just where that plant might be, but they are smart enough to know that if I'm alive, I'm planning a way to get it and take it to my lab. I don't know who in my organization could be in their pipeline. If there is such a rat, he doesn't know that I contacted Isis. Or, doesn't know yet."

"A leak? You know, François, it may not be a traitor in your operation. Isis is not the only expert tracker for hire. After all, we're certain that those Algerian twins are involved."

"Yes, I see your point, Jean-Michel, and that makes my contacting Isis all the more crucial. She'll know better than anyone whose trackers are in the game and how they operate. I really must have her knowledge of how the

Titans operate in order to get back into that hostile part of the world. If they learn that Isis is working with us, they'll hunt her down; they know her almost as well as she knows them. She was once the lover of the second-in-command, who is so psychotic that he'd either enjoy killing her or enjoy protecting her. Take your pick."

"Why do you suppose she was eager for me to go to Lima and take Amy?"

"Probably a deal, a trade-off of some sort. I'd guess that she planned to arrange a kidnapping, the ransom being an agreement that all efforts to locate *nadamtha* be dropped. You would also be told that the gang of four was using the Ile Saint-Louis as a safe haven for various criminal activities and that you were to see to it that all four left the Ile. Then we'd be taken out one by one. The drug trade would grow, but you and Amy would go on living in peace and calm on the Ile, and Isis would either return to wherever she is living or be executed. End of story."

Both men fell silent.

Hundreds of questions whirled around Jean-Michel's head, but he decided they could wait. While he'd learned a lot tonight, he knew that there was more. At least, he now knew in general the who, what, why, and where, but many of the details were missing. Lacour had identified the Irish watchers, but he didn't mention the Oriental ones. Were they actual watchers or wasn't he informed about them? Was Isis's double game really based on old jobs and an old love affair? Jealousy? Revenge? Was there really a rat within the gang of four's operation? Just where was this fabulous plant? What was it like? How did Lacour know that *nadamtha* had such properties? The details would come. Serge, Justine, and Gabriel were all back from their missions. When Luiz returned in a few days, they would sit down in this very room and hopefully work out a plan that would bring to an end the attention of the Titans to the Ile.

"I'll take the Métro back, Jean-Michel. We'll be in touch. By the way, your uncle Roger is probably the best undercover operative I've ever encountered. He's so transparent that one would never think he was actually on a mission. Botanical charts, no less! I actually enjoy his visits. He's both charming and knowledgeable. *Au revoir!*"

Jean-Michel poured another glass of wine. It had been a long conversation, but this time another veil was lifted. He had no choice but to play the game that the gang of four had devised. He took out his cell phone and made a series of calls. The last number was Amy's.

"*Allô, chérie.* Did I wake you? I'm sorry. Listen. I need you to cancel your plans for tomorrow. I have to go to Brussels. We'll take the early train and I promise you a large bowl of mussels and a huge platter of *pommes frites* as only the Belgians know how to make them. *Non, chérie,* that's outlandish. Yes, of course I know that history says that the first cut potatoes were fried with horse fat and that this is still the best way to prepare them, but I honestly don't think anyone has done them that way since the nineteenth century. I'd guess that today it's beef suet that makes the difference. Okay? I'll be home soon."

Jean-Michel knew that it was a long shot, but he thought it was worth a try. He wasn't the only one who knew a retired spy. Besides, Amy never tired of going to Brussels. Léonore's upcoming wedding would probably merit a trip to her favorite lace shop and he knew she wouldn't leave without buying several boxes of chocolates.

As Jean-Michel drove back to the Ile, he found himself thinking back to the first time he had taken Amy to Brussels. She had actually bought a miniature of the famous Manneken Pis statue, which continued to delight visitors. He'd never paid attention to that bronze fountain; a naked little boy spewing forth a continual stream of supposed urine seemed silly to him, but Amy loved it. She insisted on visiting it every time they went to Brussels. She would promptly burst out laughing. Jean-Michel just stood there, amazed that anything so small and so lacking in artistic merit and stuck in an out-of-the-way corner could attract so much attention. Yet crowds were always gathered in that out-of-the way corner to laugh at it and admire it. The statue was so popular that it was said to have a wardrobe of hundreds of costumes. During the return to Paris, he had asked her why it so appealed to her.

"Oh, Jean-Michel, it reminds me of my son Jack. Surely you know that it's typical of little boys. They love to see just how far they can spray. The first rule of toilet training boys is not to have a carpeted bathroom. I'm sure that when you were little, you were just as proud of your personal . . . um, hose as Jack was and as that Manneken Pis is."

Suddenly, he remembered his son Paul, killed by a car bomb many years ago. Yes, the Manneken Pis captured that very early rite of passage, the male discovery of his body. To this day, the statue that Amy had bought was in his study. It helped block the pain that often comes with memory by replacing it with a pleasurable moment of recall, a Proustian discovery of lost time. Amy was his *nadamtha*. He would do his best to help Lacour find his.

XII

The attacks came in the late afternoon on the last day of May. The Ile Saint-Louis was rocked by triple explosions: the wine bar on the corner of the Rue des Deux-Ponts and the Quai d'Orléans, a restaurant at the end of the island facing Notre-Dame, and the cultural interpretive center on the Rue Saint-Louis-en-l'Ile near the other end. A fourth, even more dramatic incident occurred on the Pont Marie. The unwritten message was clear.

When the explosions went off, Jean-Michel was working in his office on the Quai de Béthune. Amy was at the ATM machine on the corner of the Rue des Deux-Ponts and the Rue Saint-Louis-en-l'Ile.

Suddenly, a man on a motorcycle grabbed her and threw her into a nearby car that raced to the Pont Marie.

It was chased in turn by two motorcycles that cut in front of the sedan and caused it to crash. Several cars and trucks in turn hit the sedan and motorcycles from both sides, effectively forming a barrier across the middle of the bridge.

An artist on the bridge dropped his palette, took out a gun, and ran toward the pile-up. He was quickly joined by several people flashing guns.

Onlookers froze, not knowing what was going on, which way to run, who was a good guy and who was not.

Amy cowered in the back seat of the sedan. She knew she had been thrown against the door and had hit her head hard. She heard several men wrestling to open the front doors. They finally managed to get the driver and his passenger out of the car, but they ignored her. Later, she learned that they had immediately begun firing guns into the crowd at random in an effort to clear a path to get off the bridge. Others fired back and a gun battle was pitched. Several people were hit, including one passerby.

Suddenly, there was silence and then the sound of police klaxons filled the air. Amy heard metal hit metal as people worked to free her. She knew that the car was on its side, but try as hard as she could, she was unable to get the window down or door open. Finally, she saw a face. It was the artist, who had been painting scenes from the bridge for several weeks. Somehow, he was in the seat in front of her. "Give me your hand," he said. "I'll help you climb over and then I can get you out."

Immediately, two young men in long bright green scarves appeared and tried to pull the artist away. As they struggled, Amy heard the artist cry out in English, "Stop it, you friggin' damn Irish idiots! Don't you know I'm on your side? Mossad."

Finally, Amy was freed and lifted out of the car. She was stunned at the chaos of the scene around her. Cars and motorcycles were heaped on top of each other; people were bleeding on the street and sidewalks. Uniformed policemen arrived and tried to disperse the ever-growing crowd. Ambulance personnel in white coats seemed to be everywhere. She felt dizzy and started to fall, but several people with Oriental features surrounded her and eased her onto the pavement. Before she could say thank you, they melted away in the crowd.

"Madame, follow me," said a familiar voice. "I think you need to be checked out by a medical officer."

"Oh, Monsieur Mathieu. I'm so glad to see you. Whatever happened? This is a scene out of a horror movie! I heard gunshots, lots of them, and then all sorts of odd people seemed to be around me: Japanese businessmen, green teenagers, a crazed artist with a gun, yelling that he was Moses. I must have been hit on the head and had delusions. Good grief! I was kidnapped, wasn't I?"

"So it would seem, Madame, so it would seem. Have you any idea who your kidnappers were and why they wanted you?"

"No. I was at the ATM machine and someone grabbed me from behind and tossed me like a head of cabbage into a car and off we went. Then there was a huge bang, a collision, I guess, and I was thrown against the car door. I must have been knocked out at some point. I don't know. Maybe I should see a doctor. I am a little dizzy."

Mathieu groaned. Of course, Amy Page, now Jolivet, would be in the middle of this mess. He had received word about the three explosions on the Ile and was hurrying to the Ile when he heard the crash, screams and shouts, and then the noise of the gunfight. He already suspected that there was a major plot in the works and that the police were being purposefully sidelined.

Rémy Legrand pulled up on his Vespa.

"Bonjour, Hervé. Don't say it! Whatever you're thinking is right. I've just gotten word that there were three explosions on the Ile. Yes, three. Those events added to this incident will force Jean-Michel to bring you into the picture. It's basically an IBS case, but before you ask, yes, the Archangels are involved. Yes, it includes locals. It's my guess that he's kept you out of it until the situation is clearer. He also thinks there's a traitor somewhere and he was hoping to identify him before bringing in the police. But that's all moot now. Yes, there's a terrorist gang behind all of this. Yes, it involves French citizens, as well as foreign nationals. Yes, the Ile is the likely center of the whole affair. And, yes, our dear Amy is up to her neck in it and as usual she's the innocent victim-cum-witness or witness-cum-victim."

"I thought that something was going on. Jean-Michel did ask me to increase patrols on the Ile. He gave me some cock-and-bull story about the possibility of a gang of criminals being able to set up a headquarters on the Ile, coming in with the influx of tourists. Of all people, he knew that the police always assign extra men to both the Ile de la Cité and the Ile Saint-Louis for that very reason. Not so much to find a nest of criminals, but rather the usual ramshackle collection of petty thieves, pickpockets, and con artists who prey on the tourist trade. He gave me the impression that he wanted his precious group of ex-spies protected from suspicion whenever something happened. After all, the general was killed by mistake, and the killer was apprehended elsewhere on other charges."

There was no reason to tell Mathieu that the killer had purposefully been left at large. Sometimes it was best to let sleeping dogs lie.

"Your men have things on the bridge well under control, Hervé. There's nothing we can do about Madame Jolivet; someone will get her to a hospital to check her out. I think we need to get hold of Jean-Michel and fill him in. He's probably somewhere on the Ile, looking at the bomb sites. Let's walk over there and try to find him."

Mathieu and Legrand walked around the pile of wreckage to the Rue des Deux-Ponts. As they crossed the Rue Saint-Louis-en-l'Ile, Legrand made a note to have the area scoured for a witness to Amy's kidnapping. Just ahead they spotted Jean-Michel, standing in the middle of the next block in front of Lacour's map shop. He was taking notes on his BlackBerry while surrounded by a small crowd of shoppers and shopkeepers.

"*Bonjour*, Jean-Michel. Hervé and I were looking for you. We heard that that there were three attacks on the Ile. We've just come from the crash on the Pont Marie. While a lot of people were wounded, most can be taken care of on the spot. The more serious cases are already on the way to area hospitals. Interviews are being conducted as we speak. As you can imagine, that incident has brought out loads of curiosity seekers, not to mention the press, making a chaotic situation worse. It'll be several hours before we can even begin to clear the wreckage and open the bridge to traffic."

"So that's where all the ambulances are. One of the bombs targeted the corner wine bar. There is at least one dead and two are badly wounded, one of them being my uncle Roger. I think he's broken his leg. At least, that's the diagnosis by the retired veterinarian whose apartment is just over there on the other side of the street. Passersby just have minor cuts and bruises, which the vet has been able to treat, telling me that he had the same first aid knowledge as a doctor or nurse, or Boy Scout for that matter."

Legrand smiled.

"Maybe we should take him over to the bridge to patch up the walking wounded and relieve some ambulance personnel so that they can come here and tend to your uncle and the others. A doctor and several nurses walked over to the Pont Saint-Louis to take care of those hurt by the attack on the restaurant. I just heard from the detail that I sent to the cultural center. They reported no injuries but one dead. A Mademoiselle Darcet."

"How sad! She was the new curator. Amy will be crushed to hear that she was killed."

"Speaking of Madame Jolivet, she is okay, but she did hit her head and should see a doctor."

Jean-Michel frowned. "Amy? Where is she? What happened? Don't tell me, Hervé, that she was on the bridge! Why would she be on the bridge? She didn't have any plans to leave the Ile today. She wasn't even going to the cultural center."

Mathieu cleared his throat.

"We don't know exactly what happened, but it seems that she was the object of a kidnapping. All we know is that she was apparently in the backseat of a car that collided with two motorcycles in the middle of the Pont Marie, more cars and trucks crashed into them, and then for reasons unknown the driver of the car and his passenger started shooting. We gather that there were some armed men on the bridge who returned their fire. The long and the short of it is that one of the gunmen got away, the other was killed, and quite a few people were wounded."

"And Amy? Kidnapped? Was she hurt?"

"Somehow she got out of the car. She's got a bad cut on her temple and she's probably sore from being knocked around in the back seat. The car landed on its side and people helped her get out. She says she's fine, just a little woozy."

"Of course, she's dizzy if she hit her head! What else did she say? Does she have any idea who tried to kidnap her?"

"Well, Jean-Michel, she was probably knocked out at first, so she was bound to be a bit disoriented when she came to. She told Legrand that she saw, correct me here, Rémy, green men, Chinese, no Japanese businessmen, and a mad painter with a gun who claimed he was Moses."

"That's right. It doesn't make any sense," Legrand added. "Then again, Jean-Michel, you are the only one who's ever been able to question her and sort out her answers. But there you have it: green men, businessmen, and a painter."

In spite of the circumstances, Jean-Michel burst out laughing.

"Well, I know who the green men are, and I'm pretty sure I know who the men in dark suits and ties are. I can even identify the artist. A gun-toting painter! How very, very clever!"

"I'm glad it makes sense to you. How about letting us in on the secret?"

"Yes, yes, Rémy, I will. But first, let me tell my uncle that help is on the way and let's grab the good Dr. Landel."

When the four men reached the Pont Marie, Jean-Michel immediately spotted Amy sitting on the back step of an ambulance. She had a large white bandage around her head, and he could tell from a distance that she was trying hard to make sense out of the chaos around her. Suddenly, she saw him and jumped up to greet him. He just did manage to catch her before she fell and led her over to the curb, where he sat her down, and then sat down next to her.

"*Ma pauvre Amy*! What have you gotten into this time? I'm going to have to put you on a leash and not let you out of my sight."

"Oh, Jean-Michel, it's all a jumble. Just look around you! I don't understand any of it. There I was at the ATM machine, minding my own business, just getting some Euros for . . . well, for something important, and the next thing I knew I was thrown into the backseat of a car. Then there were green men yelling at a crazy artist, who yelled that he was Moses, and a whole bunch of Japanese, and all of a sudden I was out of the car. The next thing I knew, Hervé Mathieu appeared. I think I must have passed out. Everything is so fragmented. I just have flashes of things that don't add up to a hill of beans. Or whatever. Nothing makes sense. And I have a whopping headache. I don't want to go to the hospital. I want to go home and crawl into bed. Can't you please tell all these nice people in white coats that I live right over there, just a few blocks away? Laurent can come and look at me. I don't need to be in the hospital. Just take me home, Jean-Michel, please."

Amy burst into tears. Jean-Michel took her in his arms and held her tight. The sight of the comte de Bourdonville, sitting on the curb on the bridge, holding his bedraggled, bandaged bride tight in his arms, set off a series of flashes from the horde of journalists who had gathered to cover the scene. Their picture would ultimately appear in newspapers and magazines everywhere. It was truly written that a picture was worth a thousand words.

The veterinarian, Dr. Landel, said that Amy probably had no broken bones and might be suffering from a mild concussion. The two men convinced the physician assigned to the lead ambulance to let Amy return home. They would see to it that she received proper care and was monitored around the clock. Fortunately, the ambulance doctor knew Dr. Laurent Rochefort and remembered dealing with Amy and the family on several earlier occasions. Although most of the streets on the Ile were cordoned off to traffic, Claude and Léon managed to bring Pascal's motorized wheelchair. They quickly seated Amy in it and took her immediately to the Hôtel de Rochefort. After a hot bath and a nourishing meal, she fell into bed and promptly went to sleep thanks to a mild sedative.

Jean-Michel made a phone call and a police car picked up Victor Rochefort in Neuilly and drove him in record time to the other end of the Ile. True to form, his brother Roger was propped up on the pavement and holding court to an admiring crowd.

"Ah, my brother Victor! *Salut, mon vieux.* I've been telling these good people about canes and walking sticks. I seem to have broken my favorite one. Just look at it! The ebony is in several pieces. At least the dog's head in silver on the end is intact. Not even scratched. Now don't fuss over me, Victor. I've been assured by a veterinarian no less . . . isn't it ironic? I have a stick with a dog's head and an animal doctor just happens to come along when needed! Anyway, it's just a broken leg. I'll be fine. The blessed vet gave me some sort of painkiller. You know, there just doesn't seem to be an ambulance around when you need one and yet I've heard all sorts of klaxons wailing all around me. Look, here comes one now across the Pont de la Tournelle. That vet said he'd get one here. And there's Alain, right behind it."

It turned out that Roger's leg was broken in two places, but Victor assured Caroline over the phone from the hospital that they were clean breaks and would heal quickly. No, he didn't know how long he'd be in the hospital. Orthopedics wasn't his specialty. Alain was there and Laurent was on his way. Yes, he'd have Laurent stop by and look in on Amy. No, he hadn't heard anything about who set the bombs and why. Yes, Isabelle was mourning the loss of Natalie Darcet; she was an odd person but just right for the job and would be difficult to replace. Yes, some sort of memorial would be the right thing to do. He'd ask Isabelle to come up with something. No, he'd not seen Jean-Michel. Yes, maybe the city fathers had been wrong to close the police station on the Ile. Perhaps she should write to the mayor about it.

Jean-Michel didn't get home until dawn. He immediately went to the bedroom where Amy was fast asleep. The awkward bandage around her head had been removed and he could see clearly the laceration. Someone, probably Laurent, had placed steristrips across it. Amy would be relieved to learn that she didn't have stitches. He also noted a large bruise on her cheek. When she woke up, she would probably find several places on her body turning black and blue, and she would be very sore all over.

When he walked into his study, he saw that he had a letter in the middle of his desk: pink paper, lavender ink. His aunt Caroline, of course! Sometimes, he was grateful to have prying, meddling, caring relatives. She had written him a detailed report on what Amy had had to eat and drink, on the sedative she'd been given, on Laurent's visit and promise to return tomorrow, on Roger's condition. Appended was a list of those she had notified: his mother in Bourdonville; Amy's daughter; Margot and Agnès; Julien Turenne, who had agreed to inform the Comité des Douze, which served as the unofficial overseer of the Ile; Philippe Jammet, who said he would meet with the committee for the cultural center to discuss Natalie Darcet's death and the repairs needed; and, quite naturally, Sylvestre. On a separate sheet of paper was the notation that Chantal would be by at noon to give Amy a massage. Last but by no means least was a copy of her letter to the mayor with copies to the Minister of the Interior and several deputies to the French Assembly.

Caroline was in her glory at her command post. Her network was in full gear, notified and ready for whatever operations she ordered. He often wished he had Caroline's command of an information network; she could accomplish more with one well placed phone call than he could with several highly skilled teams and a sophisticated communications system. Notes, cards, flowers, spa baskets, and boxes of candy would undoubtedly start to overload the postal delivery system.

The large group that gathered that night at Le Singe Vert was unusually quiet. They were all there: the four Archangels along with Achille, the gang of four, both Serge and Justine, Legrand from IBS, and this time the police, in the person of Hervé Mathieu. Even Clovis, the bar owner, had been invited to join them. They were the best of the best, an elite group with sophisticated training, unlimited talent, decades of experience, and expertise in criminal investigation, field operations, weaponry, security measures, and surveillance. Most were accustomed to operating outside the law.

Jean-Michel rubbed his eyes. It had been a long night and there was very little to show for it. He had had to make a difficult phone call to Sean and tell him that one of his men had been killed in an exchange of gunfire on the Pont Marie. He went over to one of the wingback chairs in front of the fireplace and began to review the meeting he had just held at Le Singe Vert.

At least he had gotten Jacob Poncet to admit that the artist on the bridge had been one of his men, a retired agent who had come from Spain to help him keep an eye on what he suspected was Champion's team. Amy had, of course, misunderstood Mossad and thought he had said Moses. However, Poncet refused to say if he had anyone else on the case, but Jean-Michel was positive that at least two of the pedestrians were former Mossad agents.

In contrast, Paul Champion had been his inscrutable self. Why would he hire Japanese businessmen? The people Madame saw were probably innocent tourists. The Japanese were enamored of Paris and both islands in the Seine were major tourist attractions. Besides, he asked, what made Amy think they were Japanese and not Chinese? Surely, the four-star Japanese restaurant that had opened on the Quai de Bourbon drew patrons from many countries, not just Japan. He understood that reservations had to be made there several months in advance. And, as Jean-Michel knew well, there was a large Vietnamese population in Paris, so maybe his wife was mistaken in thinking they were Japanese. Was Madame an expert on Orientals? Could they have been Koreans? Or Thais?

Jean-Michel admitted to the group that he had believed that Amy was safe on the Ile. The Archangels took over whenever she went out. With Sean's Irish team, Poncet's Mossad members, and Champion's Oriental phantoms on duty on the Ile itself, how had Amy been kidnapped? Were they so busy looking for a sleeper cell that no one was watching her? There were too many teams, too many watchers, too much attention to people coming and going and too little attention to the normal hustle and bustle of daily life on the Ile. It was a wonder that the scheme to kidnap Amy had failed.

Gabriel broke the silence.

"What if the kidnapping was meant as a scare tactic? Maybe Amy would have been released several blocks away. It's impossible to think that the botched kidnapping was planned to coincide with the bombings. No one could have predicted that Amy would be on that corner at that particular moment."

"I agree," said Poncet. "Think about it. The would-be kidnappers merely tossed her into the backseat. By herself. I mean the second man was a passenger in the front seat. No one else was in the backseat to put a bag over her head, tie her up, or push her down on the floor. The only precaution taken was securing the locks. She couldn't open the window or the door. Even a bunch of amateurs would have seen enough TV to do a better job. Botching the job was part of a plan. The bombings were a stroke of luck. They just didn't count on being stopped on the bridge. Those Irish lads on motorcycles were extraordinary in causing the crash. I for one deeply regret that one of those lads had to die. Am I right to think that he was one of Sean O'Dell's group? I've never liked the IRA, but I can't fault their training."

"Sean's no longer with the IRA," Jean-Michel commented. "However, he does have a small private army to protect him and his family. I suspect that he is occasionally for hire, what he would say is a consulting job. You're quite right about the training though. You just can't beat the Israeli army system."

Everyone laughed and saluted Poncet. With the tension broken in the room, the group got down to exchanging reports and information. Tiago Luiz, Gabriel, Serge, and Justine shared what they had learned in South America. It mainly confirmed what they already knew. The Titan consortium was strong, well supplied, and well entrenched. They controlled the areas that Lacour had identified as possible places to find the plant *nadamtha*. They left alone archeologists and those researchers seeking curative herbs; they ruthlessly eradicated any they suspected of having interest in opiates. As a result, they killed scientists and shamans with equanimity and on occasion effaced an entire tribe from the face of the earth.

Uriel spoke up.

"You know that I'm a scientist, so please tell me, Lacour, have you ever actually seen this *nadamtha*? Do you know that it exists? What kind of plant is it? Is the drug derived from its flower, berries, leaves, or root? And if so, do you have any idea what its properties are? I'll be honest with you. It sounds pretty far-fetched to me. I think we all wish there were such a magic plant that could effectively block the human urge for narcotics, but I for one am skeptical."

There were nods of agreement all around the room. Everyone turned toward Lacour, waiting for him to speak.

"When I first started bioprospecting in South America, I heard about a miraculous plant that grew in, not on, trees. One tribal medicine man told me that he had never seen it, but that he had been told about it by his grandfather. It was supposed to cure all illnesses, heal wounds, ease pain, prevent the spread of disease, and do all sorts of marvelous things. However, no one knew exactly where it grew. His grandfather had told him that he had heard that even those who had seen it said that it was hard to find and even harder to harvest. It bloomed only at night during a full moon; the flower was light blue and the leaves were a blue green; all its parts were useful in medical treatment, but the most powerful drug came from the calyx of the flower."

Lacour paused and took a sip of wine.

"Ah, Clovis, I'd say this is an old expensive vintage, not your usual rot gut. *Merci bien, mon ami.*"

Clovis nodded. He had known Lacour for a long time. The world of espionage covered a multitude of sins and included a few saints, but mainly sinners.

"Anyway, I was fascinated. Bioprospecting is most often successful when it begins with shaman knowledge. Naturally, I set out to find what I call *nadamtha*, a name derived from that of my favorite professors, way back when. To make a long story short, I asked my boss, whom you all call affectionately Pip, if I could go to South America to assess the growth of the drug industry in that region. He agreed and off I went. I had a small team of genuine researchers. We came across an indigenous people who were incredibly healthy. Not one of them seemed to have ever been affected by an illness or accident. Frankly, I had never seen such a robust, hale and hearty group. One night, a full moon night, the shaman invited me to go with him on a gathering expedition. He stopped here and there, taking the leaves from one plant, digging up another for the roots, and so on. When we reached a small clearing, he went over to a tree, took the monkey off his shoulder and indicated that it was to climb up. It did and soon came back with a plant that was unlike any I'd ever seen before. It was just as I described: a light blue flower nestled in greenish blue leaves with a scraggly root. It wasn't a true parasite, such as mistletoe or Spanish moss. I'd never seen anything like it. It was quite breathtaking. The shaman gave it to me and had the monkey scamper back up for two more, which he put in his medical pouch, and we returned to the village."

"A monkey! A parasitic plant that's not a parasite! Full moon! Villagers who've never suffered from pain and injury!" The comments flew around the room. Everyone was in disbelief.

"Sounds like a pulp fiction magazine story to me!" someone shouted. "What a yarn, Lacour!"

"I know. It sounds like something out of the movies, but it did happen. I returned to London with the plant specimen and began to test it in a lab. It seems to have properties similar to the yucca or agave plant. I had just about used it all up in various tests when by accident a piece of the calyx fell onto a slide that had been used in another test. I could tell immediately that this might be the drug I'd been hoping to find. Because I had so little of the one plant left, I decided to test it at once on a person. I didn't have enough to conduct drug trials. I went out in the street, found an addict, and bribed him to taste it. I was soon rewarded by his saying he no longer craved crack. As you can well imagine, I was overjoyed. Unfortunately, the lab went up in flames within days. No, it wasn't the Titans. The lab next to mine had been working on a new explosive, which inadvertently went off, destroying half the building."

"I'm familiar with the sequel," Raphaël injected. "François went to Pip with his findings, convinced him to let him mount an operation to gather as much of the plant as he could, and back to South America he went. Which is where I came in. He ran afoul of the Titans, was captured and tortured, and

Pip asked Jean-Michel to get us to get him out because while he was one of Her Majesty's top spies, he was on an unauthorized mission."

"Yes, you're right on all counts except one. It wasn't the Titans. They weren't yet on the scene. It was one of the drug cartels. They didn't kill me because they thought I would make a good hostage, but they did massacre the rest of my team, the village shaman, and all the villagers. You know the rest. Ever since, with the help of my three colleagues here, I've been trying to locate another site where *nadamtha* grows. I can't believe it existed in just that one place. To cut to the chase, such a venture has required a great deal of time: funding, research facilities, a gathering of resources, such as a Spanish-speaking team of commandos, locals to scout the area, and so on. While I was readying things on my end, the Titans came into existence and made their deal with the cartels. They have way more manpower, arms, and financing than my organization and I can muster. The reports given here tonight by Tiago, Gabriel, Serge, and Justine support that conclusion. Not even Isis has been able to find us a way out of this impasse. And now it would seem that there is a traitor among us. The Titans always seem to be a step ahead, knowing what we are going to do before even we do. There's no other explanation for what happened on the Ile Saint-Louis today."

The room fell silent in tacit agreement. Jean-Michel interrupted everyone's thoughts: "Are we then saying that what happened today was a warning?"

"You tell me, Jean-Michel. You tell me."

No one spoke for a few moments. Mathieu volunteered the information that the police lab was working on the fragments of the three bombs, but so far they were made of ordinary matériel easily obtainable, and literally untraceable.

A preliminary report from Ballistics offered nothing new: involved were several different guns, including an old Beretta and a German Walther. Chances were none of the guns were registered and all were now resting somewhere on the bottom of the Seine.

The fingerprint unit had more fingerprints than suspects, and there were too many witnesses; the only points of agreement were loud noises, metal crushing metal, screams, muzzle flashes, yelling, a veritable Babel of sounds.

The young men on motorcycles and the artist had completely disappeared. No one had had the presence of mind to take a photo on a cell phone.

So far, there didn't seem to be a single reliable eyewitness, except for Madame Jolivet, whose testimony so far had not been helpful. The one dead kidnapper had yet to be identified.

Jean-Michel summarized what they knew to date.

First, the timing of the explosion demanded a well-trained team with expertise in bomb placement. They had done it without drawing attention to themselves and were able to synchronize the blasts.

Second, the construction of the bombs themselves pointed to a high level of sophistication, particularly the skillful use of common elements to prevent discovery of place of origin. The bombs were small, designed to be disruptive, but not destructive. The bombers wanted to create a sense of panic on the Ile by proving that no one anywhere was safe.

The death of Natalie Darcet was unintentional. No one was supposed to be killed, just scared. The bombs were meant to generate more noise, smoke, and alarm than outright mayhem. Eight people had been seriously injured and three killed; most of the victims had simply been in the wrong place at the wrong time. Killing had not been intentional. Everyone else within range suffered minor cuts from flying glass, bruises, a few sprains from running and falling down, and, of course, one broken leg.

When it was clear that no one wished to add a comment, Jean-Michel continued with his third point: financing. The money behind the operation had to be respected because it was not just a matter of bomb design, buying the materials, and then placement of the explosives, but also because of the use of a large number of professionals to carry out the plan.

Last, but not least, there was the matter of transportation of both personnel and matériel. The planners had to have an on-site location for the actual building of the bombs, and it had to be a place that would not attract attention, yet be central to the objectives of the operation. Indeed, there had been a sleeper cell on the Ile, maybe even two. He was positive that they would eventually locate the place or places, but no one would be there. Whoever was involved had probably already left. The diabolical nature of the three explosions demonstrated the power of a group that could only be the Titans. It was most definitely a warning.

The gathering at Le Singe Vert had been unusually long and Jean-Michel went home exhausted. When he woke up in the morning, he could hear Claude and Aline in the kitchen. He knew he should tell them he was home. As he walked toward the door, he spied a long cardboard box standing up against the bookcase. When he opened it, he found a large branch covered with leaves. There was no note, just a photograph of him holding Amy on the curb on the bridge. Looking closely, he realized that what he had been sent was an olive branch. He now knew who the traitors were. He also knew what they would do next. He too was an old spy. For the first time since he was eight years old and was stung by a swarm of bees, Jean-Michel Jolivet, lawyer, titled member of the old French aristocracy, retired IBS director, founder and CEO of a security service with clients in all parts of the globe, part owner of a vineyard, winery, and rather large château in Burgundy, sat down and cried.

XIII

The next ten days dragged by for Amy, but flew by for Jean-Michel. It was as though they lived in different time zones in different spaces. While he spent long hours at his office and in meetings in the back room of Le Singe Vert, she stayed in their apartment and nursed her many aches and pains. The headaches quickly went away, leaving her to cope with many bruises, which were changing hues: black, blue, yellow. Where she wasn't sore, she was stiff. She told Jean-Michel one night that she hurt in places she didn't even know she had.

Amy passed the hours talking on the phone with her daughter and sister, leafing through magazines, going through her notepad of ideas for food articles, and chatting with occasional visitors. Laurent came every day on his way home and Caroline came every day for lunch. She gave her the latest news about Roger and meticulously wrote down who had sent what so that Amy would be able to write the appropriate thank-you notes when she felt better. Caroline would then decide which flower arrangements should be sent to a hospital, and sent Léon and Claude to deliver them.

Among the gifts Amy received were a copy of Brillat-Savarin's 1825 *La Physiologie du goût* from Julien Turenne and a large cactus dish garden from Véronique and Sylvestre with a small cowboy on a horse in the center and a coyote on a rock. Marianne and Mireille sent her a beautiful multi-colored cafetan with raglan sleeves and shirring at the neckline. Caroline had snorted at the extravagant gift from the interpretive cultural center committee: a large ten-pound box of chocolates. Amy guessed that the large Limoges basket full of fruit came from the mysterious Artemis; there was no card and it had been hand-delivered by Florian.

Amy's favorite gift came from Charles Pichon: a rare silver absinthe spoon with the directions on how to make *La Fée Verte*, which was probably the most potent drink ever created. It was based on the bitter herb wormwood and was in vogue at the end of the nineteenth century. Fans included Manet, Baudelaire, Oscar Wilde, Van Gogh, Rimbaud, Picasso, Gauguin, and Verlaine. The Degas painting *L'Absinthe* featured it. Toulouse-Lautrec was said to keep it mixed with cognac in his hollowed out cane.

Preparation was a ritual. Step One: place a sugar cube on the flat perforated absinthe spoon. Step Two: balance the spoon with the sugar on the rim of a bell-shaped glass into which one has already placed some absinthe. Step Three: slowly pour iced water over the sugar cube to dissolve it. As the water drips into the absinthe, it will turn green, hence the name, Green Fairy. Although Amy was delighted to add the spoon to her silver collection and thoroughly enjoyed the story, she doubted that she could use it for one of her food articles. Jean-Michel had agreed.

One afternoon, Jean-Michel arrived with René Legrand and Hervé Mathieu, who brought Amy a box of palmiers, her favorite pastry. She was touched that the two policemen remembered. They needed to question her about the incident on the Pont Marie. Could she describe her kidnappers? No. What about the one who grabbed her? No. He had been on a motorcycle and had been wearing a helmet. She guessed he was wearing a helmet. He had grabbed her from behind. No, she could not describe the motorcycle except that it was black. Black and silver. Lots of silver, she thought. The motorcyclist was big, very big. He picked her up easily and just threw her into the back seat of the car. He never said a word. Well, he might have said something, but she didn't understand it. What did it sound like? Sound like? Yes, did he say, for example, "Here she is! Go on, get going, take off, anything like that?" "No, but it was a command of some sort," she replied. "I don't even remember hearing him take off, but he must have."

The two policemen persevered, asking where he was when he grabbed her. "Well, I suppose he had gotten off the motorcycle," she answered.

"*Non*, Madame, I mean can you remember on which street he was when he was on the motorcycle?" And so the questioning went. They sent Jean-Michel a pleading look. Maybe he knew the right questions to ask.

"Let's think back, Amy. You were at the ATM machine on the corner of the Rue des Deux-Ponts and the Rue Saint-Louis-en-l'Ile."

"You already know that, Jean-Michel," she replied. "That's where the ATM machine is."

"Yes. Where had you been before you went to the machine? From what direction?"

"Oh, I see. Well, that day, I went first to Charles Pichon's antique shop to look at some wine goblets for us to give to Léonore. Then I went to Chez Ma Tante to finalize the menu with Auguste. I really don't know why he is so insistent on doing the wedding dinner himself at the restaurant. You know that I—"

"*Oui, mon amour.* What did you do when you left the restaurant?"

"Oh, I crossed the street and went to Berthillon's to buy some ice cream for our dinner. My goodness! What happened to the ice cream? It was a greengage plum. That's it. Greengage plum. It was a new flavor. I tasted it in the shop and it was delicious. Maybe you could stop by and get some."

"I'll bring some home tonight. Let's get back to my question. You were in the ice cream store, so when you left, you crossed the Rue St-Louis-en-l'Ile to get to the ATM machine on the other side of the street. Did you just cross the street or did you walk up to the corner and cross there?"

"Okay, I confess. I jaywalked. I just crossed the street. You know there's hardly ever any traffic on that part of the street. There really wasn't any reason for me to go to the corner and wait for the light."

"So where was the motorcycle, Amy? Surely, you noticed it. Surely, you looked both ways before crossing the street. It had to be in your line of vision."

"Yes, yes, it was. I remember! When I came out of the restaurant, it was parked right in front. I didn't pay much attention to him. I just thought at the time that he was probably waiting for someone. Do you think he was waiting for me?"

All three men nodded yes.

"So he was facing the Rue des Deux-Ponts?"

"Yes, he was."

"Was the engine on or off?"

"It was on. It was running. Yes, it was idling. I do remember that."

"I'm going to assume that he moved up the street on that side while you were walking on the other side."

"I think that's right. I know that I was glad he was moving on."

"Have you any idea from which direction the car came? Do you think it came from the Rue des Deux-Ponts or across the street on the Rue Saint-Louis-en-l'Ile? Did you hear it turn a corner? What did you hear, Amy? Think hard."

Amy frowned. A headache was starting to come back. She knew that it was important for her to remember every detail, but it had been a frightening event and she had been completely surprised. It seemed to her that she had no sooner been thrown into the car than the car crashed. There was a time gap in her memory.

"You know that I wasn't kidnapped very long, so there really isn't very much to remember."

"Just try, Amy."

"The best I can do is say that I think the car turned onto the Rue des Deux-Ponts from across the street. I had set the ice cream on the sidewalk in order to put my card in the ATM machine. I had already gotten my card back and was counting the money. You always have to double-check that you get the amount you asked for, you know."

"Quite right. Go on."

"I hadn't yet picked up the ice cream when I was grabbed. That's where I left it! On the sidewalk! I hope someone picked it up before it melted and enjoyed it."

Amy's recall provided a rough time line. They would reenact the scene, but they already were able to begin to put the pieces together.

She had had the time to complete her transaction, but not enough time to pick up the ice cream. Someone had followed Amy, with the intention of kidnapping her. This incident couldn't possibly be related to the three bombings. That came about by chance. It was possible that someone might have noticed the black and silver motorcycle idling in a no parking zone outside Chez Ma Tante.

Because of the death of one member of his team, Sean had ordered the rest of them back to Ireland. Jean-Michel would have to call him to see if any of his team had taken note of the motorcycle. They had been tailing Amy and so knew to rescue her. There had never been any mention of a motorcycle, although one person he had interviewed after the bombing of the wine bar had said that he had seen a black and silver motorcycle speed down the Rue des Deux-Ponts and cross the Pont de la Tournelle. Jean-Michel would reinterview him, but he was already sure that he hadn't noted the license plate. Maybe one of the many watchers had seen it and could recall it.

René Legrand coughed.

"I'm wondering, Madame, if the two men in the car said anything at all?"

"Well, yes and no. Not at first. The car just took off and I heard the locks lock. I struggled to sit up and saw a motorcycle pass and one of the men did yell at the other one, but I don't know what exactly. It wasn't a language I know. It was a singsong, you know; it sounded like the people in that Japanese film we saw last week. They certainly weren't English-speaking, nor were they using a Germanic or Romance language."

Jean-Michel nodded.

"Yes, that makes sense and goes far in confirming one theory. Thanks,

Amy, you've been very helpful. Get some rest. I'll be home in time for dinner and I promise I'll bring you some greengage ice cream."

Amy frowned.

"I don't see how that helped. I couldn't understand a single syllable."

"I understand. Right now I'd rather not go into details. Just know that we have a pretty good idea about who was responsible for your kidnapping, and we're now going to check it out. Ah, here comes Claude with another bouquet of flowers. How many does that make to date? You're a very popular woman!"

Jean-Michel and the two policemen quickly left the Hôtel de Rochefort and held a short conference on the street. Jean-Michel then left the two men and walked down the Quai de Bourbon to the Rue des Deux-Ponts, where he turned right and walked to the map shop. Late that night, he and François Lacour flew in a small private jet to a small landing field near Basel, Switzerland. They were met by a black limousine driven by a formally attired chauffeur. Soon they were drinking coffee in front of a marble fireplace in a book-lined library, deep within a small castle.

When Amy awoke, she grumbled that Jean-Michel wasn't there. At least, last night he had brought her the greengage ice cream as promised. She had complained that she thought he was out of the spy business and was no longer going to have to go off on secret missions anymore now that he had Serge and Justine. He had merely laughed and told her that sometimes it was a matter of a friend in need, most often an old spy.

"I guess old spies are people. Funny. Somehow one doesn't think about them as having private lives and what they do in retirement. I know that Pip grows roses, but some probably don't know how to do anything else. Just like criminals. You really know some strange people, Jean-Michel. I know that Clovis and your Archangels were once on the wrong side of the law. Tell me, is Francois Lacour an old spy or an old criminal? I know he must be one or the other."

"That, *chérie*, is a very long story. When this business of your kidnapping and the bombings is over, I promise to tell you all about him. When I do, you might consider writing a novel instead of food articles. His is a strange tale indeed."

Amy got up and realized that she ached less. After eating breakfast in the Tuscany-style kitchen, she decided that she could surprise Jean-Michel by finishing several food articles for the South Carolina *County Chronicle*. If she could clear her desk of deadlines, maybe they could go off somewhere together for a few days. Basque country! That was it! She would greet him with several completed items and that folder on the Pyrenees. Yes, they could take the

TGV or fly to Bayonne or Biarritz, rent a car, and drive to . . . to someplace like Narbonne and return to Paris from there, by train or plane.

Enthusiastically, Amy went to her desk in the Provençal suite and turned on her computer. Speaking to herself, she said, "Hmm, I don't really feel like writing a whole article. These notes are just that. Notes. Random pieces of information. Aha! That's it! I can do several articles on trivia. I'll just make a list:

*Lettuce was cooked as a vegetable until the eighteenth century.

*Crème brûlée was created at the University of Cambridge, England.

*Mayonnaise dates back to the first century, AD.

*Vichyssoise was created in New York in 1917 by a French chef.

*If the tips of a croissant point outward, the croissant was made with butter; if they point inward, it was made with margarine.

*The spoon is the oldest eating utensil.

*Wine is named for a place; food is named for a place, person, thing, event.

*The potato was strictly ornamental until 1771 when Parmentier convinced King Louis XVI that it was safe to eat.

*Margarine was created in 1868 by a French chemist.

*In France, a charlotte is unbaked; in Britain, it is baked.

*The fork was popularized by Louis XIV.

*Meringue was first created by a Swiss chef in Germany."

Amy sat back and smiled.

"That's one done. Let's see . . . Another list. I'll try one on doubles. No, that's not right. Double entendres. Well, whatever. Some foods in French have rather sexy names. I know, I'll call it 'Food behind Closed Doors.' I'll see what I can come up with:

*robe de chambre (bathrobe) = potato skin

*vierge (virgin) = whipped butter

*au naturel (naked) = on the half shell

*reine (queen) = chicken

*Vénus (Venus) = mollusk

*Jésus (Jesus) = sausage from Lyons

*bâtard (bastard) = irregularly shaped loaf of white bread

*bâtarde (bastard) = butter sauce

*pomme d'amour (love apple) = tomato

Oops. I forgot that a demoiselle is also a small lobster and that preserving was developed in 1810 for Napoleon's army. Oh, and it's an odd fact but lemon grass is an herb, while wild rice is a grass. I think two lists are enough. I wonder if my readers would like to know that the English word chowder comes from the French chaudière, a pot, and that hash is from the French *hâcher*, meaning to chop up. Just because I think it's fun to know that tarragon gets its name from *estragon* or little dragon because its roots are twisted like a snake. On second thought, probably not. So now what? Aha! The napkin and the tablecloth! That's it!"

The telephone rang.

"*Allô!* Oh, hi, Foster. I was just working on items for you. I've done two. They're lists. Interesting lists. You'll see. Now I'm doing an article on linens. I'll bet you didn't know that the tablecloth was used during the Middle Ages and that one wiped one's utensils and hands on it. What? Utensils? Just the spoon to scoop things up and the knife to spear things like hunks of meat. The fork came along later. Henri III tried it but it became a laughing stock, so the preferred etiquette of the day was to use three fingers delicately. Anyway, what's really interesting is the napkin. In French, it's *une serviette*, which is based on the verb *servir*, to serve. That's where the word *dessert* comes from: to take away or *desservir*. But that's beside the point. The individual napkin entered the scene in the sixteenth century. It was hung over the left arm or shoulder, much as waiters do to this day; then it was put around the neck because the fashion of the time was a large ruff around the neck. In fact, they changed napkins with every course."

Amy listened and nodded her head.

"French pre-dinner drinks? Do you mean *apéritifs*? If so, that's easy. There are just a few in the traditional sense. In addition to a Kir, which is white wine with a splash of cassis, or a Kir Royal, which is champagne with a splash of cassis or just a glass of champagne or any sparkling wine, the French mix Pernod with water or mix Dubonnet, Campari, or British Pimms No. 1 with soda and serve it on the rocks with a twist. There's also just dry vermouth, which goes by *martini sec*. That's really just about it. After all, an *apéritif* is just to whet the appetite, and dinner always includes wine, often more than one kind of wine, so strong spirits such as bourbon, scotch, gin, and so on, what Americans call cocktails and highballs, are more likely to be served late in the evening, not before dinner. So if I write up and send you the one on napkins and the one on pre-dinner drinks in addition to my two trivia items, I'll be pretty well caught up, right? I'll get these off ASAP! Say hello to Dory. Bye, Foster."

She was tired and the headache had returned. Amy guessed she had overdone it. Sometimes she was her own worst enemy. Maybe she should lie down and rest. She wondered just where Jean-Michel was and just how long he'd be gone. She'd overheard him on the phone, saying something about a pirate, although that didn't make any sense. It had been over twenty years since he had dealt with maritime law, salvage operations, even piracy. Of course, there were all sorts of modern-day pirates: music, films, all sorts of businesses. Pirates used to have peg legs, eye patches, rings in their ears, and parrots on their shoulders. She'd even dressed her son Jack as a pirate one Halloween. Now it was in the news that there were actual pirates raiding and capturing ships in the Indian Ocean. Surely, Jean-Michel didn't know a real honest-to-goodness pirate, although some of the people he knew could easily pass for one: Clovis, Raphaël, and most certainly that odd map man, François Lacour, who might not have a peg leg, but he did wear a black eye patch.

The sound of sirens startled Amy awake. At first she was disoriented. She quickly realized that she had fallen asleep on the bed and had slept several hours. Walking over to the long French window that overlooked the Quai de Bourbon, she saw several police cars turn off the Quai de l'Hôtel de Ville and cross the Pont Marie toward the Ile Saint-Louis. She wondered what had happened. She quickly called Caroline. Caroline would know. She had a police scanner in her media room. Absolutely nothing went on in and around the Ile without Caroline's knowledge.

"Caroline, it's Amy. What's going on? I'm hearing sirens and can see police cars racing across the bridge. A body? A corpse? Found where? Really? On the Quai de Béthune? On one of those benches just across from Jean-Michel's office, you say. *Ma foi*! I'll be up in a few minutes."

Amy changed her clothes quickly. She couldn't go up to Caroline's in her nightgown and robe. She found Caroline in her media room, talking to someone on the phone. Caroline motioned to her to sit down. Next to her was a tea table with leftover lunch dishes. Still on the tray were several sandwiches, a small ice bucket, a half-empty crystal carafe of water, and a silver coffee pot, creamer, and sugar.

Amy suddenly realized that she hadn't eaten any lunch. She picked up a small triangle and smiled as she tasted a spicy pork rillette. A second triangle proved to be smoked salmon and a third yielded an herbed goat cheese with roasted red bell pepper. Also on the tray were a small dish with several spring radishes along with a tiny condiment dish of sweet butter and a small shaker of sea salt. There were also several clusters of red and green grapes, as well as three miniature lemon curd tarts.

It was obvious that Caroline and someone had shared an upscale but not overly formal lunch. Amy wondered who.

"*Alors*, Amy, the preliminary report is that the body is not that of one of those homeless creatures who live under the Pont Sully. It seems that it's the body of a German national. Inspector Mathieu is turning the case over to Inspector Legrand at IBS, so we'll have to wait a bit longer to have the identification."

Amy picked up a tartlet and nibbled on it thoughtfully. A German. Could it be that waiter from the Café du Coin, the one that poisoned the general by mistake? Surely not. He was not on the Ile and probably not even in Paris." It could be a coincidence. There were lots of German tourists in Paris, students too. Not knowing what to say to Caroline, she picked up another tartlet.

"Did you forget to have lunch today, Amy?"

"Yes, yes, I did. I finally felt so much better. Jean-Michel is out of town and I thought I'd take advantage of feeling better and being alone, so I decided to get some work done."

"And did you get a lot of work done?"

"I did, I really did. Maybe tomorrow I can tackle all those thank-you notes and feel like taking a walk around the Ile."

"So where has my nephew gone this time? I thought he was retired from all that sort of thing. I've never understood why he's always taking off on mysterious trips. Didn't he bring that young nephew of his here so that he could stay home? Tell me, Amy, how do you think that young couple is finding life on the Ile? They're in an age group that usually settles in other quartiers of Paris."

Amy bit her tongue. Serge was also Caroline's nephew, great-nephew in fact.

"I think that Serge and Justine are enjoying their apartment and the Ile. When Jean-Michel gets back, we'll have to have a dinner party so that you can get to know them and they can get to know you. Maybe when Roger gets out of the hospital. That's it! A welcome home family dinner."

"We'd have to include Margot. Agnès, if she's back in town. Tristan too. He is a cousin. Then there's the family on Cité and of course Sylvestre and Véronique."

"Don't forget Alain! What about Mireille and Alexis?"

Caroline laughed.

"*Bien sûr.* We're already up to eighteen. With the young couple, we'll be twenty-one. I think twenty-four is a nice size. We'll think about three more. I just remembered. Eugène will have closed down his dig in Egypt, so we can include him and his wife Renée, so we'll just need one. Agnès will simply have to return from Canada in time. We'll use my grandmother's Haviland and my mother's sterling and silver water goblets."

"I'll work on a menu. For the *apéritif* only a Kir Royal will do and maybe some *gougères* and some marinated olives. I like a nice foie gras for the first course. What a great project!"

"Just make sure that it's seven courses."

"Of course. By the way, one of the sandwiches was made of a particularly delicious rillette. Do you know if Yvette or Léon bought it on the Ile?"

"It was sent by Auguste from Chez Ma Tante. I too thought it was special. I wonder if he's planning to use it for Léonore's wedding dinner."

Suddenly, Amy knew who had been the lunch guest. It wasn't the bride-to-be, Léonore, because she was still in Dijon. It had to have been Justine! How typical of Caroline! She immediately put Justine at ease by having a casual lunch in the media room, a place which testified to Caroline's being "with it," as indeed she was. Caroline's communication center kept her in touch with the latest in all walks of life: film, music, stock and bond markets, fashion, best sellers, dance, economic issues, politics, world events, and athletics. It was well known that Caroline enjoyed pâtés, terrines, and potted meats. How thoughtful of Auguste, the chef at Chez Ma Tante, to help Justine by giving her a pot of rillettes to take to one Caroline Rochefort, doyenne of the Ile! No, it wasn't for a wedding dinner at all. It was pure Jolivet. Amy had forgotten that Auguste was a Jolivet and Serge's cousin, as well as Jean-Michel's.

One of three cradle phones rang. Caroline picked up the receiver on the burgundy one and listened. Amy couldn't figure out who was on the other end because all Caroline said several times was "*Oui.*" Finally, she hung up and turned to Amy: "That was the police. It was the substitute waiter who killed the general. There was no note on the body, just his identification. The police think it was a message meant for Jean-Michel. *Dieu merci*, that distasteful matter is now behind us and the case is closed. Now we can all return to normal."

Amy wondered just who in the police department called Caroline. She doubted that Jean-Michel even knew she had a well-placed informant there. Then again, Jean-Michel had once told her that nothing about his aunt's spy network could surprise him. After all, she was on a first-name basis with one cabinet minister and exchanged New Year's greetings with the deputy mayor and his wife.

"I know that you're Serge's great-aunt and that you already know him from your visits to Bourdonville. Have you met Justine? She's a beautiful girl, very bright, and extremely capable. I think she's a perfect match for Serge."

Caroline smiled. She and Amy were so much alike in so many ways. She knew that Amy had figured out that Justine had been the guest at lunch. Indeed, Amy was the right one for her nephew. She had finally come to terms with the importance of having a title and no longer objected to being referred to as "Countess," but, to her credit, she didn't consider her new status as her just due. She had somehow managed to remain Amy Page. Several years later, she still reveled in the special wonder that was the Ile Saint-Louis. What truly endeared her to Caroline was her awareness that she was not and never could be a *ludivicienne*, one descended from the first families of the Ile, yet she embraced the Ile just as much.

In Caroline's world, Amy was the only one who shared her deep lament that the original *ludiviciens* were selling out or dying off. Menus were posted in English, there was a gas station on the Boulevard Henri IV and a dental office on the Rue Budé, motorcycles parked regularly at the end of the Rue Jean du Bellay, a cheap trinket shop had recently opened on the Rue Saint-Louis-en-l'Ile, an ethnic restaurant was on the Quai de Bourbon, mounted police regularly patrolled the main street, an Italian gelato counter catered to foreigners walking by, and Berthillon's had added a room for *le brunch*, which was simply outrageous.

At least, the Opentour Bus was not allowed, and there were no sleazy nightclubs, just the old jazz bar on the corner of the Rue des Deux-Ponts and the Quai de Bourbon, but everyone knew that the "Franc-Pinot" dated back to 1640 and its iron gates were a historical monument. The interpretive cultural center would be a discreet highlight, which would preserve and perpetuate the rich heritage of the Ile Saint-Louis. If tourists were going to come, then they should be made welcome. The Ile de la Cité could continue to shout that it was the geographical and historical center of Paris, but to Caroline and her cronies, including the new Countess of Bourdonville, the Ile Saint-Louis was its very soul.

"Yes, I've met Justine. After all, she's living under my roof. Did you know that I went to school with her great-aunt Germaine? She was two years behind me, so I didn't know her very well, and then there was the war and everything changed. Imagine! After all these years, her great-niece is . . . Can I say engaged to my great-nephew? She's apparently in poor health and now lives in Poitiers with an unmarried daughter. It's the daughter who wrote to me. I guess they aren't e-mail users. So naturally, as soon as I learned just who Justine is, I called and invited her to lunch. She doesn't look a thing like Germaine. And guess what? She's never heard the family story about being related to Jeanne Laisné!"

"Jeanne Laisné! Louis Le Vau's wife?"

"Yes, the very one. It's never been documented. So many important papers were lost during one war or another, but it's a family legend. I heard it from Germaine herself. She was fascinated to meet someone who was a real *ludivicienne*. If indeed Justine is descended from the first architect on the Ile, then she is one of us. Isn't that extraordinary?"

Amy couldn't think of an answer. It was most extraordinary. Truly bizarre. But then again her life on the Ile had been anything but ordinary. Attempted murders and actual ones, kidnappings, illness, treasure hunt, cooking in a restaurant kitchen, gala parties, gossip in cafés and at high teas and just plain teas, moments of fear, pain, anguish, joy, happiness, and pure ecstasy. In just a few years, Amy thought she had been through the whole gamut of human emotions from discovery to loss to recovery. She had laughed and cried, been hurt and been healed, known anger and come close to hatred, sought justice and learned forgiveness. She had witnessed violence and life at its worst and experienced passion, life at its best.

"It is indeed extraordinary that Justine might be an Ile native. I hope you gave her an autographed copy of your history."

"Yes, I did and she seemed truly appreciative."

"Knowing what I do about Justine, I'm sure she'll read it from cover to cover, but don't go quizzing her like you did me! Promise?"

Both women laughed at the memory of Amy's first time at one of Caroline's famous teas.

"Well, there is a difference. Before I first met you, you had already conquered the Ile. You had a local reputation, so to speak. And then there was my nephew. I needed to do something about his lifestyle."

"And now you want to do something about Justine and Serge," Amy teased. "I get it. And, yes, of course, I'll help. There's a big unused nursery in this building!"

The two women were interrupted.

"What are you two plotting? Nursery? Is someone pregnant? I know it's neither of you, and it's surely not Yvette. I doubt that it's Aline. Is it Chantal? I know that Pascal will easily go to the altar, but she's always told him no. Maybe a baby will make her change her mind."

Amy jumped up and hugged Jean-Michel.

"No, no, *chéri*, nobody's expecting a baby. At least not yet. We were just chatting about this building. Caroline was telling me about how she had tea parties in the nursery with all those dolls that are now being repaired for the cultural center displays."

Caroline nodded in agreement.

"I remember having a tea party with you and Emilie. Only you insisted on no dolls, so we just invited some of the animals. Enough of that. We're glad you're finally home."

"Well, ladies, I'm tired. It's been a long trip and I've had very little sleep. So, if I can claim my wife, we'll go downstairs where hopefully she'll fix me an omelet and I can then go to bed and sleep the clock around."

Later that night, when Amy got up to find a nightgown, Jean-Michel turned over and fluffed his pillow.

"Amy, don't tell me that you and Caroline are conspiring to get Justine and Serge married."

"Why, Jean-Michel, what made you think of that? I don't have time to be part of one of Caroline's schemes. I have lots of other things to do, like my food articles, Léonore's wedding, the center opening, and—"

"And me?

"Always and forever you, my love."

Jean-Michel smiled. He knew she was avoiding the issue, which in Amy speak was a form of confession. Let them plot and plan, he thought. It really wasn't a bad idea. He enthusiastically recommended wedded bliss. He had already heard about the body discovered opposite his office on the Quai de Béthune. It was a message. The case was closed and the Ile was now safe and secure. Tomorrow, he would tell Amy all about François Lacour. Once again, she had been the key witness. This time it was from a café. He hoped it was the last. With Serge and Justine in Paris, perhaps he truly could retire and do what he'd always wanted to do: write the history of the Jolivet vineyard and winery. Wouldn't Amy be both pleased and amused?

XIV

"My God, that's quite a story! It's just like something out of one of the novels I'm always reading. Just think! The Ile Saint-Louis has become a safe haven for retired spies! I always wondered about that old man with the dog, but I don't think I ever met that chess player or the Vietnamese fisherman. Where do they live? Come to think of it, there are very few fishermen on our quays compared to those along the Ile de la Cité."

Jean-Michel looked at Amy. She had hardly moved while he told her François Lacour's history, leaving out how Lacour was family in that he was related to his brother-in-law, as well as to Serge. There was no need for Amy to know that he was fairly certain Lacour was Serge's biological father. There was no reason for anyone to know that. He had not read the DNA report and in his presence Lacour had burned it. Pip had assured them that he hadn't read it either and the lab had destroyed its record of the test. The secret would be safe for all time. At the moment, Jean-Michel was the only person in Paris who knew Lacour's true identity. Ultimately, Serge would have to be told that the two were related, but just as cousins. However, that revelation would have to come from Lacour.

Outside, it was raining gently, what Amy described as the perfect spring rain, whatever that meant. The couple was seated in twin wingback chairs in Jean-Michel's study. On the table between them was a large silver trey with a plate of sandwich crumbs, a few grapes, two demitasse cups, three small pieces of lemon rind, a small coffee pot, and the inevitable glass of Diet Cola that Amy favored.

"I don't think you'll ever meet Tiago Luiz or Paul Champion. They've permanently left the Ile. The old man is Jacob Poncet and the dog's name is

Andromaque. He would prefer it if you didn't acknowledge him. He enjoys keeping a clandestine eye on the Ile and that really is a service to those of us who live here."

"Of course, I'll respect his wishes. I just never thought about what old spies did when they stopped spying. It's obvious that Pip isn't really out of the business despite his greenhouse of incredible roses, and that odd redheaded Irishman appears at the strangest moments. Then there's Lacour. I always thought there was something strange about him. Isn't it amazing that you knew him many years ago when you lived in London? Wonders never cease! You must have led quite a life before I met you. It's hard to imagine that you really know all those strange people. I mean, I knew that the Archangels had once lived on the other side of the law, but I thought it was because they were political rebels or revolutionaries or something like that, not outright criminals."

"You have to remember, Amy, that the world is made up of all sorts of people. Historically, the first members of the criminal division known as the French Sûreté were reformed criminals. Then there's the history of the French Foreign Legion."

"And pirates too! We can't forget those swashbucklers. Sir Francis Drake was actually authorized by the Queen of England to raid Spanish galleons. And of course there was that rogue Maltese knight who still sends me a gift from time to time. Speaking of pirates, who is the Pirate? It's obviously someone you know. I overheard you mention the Pirate on the phone. Was that who kidnapped me? You didn't mention him in the Lacour story. I know that pirates are known for kidnapping people and holding them for ransom."

Jean-Michel thought quickly. How much should he tell Amy? She had an illogical way of putting odd pieces of information together into a meaningful pattern. He guessed he would never understand how her mind raced from incongruity to incongruity and somehow came up with a rational explanation or simple solution.

"Ah, the Pirate. First of all, I don't think you can compare Sir Francis Drake to the Somali pirates. But it is true that we tend to think that pirates merely seize ships and their crews for money, and we forget that throughout history they were ruthless invaders who raped, looted, and burned villages. Remember the history of Paris. When the Parisii tribe was living on the islands in the Seine, they were brutally attacked by Vikings, who were no more than organized barbarians. Your Jack Sparrow of the "Pirates of the Caribbean" has truly romanticized the very idea of piracy and fostered some sort of mythology about the wonderful life that comes with being a pirate. Reality is quite different. But to answer your question, no, the one referred to as the Pirate was not responsible for your attempted kidnapping. In fact, Amy, we're never going to know exactly who ordered it. We only know who was behind the three bombings and they aren't related to what happened to you."

"But, Jean-Michel, I can't believe that you, the police, the Archangels, and all those retired secret agents don't know who tried to kidnap me. One of them was killed. Surely he was identified."

"Yes, he was. We think we know who was behind it, but we have no hard evidence."

"Well, who do you think did it? You must have a theory, and I think I have a right to know."

"It's another long story, Amy. It was a long time ago. Bear with me. When I was living and working in England as a maritime lawyer, I was sent by the London office to negotiate a ransom . . . well, those details are beside the point. Anyway, I wound up in a jail cell in the old Czech Republic and my cell mates turned out to be Gabriel and the man we call the Pirate. Yes, Gabriel. Both my employers and the Pirate's contacts were working out a ransom—gold in his case, an exchange of a certain prisoner in mine. Whoever Gabriel was working for decided to throw him under the bus and just leave him to fend for himself in prison, so he had no one. In a nutshell, the Pirate decided to pay for Gabriel's release, provided I set him up somewhere in the West. With Pip's help, and probably Lacour's, I sent him to a contact in Brussels and he lived there until I moved to Paris. By the way, Gabriel has since repaid the Pirate. With interest, I might add."

"So everybody knows everybody in that underground world."

"That's how one survives. Contacts. Who can be trusted. Who cannot. Who has a specialized knowledge, who can tap into a given network, who has entry into officialdom and vice versa. What works for spies often works for criminals. Spies spy upon spies. Agents direct agents. Counterparts know counterparts. Just as you, Amy, know which chefs specialize in which foods, know which pastry shop has the best palmiers, which bistro has the best cassoulet and which café makes the best croque monsieur sandwich. It's a question of professionals knowing their profession and their colleagues, but even more important, knowing their competition and their rivals. Sylvestre and his brother work overtime to remain the best in their industry of tooth products. Toothpaste alone wouldn't keep them at the top; they had to branch out into whiteners, floss, picks, electric brushes, travel brushes, child-friendly brushes and gels, mouthwashes, on and on."

"I gather that after you got out of jail, you stayed in touch with the Pirate."

"No, not really. Actually, once I took care of Gabriel, I really forgot all about the Pirate until the murder in the Café du Coin and I had figured out that Lacour was the real target."

"In London, you were involved with maritime law, so why didn't you hear about the Pirate? Surely, he was still raiding ships."

"No, Amy. He was never that kind of pirate. He was a hijacker, a bootlegger, a smuggler, a robber, but not a kidnapper, and he never dealt with ships. Today we talk about organizations that pirate music and films. The Pirate worked in contraband, selling stolen property, both actual property and intellectual property. He was behind the scenes in most black market operations in Europe, the Middle East, and parts of Asia. He was a premier arms dealer and often sold to both sides: guns, ammunition, rockets, tanks, bomb materials, and on down the line. Ultimately, he amassed a huge fortune and so turned to being the banker for all sorts of illegal operations, including armed uprisings, corporate takeovers, bootleg films, extortion rackets, and parts of the drug trade, mainly the finances involved in its cultivation, manufacture, and distribution. He claims that he has retired, but he could very well be the one who's financing whoever is providing the Somali pirates with the latest guns and technology—"

"So people who rip off Gucci handbags and Hermès scarves are pirates!"

"Yes. Think of it this way. A pirate takes and sells stolen property, but he is not necessarily a brigand on the high seas operating outside territorial waters. I don't know how the Pirate got his name, but I've heard that he considers himself a modern-day privateer who operates with letters of authorization, meaning that he is legitimately hired. How that gives him a degree of legality and jurisdictional approval is beyond me, but he thinks that his illegal acts have some basis in morality since he does not rape, loot, kill, maim, plunder, or destroy like the Vikings of old or Bluebeard or the Barbary Pirates. And he most certainly doesn't kidnap, which is an interesting point. You see, most modern sea pirates seize ships and kidnap crews for financial reward, but they rarely kill their victims because they want the owners and families to know that in their negotiations they keep their word. In a nutshell, it's a business, with rules and policies and a reputation to maintain, so they usually release whatever and whomever they capture once they are paid. It's their badge of honor."

"But not the Pirate! How very strange! It's really an odd word. Pirates are the ones who have morals. They keep their word. You make them out to be no different from businessmen and politicians who pay people to spin webs of deceit. You're actually telling me I can always trust people who live outside the law."

"No, Amy. I'm just trying to tell you about the Pirate. He sees himself as some sort of Johnny Depp character: a privateer whose illegitimate business is legal. That's all. I see him as a cunning, ruthless manipulator. He doesn't really care who gets hurt as long as he's removed from the actual deed and gets paid. In my dealings with him, I've always found him to be . . . up-front. That's as good a term as any. I think we respect each other, and respect is the basis of our business. I haven't had to deal with him very often, but I did this time because I had reached the end of my rope. There was nowhere else to go. He has a finger in every major dirty deal in the world."

Amy fell quiet. She was uncomfortable knowing that the universe had a dark side in which her lover and husband was at ease, a world of spies and criminals. She found some comfort in the fact that the gangster who was known as the Pirate and was apparently one of its kingpins respected her Jean-Michel.

Now it turned out that she didn't know the Ile after all. Lacour was probably the most interesting citizen on the Ile, and he had certainly earned every right to be as odd as he wanted. The dog walker was an ex-Mossad agent, of all things, while, overnight, two spies had simply taken off and left no traces. No one seemed to know who had tried to kidnap her, yet it was commonly agreed that her kidnapping hadn't been planned to be a real kidnapping. Now, who planned a kidnapping that wasn't supposed to be one? Were the inmates running the asylum?

"I'm still confused, Jean-Michel. Why was I kidnapped when I wasn't supposed to stay kidnapped and be ransomed? What makes you and everyone else think that my kidnapping wasn't a serious one? That doesn't make any sense. It was certainly serious to me. And there was the gunfight on the bridge. You can't overlook that. People were wounded, three were killed, I was concussed, lots of vehicles were damaged. If that wasn't serious, I give up."

Jean-Michel knew that Amy wouldn't give up until she had an answer that satisfied her.

"In brief, the Pirate has a sister, actually a half-sister, who goes by the name Isis—"

"Isis! You mean the Egyptian goddess? Surely you're kidding. First there's Artemis, now there's Isis. Really, Jean-Michel, next thing you'll be telling me that you know an Amazon queen, like Wonder Woman!"

Jean-Michel was amused. It made sense for Artemis to adopt the name of a goddess of love for her erotic theater performances, but Amy was right. To adopt the name of Isis and then to do everything possible to look like Cleopatra was ridiculous. In fact, on the way to Switzerland, he had said as much to Lacour, who had burst into laughter.

According to Lacour, Isis had bright blue eyes, flaxen hair, a fair complexion, and a Junoesque or in her case Teutonic build. Disguising herself as an Egyptian of old was the perfect cover in a world of subterfuge and deceit.

Everyone had special nicknames, aliases, code names, and various identities, just as all operations, especially military ones, had special cover names. No one questioned names. It was a given that no one used his or her real one. In one group, he himself was referred to as the Unicorn because that image appeared on his family coat-of-arms and on occasion he had traveled with a false passport.

Indeed, how should he respond to Amy? He thought about telling her that the Archangels's code name for her was Princess, while the police most often referred to her as Milady and the gang of four had nicknamed her Minnie Mouse. No, he decided. She probably wouldn't see the humor in those names.

"It so happens, Amy, that I do know Wonder Woman. It's you! You're a wonder and you are all woman!"

Amy laughed.

"Flattery is not going to get you out of telling me what this Isis person is doing here and what she has to do with my kidnapping that wasn't one."

"Isis is her cover name. I don't know her real name. I'm sure she has several identities. Most spies do. She's a huntress. She can track down anyone anywhere and she commands extremely high fees for her services. She's the one who found the man responsible for the general's murder and probably arranged for his execution."

"You mean she's an assassin?"

"She may have been one at times in the past, but she's never been known as a contract killer. In this case I believe that she located the killer and as part of her payment asked that the body be placed on a bench on the Quai de Béthune opposite my office as a message: job completed. Yes, Lacour and I did hire her to find him. We did not hire her to assassinate him, but whoever did, saved the country time and money. It's now officially a closed case."

"I see, but what does Isis have to do with my kidnapping?"

"It seems that she did some work for the drug lords in South America. I don't have all the details, but what Lacour and I learned from the Pirate was that she was working for the drug consortium that wanted to locate Lacour. She fingered him without realizing who he really is. She had known him under his real name in London and thought, as did many, that he was dead. It was the first time that her homework on a target was sloppy. When the general was murdered by mistake, it became clear to a few of us that only Isis could have somehow set it in motion, so only she could find the actual killer. As a result, we hired her. What we did not know was the extent of her involvement with the South American drug consortium, nor the fact that she and Tiago Luiz were once married."

"You've got to be kidding!"

"It's true. They even have a child who is severely retarded and requires special care. Isis herself has developed a rare neurological disorder that is beginning to take its toll and slow her down, which is probably why her planning of the attack on Lacour was somewhat careless. In a nutshell, she needed to extricate herself from working for the drug consortium and she wanted to protect Luiz, who is still her legal husband and the father of her child. And, of course, Luiz and Lacour have been associates for years. In a deal that can only be described as one of Chinese nesting boxes, she saw to it that the consortium set those bombs on the Ile in order to scare off Lacour and force him to stop his research for an anti-narcotic drug—"

"So that's why you said those bombs weren't designed to kill anyone? That's why they were so loud. And Natalie Darcet wasn't supposed to be there."

"Yes. That's right. The bombs were meant as a warning of what they could do."

"So why kidnap me?"

"We think that was a separate issue. Tiago Luiz was trying in his way to help both Lacour and Isis by forcing me to bring pressure on Lacour to stop his work in South America. He and Paul Champion arranged to kidnap you to get me to see how vulnerable you were, even on the Ile. It was a form of blackmail. You would have been released several blocks away. I think it was Luiz himself who was on the motorcycle and grabbed you. The driver was from one of the Asian gangs in Paris."

Amy sputtered.

"Jean-Michel, do you know how ludicrous this sounds? A pirate, an Egyptian goddess, drug lords, Asian gangs, a Russian chess player, and a fisherman, all highly trained secret agents, skilled in assassination, kidnapping, setting bombs, and who knows what? I really should give up writing about food and take up writing novels. It would have to be fiction because no one would believe the truth."

"I can't help it, *chérie*. You asked for the story and I'm doing my best. It is what it is."

"Okay! Go on. You were saying that the driver of the kidnap car belonged to an Asian gang in Paris."

"Yes. He was hired no doubt by Champion, who doesn't drive, preferring a bicycle and on occasion one with a motor. My guess is that Champion was the passenger and he was the one who got away. I had noticed a sudden increase of Oriental students and tourists on the Ile, so I asked my friend

Sean to send a team over to keep an eye out. However, neither I nor the Luiz-Champion team took Jacob Poncet into the plans. On his own, he got into the act with his own spy, namely that artist. The gunfight broke out because the Irish and the artist didn't know that the kidnapping was a fake. You heard him say Mossad, not Moses. By the way, that artist is also a Mossad agent who in retirement is a real artist who lives on the Costa del Sol in Spain."

"And that's it? I mean that's all. It was just one big mix-up?"

"That's what happened."

"Surely there's more. There has to be a grand finale."

"Isis has gone back to wherever she lives. I imagine that Luiz is with her and will look after her as her disease becomes worse. Then there's the child. Champion is probably somewhere in Asia. Lacour has agreed to stay out of all of Latin America. He's going to stay here and work with me, Serge, and Justine on the days when he's not doing his map business. He says he's going to set up a lab in the Azores and the first priority will be to work on *botrytis ceverea*."

There was no reason for Amy to know that Lacour was already a silent partner in the security business or that he and Jean-Michel had sent Sean a considerable sum for him to give as an insurance payment to the family of the young Irishman who had died on the bridge.

"*Bo* . . . what?"

"It's a terrible fungus that rots grapes. It turns them to mush at harvest time after the fall rains. Right now, vineyards rely on fungicides and thinning the number of clusters so that there is more air around the grapes. As a matter of fact, that's what your son Jack is going to do this summer, thin the vines. Of course, reducing the number of clusters reduces the number of grapes and in turn that means less wine will be produced that year. When that fungus attacks, it can be devastating, so any new treatment to avoid harvest rot would be welcome."

"My head is spinning. I really have information overload. I guess I was somehow in the middle of it all, wasn't I? Ever since I met you, I seem to be involved in one crime after another. My life here is certainly different from what it was in South Carolina."

Jean-Michel smiled. Amy was satisfied that she now knew all there was to know about the case, which Mathieu and Legrand had jokingly named "Milady from the Café." He stood up and held out his hand to Amy.

"It's still raining outside. Let's go down the hall to your study and you can show me all those brochures on Basque country. I think we both need a change of scene."

An hour later, Jean-Michel and Amy were hastily packing their bags. While they were planning a vacation to the French Pyrenees, Jean-Michel's cell phone had rung, interrupting a light-hearted argument over how many days to stay in Saint-Jean-de-Pied-de-Luz. Amy noticed that Jean-Michel had immediately turned white. The caller was Robert Petit, Jean-Michel's brother-in-law. There had been an explosion at the Jolivet vineyard office. Several people had been killed outright, among them Jean-Michel's uncle Antoine, the office secretary, and the accountant. The blast had happened during a monthly meeting, so everyone was there. His mother was in the hospital and not expected to live. His brother Alexandre had been critically wounded and was in surgery; all that was known was that he had lost one leg. Yves, the other brother, had also been hurt, but Robert didn't know the extent of his injuries. Several workers had also been injured, but he didn't know how many. As far as he knew, Amy's son Jack had been out in the fields, so he wasn't hurt. Would Jean-Michel please come at once? He was urgently needed. Bourdonville was in chaos.

For the first time in her life, Amy found herself behind the wheel, driving out of Paris, while Jean-Michel worked on his laptop and talked on his cell phone. She had no idea when they'd be back on her beloved Ile Saint-Louis. She suspected that it would be a long, long time. Maybe it was time to close that book and start a new one.

The Ile would always be there, imperturbable, solid, unchanged and unchanging in a changing world. From cows on its pastures to mansions along its quays to motorcycles on its streets, the Ile managed to retain its separateness and its urbane elegance. It preserved another time and another place without any loss of its sense of self. It simply held its own against floods, ice storms, wars, revolutions, political controversy, crimes, big business, economic ups and downs, even consumerism. It patently and patiently avoided all extremes.

As Amy negotiated the outskirts of the city, she reflected on how the Ile had provided comfort and security to those who chose to live there. It protected Caroline Rochefort and indulged her brother Roger's foibles, provided the hunchbacked dwarf Margot with a life of normalcy, kept the industry magnate Julien Turenne modest, tolerated the flamboyant actor Florian Renan, and ignored the odd map man François Lacour and the dog walker Jacob Poncet. It supported local restaurants, cafés, grocery stores, pastry shops, and small boutiques. It was proud that the world-famous ice cream shop, Berthillon, was located on its main street and didn't find it in the least peculiar that it always closed in August at the height of the tourist season and summer heat.

Through the centuries, all manner of persons had sought haven there: poets, artists, scientists, American ex-patriates, even a former President of the Republic and ex-spies. When Jean-Michel had been struck by personal tragedy, it became his refuge. When she set out on a voyage of personal self-discovery, it became her guide. The Ile had nursed him, nurtured her, and brought them together. The Ile would always be a part of her.

Suddenly, Amy spotted the crumbling walls of the medieval town of Bourdonville. The town was now on the UNESCO list and restoration of the ramparts was underway. They would be at the hospital in a few minutes. She didn't know what awaited them. All she knew was that they would meet the challenge. After all, they too were survivors.

Perhaps in its own way life on the Ile had prepared them for this next chapter in their lives. As Amy looked at the crowd in front of the hospital, she realized that it was not so much a crowd of curious onlookers as it was a welcoming committee. She sensed that everything she had ever done had been leading to this time in this place with this particular man. As Amy stopped the car, she took a deep breath and looked over at Jean-Michel, who seemed unable to move.

"We're here, Jean-Michel."

Amy and Jean-Michel slowly got out of the car and walked into the crowd milling about the hospital steps. As if a signal had been given, the crowd immediately fell silent and made room for them to pass. Amy felt those around her breathe a collective sigh of relief, as she and Jean-Michel made their way up the front steps. She later compared that moment to the first time she stood at the very end of the Square Barye on the Ile: the swirling waters of the Seine seemed to come to a halt and then parted in order to go around that marvelous bastion in its center. The Seine paid homage to the Ile, just as the throngs of townspeople now were paying their respects to them. The Count of Bourdonville had come home, accompanied by their new countess. It was a foregone conclusion that they would stay. She understood that she and Jean-Michel were experiencing a homecoming. A strange one, but a homecoming, nevertheless. Even stranger was the knowledge that she was where she wanted to be. Not in sophisticated cosmopolitan chic Paris, but in a small provincial town in the southern part of Burgundy. She would no longer be living in a discreetly luxurious old mansion with the latest modern conveniences, but in a spacious rambling old château in serious need of updating.

Naturally, she would go back to Paris for visits, but this medieval town with its ancient ruins and medieval rooftops was now her world. Regardless of what might lie ahead, she thanked her lucky stars that she had undertaken the journey that had led her to the Quai de Béthune. So much had happened. She had begun as a witness to the people, places, and things around her, taking notes and pictures, recording in her journal events as they occurred. Somehow somewhere along the way, she had stopped being a passive observer and become an active emissary of change. But, of course, it could have only happened on that wondrously magical island in the Seine, the Ile Saint-Louis.

8123542R0

Made in the USA
Lexington, KY
06 March 2011